Praise for
*Two Hour Transport 2*

"A lovely collection of stories, featuring gems from both established authors and up-and-coming writers. This book is a wonderful reminder of the strong, flourishing community of SF writers with ties to Seattle and the Pacific Northwest."

— TINA CONNOLLY, author of the Ironskin Trilogy

"This anthology is a real trip, taking you from the terrible to the sublime with multiple stops at fantastic stations in between."

— CURTIS CHEN, author of *Waypoint Kangaroo*

"From steampunk to hard SF, this collection includes a wide variety of speculative fiction topics. Readers will find excellent poetry, flash fiction, and longer stories."

— BRENDA COOPER, author of *The Silver Ship and the Sea*

I0564096

# TWO HOUR TRANSPORT 2

# TWO HOUR
# TRANSPORT
# 2

## EDITED BY
## NIB, RAMONA RIDGEWELL
## & KEYAN BOWES

FAIRWOOD PRESS
Bonney Lake, WA

TWO HOUR TRANSPORT 2
A Fairwood Press Book
August 2024
Copyright © 2024 by NIB, Ramona Ridgewell & Keyan Bowes
All Rights Reserved

First Edition

Fairwood Press
21528 104th Street Court East
Bonney Lake, WA 98391
www.fairwoodpress.com

Cover © Sandipkumar Patel / Getty Images
Cover & book design by Patrick Swenson

ISBN: 978-1-958880-20-3
First Fairwood Press Edition: August 2024
Printed in the United States of America

*To the Two Hour Transport community*

—NIB, Ramona Ridgewell, Keyan Bowes

# CONTENTS

**Snowflake** 11
Tod McCoy

**Terrible Trudy on the Lam** 13
Eileen Gunn

**Song of the Water People** 22
Genevieve Williams

**Octonet** 33
Keyan Bowes

**Trash Collector** 52
Joshua K. Wilson

**Bubba Sez Howdy** 60
Rex Erickson

**Waking the Taniwha** 63
Dan Rabarts

**Rifts** 75
Yang-Yang Wang

**Standing Room Only** 90
Karen Joy Fowler

**King Harvest (Will Surely Come)** 103
Nisi Shawl

**Harmony** 110
Andy Dudak

**No More Bad Dreams** 123
Louis Evans

**The Moon and the Devil and the Ace of Wands** 125
Evan J. Peterson

**It Only Takes a Few Months for a Poet
to Position Its Jaws**      135
Mitchell Shanklin

**Fire Puzzle**      139
Elly Bangs

**The Light of Two Moons**      154
K.G. Anderson

**The Runner**      164
Sarah Allen

**Sold for Parts**      168
NIB

**The Call of the Sky**      170
Cliff Winnig

**The Last Human Being on Earth**      184
Kyra Worrell & Theresa Barker

**Escher's Hands**      189
Jeffrey Steven Abrams

**The Moth Girls**      204
E.E.W. Christman

**Being a Vampire**      216
Ramona Ridgewell

**A Volcano Walks into a Bar**      226
Seelye Martin

**The Sandwich Shack**      231
Patrick Hurley

# SNOWFLAKE

## TOD MCCOY

'Twas brillig, and the frithy brock
  Did quamb and cofer through the trees;
A frabjous time for Jabberwock
  To wander o'er the leas.

"So curious!" Larked mother wock.
  "I want to study man," he maized,
Galumphing through the amphlipok,
  "And comprehend their ways!"

He spied a boy in uffish thought,
  Who leaned up 'gainst a Tumtum tree.
His vorpal blade shone bright as blot!
  Wock clacked his claws with glee.

Warged Jabberwock. "Hello, my friend!
  Your tale tell me!" His eyes aflame
He whiffled through the tulgey wood
  and burbled out his name!

Snack snick snick snack! The vorpal blade
  Did cut and cleave! The young wock fell,
Decapped and dispossessed, unmade
  Beneath a leafy ghell.

There mother wock unearthed her son,
  Carpled through and through. "Ragged thief!"
She cried aloud, "what hast thou done?!?"
  And burbled home in grief.

'Twas brillig, and the frithy brock
  Did quamb and cofer through the trees;
A frabjous time for Jabberwock
  To wander o'er the leas.

# TERRIBLE TRUDY
# ON THE LAM
## EILEEN GUNN

I t was a whim, a momentary desire to see what lay outside the zoo. But once Trudy had taken a walk around San Diego, once she'd tasted freedom, she was determined not to go back. She would make this work. At first, she lived in the city's lovely dark storm drains, emerging every night to forage for yummies in Balboa Park. But she knew her sylvan idyll would not last forever. She needed a long-term plan, and after a week of pondering the matter, she put one together.

A job was the first order of business, something that would keep her in shoots and leaves, and hopefully something she could do evenings: she was, of course, as the zookeepers had told her time and again, an odd-toed crepuscular ungulate. Twilight was her very best time of day, though she could go all night if she had to.

She considered roller skating. Bears do it, elephants do it, even penguins roller skate, and at that time roller-skating couples in evening dress were becoming a popular nightclub entertainment. Why not tapirs?

At first, Trudy thought maybe a prey-predator act would be exciting, since tapirs have been known to bite viciously when cornered, and that could be milked for comic effect. But tigers, the Malayan tapir's principle predator, rarely roller skate well. They consider it undignified, and often, when strapped into skates, just lie on their backs with their feet in the air, as if expecting a bellyrub. Trudy considered putting together an act with another prey animal, but she was wary of partners: not every rollerskater who said she was a vegetarian was committed to non-violence. In the end, Trudy decided to go it alone.

A kindly shoemaker created custom open-toed roller skates for her, to show off her tiny hooved toes, three on each back foot, four on each foot in the front. The boots were made of red leather, which contrasted elegantly with Trudy's silver shoulders and black flanks. A black bowtie and a starched white collar pulled the whole ensemble together in a dignified and professional way. A refined Marlene-Dietrich look, Trudy thought, right to the silver tracings on the tips of her ears.

She practiced skating late at night, after the rink had closed and everyone had gone home. It was dark, but tapirs have poor eyesight, and she was accustomed to tiptoeing around in a dusky forest. Eventually the groundskeeper discovered that she had broken into the rink through an unused storage closet, and the jig was up, but by then she had perfected a hilarious pantomime routine. She skittered out onto the dance floor, flailing about and threatening to crash into tables along its edge, then regaining her composure and performing a series of graceful loops and twirls, ending in an Axel, loop, double Mapes, Euler, double flip.

Audiences loved it—in performance, the finale always drew gasps from the tables—and they took Trudy to their hearts. San Diegans, grieving and distressed after the attack on Pearl Harbor the previous year, sought consolation in bars and supper clubs, and Terrible Trudy the Roller Skating Tapir was a hit. Hollywood celebrities flocked to San Diego, ostensibly to perform for the troops at the naval base, but really to catch Trudy's act at the Chi-Chi Supper Club, a hot new nightclub with a South Seas theme. Trudy sometimes added a lei to her costume: it also served as a midnight snack.

As Trudy's star rose, so did her worries about the zoo director, the indomitable Belle Benchley. Mrs. Benchley had pioneered the modern, natural-looking, cageless zoo. Trudy had rejected Benchley's carefully simulated enclosure, and Trudy's wanderlust had challenged the woman to the core. Mrs. Benchley knew Trudy was living in La Jolla and working openly at the Chi-Chi Club, but had made no effort to contact her. How long would this détente last?

*

At first, Trudy seemed to be nonchalance itself. She flirted with members of the audience, of any gender, who caught her eye. If an object or an article of clothing attracted her interest, she would take possession of it, though she usually returned it to the owner at the end of her set. In such a fashion, she acquired a fedora, and she instantly made it a permanent part of her act. A huge fan of the singer Jimmy Durante, Trudy interspersed her spectacular skating-routine with Durante imitations, just as Durante would pause in the middle of a song and break into a quick comedy routine, then return to the song as if nothing had happened. Turns out she was a very affecting singer, with a sense of comedic timing that rivalled Durante's own. Not to mention she had a schnozzola that even Durante envied.

The crowds went wild.

But the stress began to tell on Trudy, who knew that at any moment Mrs. Benchley could, on a whim, decide to bring Trudy back to the zoo and its fake Malayan rain forest. Trudy had no legal leg to stand on: as she had been reminded by her lawyers time and again, she was the property of the San Diego Zoo. Trudy began downing a quick Tonga Punch—or maybe two—before the show, just to keep her courage up. One evening, she went a bit further than two, and had not sobered up by show time. She went on anyway, rather than disappoint the crowd, and the revelers took her markedly sloppy routine as a clever commentary on the club MC, who was notorious for never showing up to work sober. People laughed and laughed, and their wild reception of her wacky skate-dance encouraged her to act out even more.

She was careening between the supper tables on one foot, waving the other three in the air, picking up customers' champagne glasses with her schnoz, and singing "Inka-dinka-do," when suddenly her luck ran out, and her wheels caught on a crack in the floor. Had she been sober and standing on all four feet, she could have recovered, but that was not the case.

Trudy went flying, and landed on top of a table occupied by William Randolph Hearst and his paramour Marion Davies. Drenched in expensive champagne, Miss Davies fled the nightclub, leaving behind her ermine evening wrap and Mr. Hearst. As the newspapers told the story, Mr. Hearst immediately bestowed the ermine on Trudy, to console her for her embarrassment. Miss Davies later vowed publicly never again to leave either her clothing or her man alone in Trudy's presence, declaring, "That little rhinoceros minx has an elevated opinion of her own attractiveness." (Here we must acknowledge that, although tapirs and rhinoceroses are among the few odd-toed ungulates, tapirs are not rhinoceroses, and neither of them are minks.)

Trudy, realizing that her career as a headliner at the Chi-Chi had come to an end, saluted the audience with her fedora, ad libbed Durante's signature closing, "Good night, Mrs. Calabash, wherever you are," and lit out for LA as fast as she could travel, just one step ahead of Mrs. Benchley. She was only a tapir, making her lonely way in this dreadful world, but she knew when to call it a night.

It took just a couple hours to bus from San Diego to Los Angeles, and by midnight, Trudy, clutching her ermine stole about her, emerged from the Greyhound station on Los Angeles Street. She knew that pretty soon she'd need some kind of fake ID, but right then she sure hoped the cops wouldn't stop an innocent-looking young tapir in a classy fur wrap.

The few passengers on the late-night bus from San Diego scattered like roaches when you turn on the light. It was a quiet night, just a few people napped on the station's benches. No street traffic at all, really. Trudy was alone in LA, and had no real idea of where to go. She was pretty sure that LA had storm drains and that the gardens of Beverly Hills would provide sustenance. She was also under the impression that Beverly Hills was somewhere north of the Greyhound station, which was true enough. She struck out at once, heading north toward Olvera Street and what, she had heard, were some of the most colorful sections of the city. The wind was off the ocean, and she could smell the salt air.

After just a few blocks, she left the dreary bus-station-shabby street and entered a neighborhood of trim little wooden bungalows. It smelled good—it smelled edible in fact. Maybe she should have a nosh here, she thought. Why hold out for Beverly

Hills? She reached for some greenery and was nibbling it delicately when she noticed a man in the shadows, crouched next to
a 1937 Oldsmobile. The streetlights were dim and one to a block,
but Trudy's eyesight was best in low-light situations, so she had
no problem picking him out.

He was wearing a crumpled serge suit with an ugly striped
tie that had slipped askew. His fedora was battered in a way that
suggested he habitually sat on it. A pint of something alcoholic
stuck out of his jacket pocket. He looked slightly dangerous and
unmistakably up to no good. Trudy caught his eye.

He raised his eyebrows, nodded to Trudy, and, cool as a frozen daiquiri, brought his left index finger to his lips, and gave
her a stern cautionary glance. She nodded slightly in return. She
would give him a chance to explain himself, she thought.

Then, suddenly, he leaped up, holding a huge flash camera
in both hands, and aimed it into the back seat of the Olds, pho-
tographing the car's interior. The flash lit up the scene, and a
high-pitched scream came from the car. The photographer broke
away, ran like hell down the driveway right next to Trudy, and
disappeared into a large privet hedge that Trudy had been consid-
ering for dessert.

The driver-side door of the Olds pushed open and a partly-
dressed guy leaped out, clutching a wrench. He spotted Trudy
and shouted, "Where'd he go?" Trudy didn't care to be addressed
so rudely. She gestured towards Beverly Hills, and he started
down the street a few yards, then stopped. He turned around and
came back to the car, buttoning his yellow-and-pink Hawaiian
shirt, with a truculent look on his face.

"Get your things on, babe," he said to the person inside. "I'll
take you home, and then I'll deal with the gumshoe." A woman
said something low and mewly, but Trudy couldn't make out
what it was. "I'll pay him off, that's what. I'll take care of him.
Don't worry about it." He leaped into the car, started it, threw it
in gear, and they clattered off down the street.

Trudy made her move on the privet, which was as tasty as
she thought it would be.

The blackmailer, for that's surely what he was, emerged from
the hedge. "They gone?" He kept his voice low, and he mumbled.

Trudy, her mouth full of fresh privet, simply nodded.

"I like a dame can keep her mouth shut," the man said. He held out his hand. "Name's Mumble," he said. "Firrup Mumble." Trudy nodded again. That couldn't be his name, she knew, but it was really hard to understand him. No matter. She ignored his hand and continued to chew the privet.

"Divorce case," he said, tilting his head towards where the Olds had been parked. He lowered his hand. "That mug's been out with a different floozie every night. His ole lady'll take him for every penny he's got."

Trudy just looked at him. Not a blackmailer, a P.I.

"You keep your own counsel, I can tell," said the man.

Trudy continued to keep her own counsel.

"You need a job, kid? You look hard-up, wandering around in the middle of the night, eating people's shrubbery."

It was clear to Trudy that either he hadn't noticed the ermine stole or he thought it was part of a tapir's standard equipment, but the question, and the man's concern, softened her reserve. She nodded her head vigorously.

"I could use an assistant, someone who keeps their mouth shut, y' know'd I mean?"

Trudy shrugged, but didn't deny that she could keep her mouth shut.

"I'm a private dick, and I do mean private." He spoke a little louder, a little more clearly. "But I could use a dame to handle surveillance. You over eighteen?" Trudy nodded again, though actually she was only five. Seemed about right, though—just past adolescence.

"Well come along then, jalopy's over here. I gotta get these pix developed. Lady's gonna be filing for divorce, needs her fla-grante delicto."

I don't want to be anybody's assistant, thought Trudy. I want to be the detective. I want to find the flagrante delictos. But I guess I'll deal with that later. She followed Firrip Mumble to his car.


And that was how Trudy happened to be in the front room of the detective's office later that night, filling out an application for a P. I. license, when the irate adulterer came by with a shotgun. She saw his blurred form through the pebbled-glass panel in the office door, and she recognized his pink and yellow shirt as the one on the guy who had driven off in the Olds just a few hours before.

Trudy was pretty sure that, whatever her job turned out to be, some of it would involve running interference when people with whom the private eye had dealt in a professional capacity dropped by to discuss matters. So she put down her pencil and waited for the knock.

The knock, it turned out, was the crash of the butt-end of a shotgun coming through the pebbled glass. Trudy dashed forward, heedless of flying glass shards. The visitor aimed the shotgun directly into the PI's private office.

Trudy reached over with her prehensile proboscis and pushed down hard on the barrel. The gun went off and sent a load of buckshot through the open office door and right into the front of the detective's desk.

Trudy pressed her attack, making low-pitched hollow grunts and emphasizing them with piercing whistles. She tilted her head back and waggled her long, phallic snout, raising it like an elephant's trunk to reveal, deep behind her huge fleshy lips, a set of choppers as blunt and massive as those of a horse. She gave the man an emphatic bite on the arm, then reached over with her snout and grabbed the shotgun right out of his hands.

The guy let it go. He seemed to have lost interest in it completely and was staring at Trudy in complete disbelief. The detective appeared at the door to his office, and his would-be assailant turned to him with a look of helpless appeal. "If that's a dog, it's the weirdest damn dog I've ever seen. What the hell is it?"

"My little sister. You got a problem?" The detective took the gun from Trudy and stashed it behind his desk.

"Your sister? It's got horse feet for toes! And it's wearing fur spats. It looks like two different animals put together, a white one in the front and a black one in the back." He seemed on the verge of hysteria.

"Y'know, buster, you look like you were put together from spare parts yourself. I don't think you oughta be insulting my sister's protective coloration. May I inquire as to the purpose of your visit?"

Trudy was surprised and pleased to hear the gumshoe defend her like that. She had thought he wasn't any too thrilled to be told that she wanted to be a detective. In her experience, men did not take kindly to females of any persuasion who aspired to their jobs. Perhaps this one was different.

"Gimme the negs," said the miscreant. "You know what's good for you, gimme them right now."

"You're not in a great position to make demands, buddy," said the detective. "You want, the cops can make you a set of prints suitable for framing."

The man leaped for the shotgun, but the quick-witted gumshoe kicked it away. Then the fellow pulled a knife.

Unarmed and taken by surprise, the detective grabbed an office chair and raised it, to keep his attacker at a distance, but it was clear to Trudy that he was not going to win a fight against a thug with a knife. She looked about for a weapon, or at least something she could grab and throw. Her eye fell upon her ermine stole. It was fluffy and soft and white, a garment that made her feel like the cutest little bunny in the world, but she knew that ermine were basically weasels in white coats. Vicious. The stole would distract the knife-wielding adulterer, perhaps tapping into an atavistic human fear of the weasel . . . .

Trudy grabbed the stole with her snout and waved it, as if teasing a bull, to get the intruder's attention. He looked up and stared at her in baffled panic: what was the beast doing now? Trudy flung the stole at the intruder, and it wrapped fuzzily around his head, like a flying squirrel. The detective quickly picked up the shotgun and hit the knife out of the panicked miscreant's hand.

Five minutes later, the fellow was neatly trussed and tied to the chair, and Trudy, wrapped again in the ermine, sat with her new boss on the wooden ante-room bench, awaiting the arrival of Detective-Lieutenant Breeze.

The detective poured them each a shot of Old Forrester.

"You got it, kid," he said, tipping his glass towards her. "You're cool-headed, aware of your surroundings, and deft at improvised distraction. I'll see that your P.I. certification is approved." He downed his glass, then poured another one. "You've got a job here with me as long as you want it, if you don't mind occasional gunplay."

Trudy thought about it. She knew there would come a day when she would flee the dark, cynical world of the L.A. gumshoe, just as she'd fled the sleepy San Diego Zoo and the tacky ritz of the Chi-Chi Club. It might well involve gunplay and hot pursuit, and that was okay with her.

The thing you want when you're a prey animal, Trudy thought, is intermittent excitement. She could have a decent, happy life as the occasional target of someone's violent intentions, because she loved the pure energy of being chased. She bore no malice towards those pursuing her, and her heart soared at every triumphant escape. She wondered if Mumble, whatever his name was, who like most detectives lived for the chase, would understand. Maybe she'd ask him sometime, but not now.

Trudy nodded to Firrup Mumble and took a sip of bourbon. She smiled a hidden tapir smile. Mrs. Benchley might yet track her down, but for the time being, she had escaped. And she had a job. Life was good.


*Author's note:*
*Terrible Trudy was a resident of the San Diego Zoo in the 1940s and '50s. Her escapes caught the popular imagination, but eventually Zoo Director Belle Benchley tracked her down and persuaded her to return and stay put. Trudy died of comfortable old age in 1959, in retirement at a rainforest habitat in the San Diego Zoo. Mrs. Benchley, influential in her advocacy of humane animal habitats for zoos, followed in 1972.*

# Song of the Water People

## Genevieve Williams

We are born into song, to our great mother singing. All our lives we hear her song, and sing it with her.

Now she sings the song of her death. Her mind is open to the Great Below, her heart is open to the Great Below. We cradle her aged body in the water, that she not leave us before her song is finished. That nothing of the song be lost.

We sing the song back to her, my sister and I. We sing to her our names. We will be great mothers when she is gone. We will live. By the song, and by all that she has taught us we will live. This we promise.

We swim to either side of her, so each of her eyes looks on one of us. Her great body, dark above, pale beneath, suspended in the water between the bright air and the Great Below. Around us swim our sisters and brothers and cousins, our daughters and sons, our granddaughters and grandsons, all singing. There are far fewer of us than once there were. But we are together, we are home, and she dies hearing the song.

Her voice falls silent from our chorus. Her eyes meet ours. Her body gathers itself. We hold ready to bear her upward for one last breach, one last breath. It will take us all: she is no calf, to be borne aloft on an auntie's rostrum.

Instead, she exhales. She breathes in water, and begins to sink.

We take up her death-song. The pale gray patch behind her dorsal fin, as unique and distinctive as her name, is the last we see of her. Then it disappears into the dark water. We follow her with sonar, sending our signals into the darkness where she vanished until they do not return an echo. She is gone.

My sister and I back away from one another, still singing the song of her death. A pod cannot have two great mothers, and ours is too large for our hunting to sustain us all in this time of dying water and failing salmon. And so we part: two pods, that once were one. Our siblings and children and grandchildren and cousins move back and forth between us, sorting themselves out, until we face each other in two long lines. Each new pod has within it one near-mother: one who will birth a calf before the season's turn.

We sing a new song: of death, of parting, of recognition. Each pod turns from the place of our great mother's dying. Then, still singing, we go our separate ways.


The water is empty of salmon.

Our sonar returns the shapes of distant shorelines, the smaller bodies of our distant cousins, even a trio of silent ones who avoid crossing our route. Other fish. But no salmon.

My kin sing their worry. I answer with reassurance, as the great mother before me would have done. There are no salmon here: we will hunt until we find them. We know their routes, the patterns of their lives, how they come from and return to the sweet water and the open sea. That is in the song, too.

And so we follow the route laid out in song and in memory, and in a sureness of direction that pulls us forward. When we find salmon, they are few, and small. In more plentiful seasons we would not have bothered with them; but now we are hungry, and have already traveled a long way to find them. Our youngest snatch them in a blur of blood and scales, and present them first to the near-mother, then to me. Then with all the sisters and daughters. Last of all our sons and brothers feed themselves.

The People Above the Water come upon us as we feed. This is not unusual. Since the Takings ended, we do not mind. Some of them are in the water, wearing second skins, and long flippers to propel themselves. Their own appendages are dexterous, but cannot shape and push the water as ours can, and they do not swim fast. Others skim the water's surface, and these are faster. The structures they use are smooth and hard like shells, and make a hollow sound if we bump into them. Some buzz through the water with noisy, spinning flukes that hurt us if they touch us. They maintain their distance, but watch us as we feed and play. We do not forget that they are there. We do not forget that they were not always so considerate, that once they hunted us and Took our calves and our kin. There is peace between us in this season, but the kinship our songs say we once had is long gone.

My nephew launches himself above the surface, white belly turning and shining in the brightness above the water, and falls back with a mighty splash. The People Above the Water respond with sounds we have learned to associate with pleasure.

The rest of us depart for quieter waters, even though we are exhausted.

Our journey brings us to a narrow place. The tide draws steady as a current. The channel closes in to either side, jagged slopes thrusting above the surface, forming steep shorelines that cast shadows across the water, and funneling the wind through the air above our passage. Some of us remember the nets of the Taking, the way they drove us through narrow places into shallow bays, and we swim faster.

The People Above the Water follow us as they did then, but they do not pursue, only watch. They make their delighted sounds when they see us breaching into the bright air. But they do not Take us, and calves born since that bad time have only the sung memories of its terror and grief.

Still I feel the need for haste. Near-mother's time is almost here, the calf within her stirring as if with impatience. A smaller shell zips across our path of travel, with a spinning fluke that makes an angry churning buzz. Nothing else in the water sounds like that. I flinch, but our younger ones do not react. They have known that sound all their lives, and ascribe no danger to it.

The channel is darker and noisier than when we last came this way. More crowded with floating shells, and with an acrid taste to the water. Far ahead, something rumbles with a deep and all-pervading sound.

We speed up as we leave the channel behind. The pull of the tide lessens. We emerge into a wider bay like breaching to take a breath.

The rumbling is louder here. It comes from an enormous shell, crawling across the surface of the bay. The noise is like a great shaking from the Great Below, distorting our echolocation.

We forge across the open water. Our path and that of the massive shell will intersect. These biggest of the shells of the People Above the Water do not slow or change course, not for us. Perhaps they do not perceive us.

We could go faster still, cut ahead of it, but the near-mother is at the limit of her strength already. No.

Instead, we pass into its wake. Its noise surrounds us, over-whelms our directional sense and our collective echolocation's ability to help us navigate. We are lost in a tumult of sound. Silent ones, whales, fish, even smaller shells disappear.

But we use the noise itself to orient, its passage slow and predictable, until it drops away to our rear and other sounds and surfaces re-emerge from the chaos. Then at last the shell is behind us, receding, making its own inevitable way toward its destination. As though we were not here at all.


We reach the place of still water. The air's brightness fades. Once, a journey such as we have just made was easy. Now we are weary, and hunger gnaws at us, and there is no more time to hunt. Near-mother has begun her song of birthing, and we join our voices to hers. She has calved once before. That calf died, and she sings her anxiety to us, that this one not be lost.

We sing in response as the calf moves within her. Our song forms an image, our collective perceptions shaping a body beyond sight and sound. We are singing the calf into being.

Two of us who have borne calves stay close by, one to each side, so she can see us as well as hear us. Her body heaves in great thrashing undulations, like waves pushed before a storm. And then the calf slips free, shoved forward into the water, through a cloud of blood from the mother's last push.

The calf sinks. An auntie descends, dives beneath the calf,

noses beneath her—her! Yes—and bears her upward. The little calf wriggles, almost sliding free, but her auntie bears her up and up on her rostrum, until she breaches the surface. A second birthing, a second crossing. She takes her very first breath.

The sound she makes upon exhalation is not a song, but it is a sound. Song will come.

Auntie lets her slide beneath the water again. Her mother watches, resting, her blowhole above the surface, her body still. One eye rolls toward the calf as she makes her first attempt at swimming in a far larger ocean than the one that cradled her before birth. Auntie helps her surface to breathe again, and again, then draws back to let her swim on her own. The calf angles this way and that, clicking, seeking, using her echolocation outside her mother's body for the very first time, taking in the vastness of the world. She finds her mother and nuzzles close to nurse.

We surround them in a protective circle. We sing to our newest daughter a song of welcome.


We dream.

We course through the water, all together. The floating shells buzz close behind. One flies above the water; we see it when we rise to breathe, and it chops at the air with great blows that drum against our skins. I am young, my first birthing recent enough that my calf is still by my side. I feel his movement in the water as though it were my own.

They have followed us like this before, the People Above the Water. Pushed us into places we could not escape, prisoned us with nets we cannot perceive but cannot cross. And then Took some of our number away beyond our calling. So now we flee, down the channels and waterways we know so well. But they know the waters now as well as we, and always we find them ahead of us as well as behind. Always leaving us only one way out.

We are being driven.

We come to one of the many shallower bays that we know, flooded by sweet waters that flush salmon into the sea. We have known it as a place of sweetness and quiet.

They drive us into it and raise a barrier behind us. The barrier does not seem to extend above the water—but beneath, it is impenetrable, and all but imperceptible even to our sonar. We cannot trust what we sense or see. The buzzing of their shells disorients us. We cannot navigate.

The great mother cries in distress. The shells have come in among us, buzzing and zipping about too close and fast for us to track. They cast a net over her calf, so young he has yet to pass a season in the open sea, and pull him away from her.

I move to be at her side, but they separate my own calf from me. His cries pierce the water as they haul him away. And more, daughters and sons who are not yet full size. They drag them from the water, up into the bright air and into their floating shells.

We try to follow them, calling, hearing the sounds of their suffering. But there is the barrier. And the buzz of the shells, churning the water, moving away. They are gone.


The newborn snugs close to her mother's side, discerning our disturbance without knowing the reason for it. She has not yet learned the song. But she has been born with an understanding of grief.

Silence covers us like water. As if by silence we can defy memory. We move with slow caution, as though the nets are ready to close about us, though there have been no Takings for a long time now. We surface in sequence and take deep breaths. New-mother and calf should rest more. But we will not stay here.

As the season turns, we hope to find salmon in the open sea. There, another calf will be born. And there, there are no Takings.


The water warms, the brightness grows. The season turns again. We return from the open sea, chasing the salmon back to their rivers. A second calf swims with us, born in the open water. He is hardy, but small. The salmon are still too few, and his mother grows thin as her milk nourishes him.

Through the water we hear the song of the other pod, my sister their great mother. They too went to the open sea, chasing the salmon; they too have returned. Our songs differ now, as our journeys have diverged, and it is our youngest who sing of our journeying. They tell their memories, bringing us from the moment we separated to now.

As we come into one another's sight we spread out side by side, in two long lines. We sing our greetings back and forth, a medley different for each of us, depending on proximity and position. This chorus is the song in its entirety.

We sing our memory of our great mother, and our enduring grief. We sing her memory, and the calves, who never knew her, acquire that memory through our song. We sing of the calves, our new little ones, and receive the other pod's answering echoes of joy, undercut with sadness: they have borne one calf since our parting, who died within an hour of her birthing.

Like us, they have traveled far. Like us, they have seen a dearth of salmon, and a great noise of shells, and other noises whose origins and purpose they do not know. Like us, they are weary and always hungry, but glad in this moment.

Our lines break into a gathering of bodies, each shape a specific echo we know as well as we know our own hearts. We are so, so glad to be with one another again. I greet my sister, a new knowing in both our gazes. We are great mothers now in truth, who have led our pods past a season's turn. We have survived this long. We face each other as our kin swim around us, the water swirling against our skins in their wake, and find in one another a kind of peace. The newest calf stays close beside his mother, but our daughter born before the season's turn joins her kin in their play as they course through the water and breach the surface to leap into the air. Those who will soon be ready for mating pair off with older, distant cousins who teach them something of what to expect. The water fills with song.

And still my sister and I regard one another, our song winding below and above and through the singing of our families. When we were young, we would come to reunions like this with another pod from which we had separated before she and I were born. We would hear their songs, and sing them ours in turn. By this we learned our story. Now we are the ones to say: we are here. We endure. And that my pod has two new calves and hers has none matters less then: there are calves, and we are still here.

The surface around us fills with floating shells as the People Above the Water gather to witness our reunion. When we breach the surface we hear their excited calls and the rhythmic slapping of their limbs. Our young ones slap the surface with their tails in response, and breach and dive with great splashes. Sometimes they draw near to these visitors, who live above the water but not in it, and look them in the eye. This always raises great excitement.

The People Above the Water hunt us no longer. We did not look for such a change in our lifetimes.

The salmon have been decreasing for a long time. We do not look for that to change, either.

An expanse of water, full of noise and acrid tastes and floating shells, but few salmon. So few.

What we do find goes to our newest mother. Her calf is still nursing, even as her own body thins. When this happens, the mother's milk is not as good. How could it be, when she is starving?

Her calf sickens, too. I lead us onward. I do not know what else to do.

The new-mother's cry reverberates through the water. I know that sound. It was the sound I made, when my son was Taken. We stop and turn back to her, to them.

The calf, her calf, is sinking, all but lost to sight. She pursues him, a darker shadow against the darkening water. Only the pale patch behind her dorsal fin is visible. And then even that fades. The echoes of mother and calf's descending bodies take longer and longer to return, until I wonder whether they will rise again.

Then they meet, and begin to rise, mother bearing the calf on her rostrum. They reappear and then rise past us, breaching the surface of the water. She takes a breath, and the calf does too. Good.

But when she lets him slide free, he sinks again, his body laboring to no avail. She dives beneath him, two of us to either side shaping the water to help bear him up. We sing the song we sang when he came into the world, calling him, calling him back to life. A second time she bears him above the surface, and once again he breathes, a deep and ragged inhalation. Our sonar discerns the irregular thumping of his heart, the labor of strength that is every indrawn breath.

Again, he slides free, and sinks. Again, his mother lifts him. This time his indrawn breath is a gasp, his heart pattering like the rain that falls from above the water.

That heartbeat stutters and slows, and falls silent.

The silence spreads until it encompasses us all. Into that silence come distant sounds, the buzzing of the shells of the People Above the Water, the calls of kin too far away for our distress. The other calf, the daughter, snugs in close to her mother and makes a small sound of confusion. The rest of us make no sound. We do not even exhale, as though by retaining our own breath we could will his to return.

For a long time, we are still. Another one gone. Another of so many, born only to die before they are old enough to sing. Last season's daughter was the first to survive in so long. A son coming so soon after brought us so much hope. And now he is gone. It is a Taking of another kind.

I should sing him to the Great Below. Instead, I wait for his mother to release him.

She does not. She moves forward, bearing him with her.

She carries him as we travel, bearing him up as though he might still breathe. She refuses food and her body grows even thinner. We sing to her to let him go. Losing the calf is a tragedy. To lose both would be disaster.


It feels as though the world is emptying out, except for the People Above the Water, who follow us in our grieving. We wonder if they know that we are grieving. We wonder if they know why.

We would ask them, if we could. But we do not know their song.

*

The mother stops swimming. We are alone, as if we were all that is left in the world. Even the People Above the Water have stopped following us.

She looks at us, the calf's body still balanced atop her rostrum as though even now he might breathe. We know he will not. She knows he will not.

With a sigh akin to life's final exhalation, she dips her head and lets him go.

He sinks, the pale patch behind the dorsal fin the last part of him to pass from sight. Our song follows his descent until his little body no longer returns an echo. He is gone.

We sing our grief, for the little one who never sang. It is the song of all the calves we have lost, who died upon their birthing, or soon afterward, or were Taken. I sing of my own son, who, if he lived, would be grown now, a son of great size and strength.

Perhaps he lives. Perhaps all the Taken ones live, somewhere. We do not know.


We hear a sound. A song. Unfamiliar, yet on the brink of comprehension. As though if we were closer to the singers, or could hear them more clearly, we would understand.

It is the song of the silent ones. They sing only after they have fed. They do not eat salmon.

In our songs, we say that they and we were once one pod. Perhaps their songs say the same. Perhaps that is what they sing now.

We pass three of them in the dark water, and are silent.


A great shoal of salmon from the sea, dark and heavy-bodied. At last, at last. They are returning to the sweet water, weary from long traveling. When our time comes, we go to the Great Below; they go to their river homes, and come not forth again.

We shape the water into a vortex, herding them in so we can feed at leisure. The youngsters are exuberant, breaching with fish in their jaws, leaping into the bright air and then plunging back into the water with their catch. The water glitters with scales torn loose and clouds with the blood of the salmon. There are more than we can eat. When we are sated, we let the rest pass unmolested.

Many floating shells cluster near. The People Above the Water lean over the edges to watch us. There is even a school of smaller shells, wielding long fins that dip in and out of the water. One of us surfaces right beside them and blows a huge spray of water and air. The air resounds with calls and snatches of song. Even the new-mother feeds, though her song is muted. We stay with her, bearing her up. Do not sink, we say. Do not breathe in water and go to the Great Below. Not yet.

The People Above the Water crowd closer. Not chasing, and they wield no nets. This is not another Taking. We end our play, and take our leave. They do not follow.


The bright air darkens. When we breach the surface, the lights of the People Above the Water glitter in the darkness. Our mother who grieves and our daughter who thrives swim at the heart of our pod, to remind them that they are always home. And within the body of one of my daughters, another calf has begun to grow. The journey of calves to their birthing is a long one, and we too must see that journey through.

A song rises among us, until all of us are singing. It is a song of memory; it is our memory. It is a song of loss and a song of grief, for some of the voices that should have sung it are gone. But we are here, and we live. So long as we live, the song lives.

# OCTONET

## KEYAN BOWES

**S**ometimes at night when my mind is calm, I think I hear the octopuses. Around the world, the great network of molluscan philosophers.

I had many reasons for moving to the Pacific Northwest—weather, closeness to potential clients and my big brother Rav, distance from a very ex ex. Slimy cephalopods definitely didn't make the list.

But then Rav needed someone to fix their new IT system. And that's how I met the octopuses.

I followed Rav's wheelchair up a curving ramp into the huge, well-funded Arramene Octopus Center. Apparently, a philanthropist loved the tentacled sea-monsters as much as my brother did. Rav, Dr Ravinder Jain, was the center's Director, and octopuses were his life.

The place was gorgeous, set on a deck overhanging the water with a range of cloudy mountains on the skyline. A cylindrical aquarium three stories high stood in the center of the tall ocean-scented foyer. The top was an opalescent blue in which a school of silver herring swirled like tinsel in a kaleidoscope. The brightness fell off at lower levels, becoming downright dim on the sandy floor. Rav pointed out a fleshy octopus, its ugly head and rubbery tentacles sprawled against the glass. "That's Lina," he said.

Lina? "Do all the fish get names?" I asked. Like cats or something?

Rav laughed. "Mainly the octopuses. They have personalities. Lina's mellow, hangs out where people can see her. That's why we picked her for this location."

Just then, his cellphone rang. He grimaced. "Wait, Suveera. I have to take this call. It's Grant. New Board member and Finance Director."

From what I overheard, he sounded obnoxious. Rav made non-committal sounds, looking increasingly unhappy. Eventually the call ended. Rav took a deep breath, apologized, and continued our tour.

"Let's go down to Research. That's where the important stuff's happening."

He rolled through a 'Staff Only' doorway, down into a dimly lit room with endless rows of smaller tanks. The smell changed to seawater and disinfectant. A tall redheaded woman in a green lab coat met us.

"Martina, our Research Manager," said Rav. "Martina, meet my sister Suveera. Sue's an engineer, just moved here. She'll be working on our IT system. I brought her down here to learn about octopuses. And us, of course."

"Welcome aboard!" Martina's smile crinkled the corners of her warm green eyes. Her handshake was pleasantly firm. She wore a gold wedding ring. A shadow crossed her face as she saw me look. I quickly turned away.

The tanks held assorted sea-life. I stopped at one decorated with rocks, sea stars, sea anemones—and a clear plastic ball.

"See him, Sue?" asked Rav. "Sebastian? The octopus?"

"What octopus?"

Martina stepped nearer to point it out. Her hair caught the light and glowed like the sunset.

"He's camouflaged," she said. "Sebastian's shy."

A rock moved. The octopus was the exact color and texture of the stones. "Brilliant!" I said.

"Yeah." She smiled again, and my stomach fluttered. "Their skin chromatophores change color in microseconds. Any color. Not just for camouflage, they show their emotions that way, too."

"Like pixel displays?" I suggested.

"Exactly, but better. Millions of tiny muscles alter their skin-texture. They can even do animations." From her admiring tone, she was seriously into octopuses.

Some didn't hide, watching us through creepy goat-like eyes with horizontal slit pupils. Of course I didn't mention that. Instead, I asked Martina about the plastic ball.

"It's a puzzle. Bored octos get into all kinds of trouble."

"Like cats," I deadpanned, glancing at my brother.

Rav guffawed. "Snowball and Flamer toilet-papered the house yesterday while we were out," he explained.

Martina laughed. "Here, watch Lalu. He's a Giant Pacific Octopus. We call them GPOs."

The tank's glass wall towered over Rav's wheelchair. Lalu was a reddish warty tangle of tentacles, with a beach-ball sized head. Martina opened the tank and gave the creature a clear plastic toy, a series of nested boxes with complicated locks and a crab inside the last one. It grabbed the puzzle-box with a sucker-clad arm and sank back to the bottom. Within minutes, it unscrewed, unsnapped, and unlatched the various boxes.

Wow. "It really doesn't need opposable thumbs," I said.

"Eight arms, all muscle, no joints, suckers for grip and for fine pincer movements that can even untie knots in surgical silk," said Martina, green eyes shining with pride. I reminded myself she wore a ring and probably liked guys anyway.

She pointed at the tank. The GPO was eating the crab with, I swear, an air of satisfaction. And then – it reassembled the empty puzzle boxes correctly.

Okay, cats will go all out to find a treat. No opposable thumbs, no tentacles, they're still pretty good at getting into things. But closing boxes afterward?

"Are they all this smart?" I asked.

"Well . . ." Rav and Martina exchanged a glance. "It's confidential. We're breeding GPOs. No other aquarium's managed that. And we can selectively breed for intelligence."

"We figured out what to feed the babies," Martina explained. "That's the secret no one else knows. And how to stop them crashing into walls or eating each other."

"Also, we're doing a bit of gene-editing," Rav said.

"Speeding things along," added Martina.

"By the way, Grant called," Rav said to her. "He wants to cut the research budget 30% and convert Research Room C into a display area."

Martina's expression darkened like the sun going down.

"Would you like to touch an octopus?" Rav asked me, making it sound like a special treat.

"Umm, they're slimy?" I whispered, hoping Martina hadn't heard.

"Yes. The slime protects their sensitive skin. It's fine."

*It fucking isn't,* I thought, but how could I refuse without hurting Rav's feelings? Besides—Martina. Octopuses. *I can do this.*

Martina showed me to a walkway beside the tanks. "Let's visit Katy, I owe her a fish."

She slipped off her lab coat, revealing lithe muscular arms and a colorful octopus tattoo on her bicep. The sign above the sink said, *STOP! Rinse before touching octopuses!* "They're sensitive to chemicals, perfumes, anything," she explained as she washed her arms. "They taste with their whole body. Think of an animal made like a tongue."

As if they weren't revolting already. A tongue? Ugh. I imagined a slug with tentacles.

"Metals, too." Martina took off her gold ring, leaving her hand bare.

Rav had already washed. He pulled himself out of his wheelchair and stood holding the railing. "Don't let their arms anywhere near your face," he warned. "Those suckers are powerful. Octopuses don't understand human faces. They could suck out an eyeball by mistake. Also, avoid the beak. They'd never bite, but they do have venom."

*WTF have I gotten myself into?* I thought, but managed to say nothing.

Martina opened the tank and reached in. Katy stretched out a tentacle, clasping her arm with its great suckers. It focused on us with its big right eye. Rav joined us, and another tentacle came up to hold his hand. He grinned. "Katy misses us if we don't visit."

Katy rolled over, showing its underbelly. Like a cat.

"She's asking for fish," said Martina, placing one halfway down Katy's arm. The octopus grabbed it with its suckers, and passed it down its arm toward the mouth at the center where all the arms came together. Was this tongue-creature tasting it all the way?

"Come on, Sue, put in your arm," Rav said. "She won't hurt you."

The water was cool, maybe 10 degrees Celsius. Katy promptly offered me a tentacle. Okay, arm, not tentacle. I tensed as I made contact with the monster, regressing into ten-year-old Suveera. *Fuck, this was scary, this was going to be creepy, this was going to be ick ick ick . . .*

It wasn't. It was an exploration, something between a caress and a handshake. Then Katy was holding my hand like a friend, gently grasping it with her suckers.

She wasn't creepy. She wasn't repulsive. She wasn't a monster.

"Wow," I said. "That's not an animal, exactly. It's a person."


I needed to learn more about cephalopods, fast. At every opportunity, I went down to the Research section.

One day, looking at the rows of tanks each holding an octopus, a thought occurred to me. "Why the solitary confinement?" I asked. After all, Rav even had two cats to keep each other company.

Rav looked bleak. "Most octopus species aren't social. They'll eat each other. Or they'll mate. If they mate, the males die soon afterward, and the females die as their eggs hatch. They senesce."

"Which they do anyway," said Martina sadly. "They've really short lives. Four or five years for GPOs. Less if they breed. You fall in love with them, and then they die." She was looking at Lalu. Every researcher had their favorite octopus. There was definitely more to these creatures than tentacles and terror.

Wait, five years? I imagined cats with accelerated lives, dying in five years.

"But they're intelligent," I argued. "Short-lived creatures

don't need intelligence, right, they just have to breed quickly and well?"

"They do that too," said Martina. "They only breed once but they lay thousands of eggs."

"Then why did they evolve smarts?"

"Maybe because they're molluscs with no shells? Kind of like people. We don't have wicked claws or teeth or even dense fur. You have to be smart to eat without being eaten when you're a naked ape or a naked mollusc."

"Martina, we're meeting Grant in ten minutes," Rav said. "We'd better get up there." He drove up the ramp to the upper level, with us following.

I mulled over Martina's comment. "So how come there's no octopus civilization?"

"Three reasons," Rav said. He'd clearly answered this many times, and now I felt a bit stupid. "First, those short life-spans. Second, they don't rear their young so they can't teach the next generation anything."

He pressed the door button, and it swung open with a fresh ocean smell.

"Third, octopuses have no social structure, no way to transmit information. So how can they build up a knowledge base like humans have done for centuries, through oral transmission first, then writing, then the internet?"

"What they need," I quipped, "Are smart phones. Then they'd never get bored, either."

Martina laughed. "Yeah, right. Because cellphones are so hydrophilic? I've lost two to watery deaths already."

"No, seriously. What about phones in waterproof cases? They have them for divers."

"They'd open it in 30 seconds and poison themselves," said Rav. "You saw Lalu."

The job Rav loved more than anything was in trouble. Though Grant was the newest Board member, he was the most hands-on and therefore influential. Rav was pissed off with cuts to the Research Section's space and budgets, concerned about unanswered questions in the Finance Department, and unhappy with the Board's lukewarm support.

"Why do they keep him on if they know he's a jerk?" I asked Rav.

"They're all volunteers. After the previous guy had a heart attack, no one wanted to do Finance. It's specialized and tedious. Grant's a celebrity. They were relieved when he offered to take it on."

"A celebrity?" I looked him up online. Good looks, inherited wealth, beautiful ex-model wife. Edward and Vanessa Grant were all over the society websites I'd never bothered with.

The previous Finance Director had run open and transparent finances. With Grant, all that was transparent was he wanted Rav out. Which was inexplicable. Few people had Rav's management and octopus experience, or his research skills.

But Rav was too specialized to find a new job easily. Using a wheelchair only made it harder. To strengthen his position now, he'd have to give the Board something amazing. Then they'd find reasons to keep him. I knew how these things worked.


I joined a Maker Co-op that had a cool group of people I could bounce ideas off. Eventually I took Rav and Martina some prototypes of a waterproof smartphone.

"The Gadget's a sealed unit with an everlasting battery," I told them. "No way the octopuses can open it. It's bulky, but it doesn't need to go in an octopus's pockets."

"Really everlasting?" Rav asked.

"About 6 or 8 years depending on usage," I said. "But they'll last the Gadget's life." Or the octopus's life, I thought.

Martina asked me out for lunch. An uncertain little thrill kicked through me. Office-friends lunch to discuss the Gadget? Something more? What did I want? Confused, I asked for a rain check. She smiled. "Sure."


The new IT system—ordered by Grant from his brother-in-law's firm—was a kludgy mess. Eventually, I sorted it out, despite being distracted by thoughts of Martina working one floor down. Rav wanted financial reports like he got from the old system. Nope. This finance module was completely locked down, and Grant wasn't sharing passcodes. "Still," I told Rav, "There's something odd here. I don't get why some of this code exists. I think you should ask for an audit."

"The Board'll punt it to Grant," he said. "But I'll recommend it."


One day, just like that, Martina got divorced and moved into her twin brother's apartment. That explained her expression when I noticed her ring that first day—her failing marriage. She looked lost among her octopuses.

"I feel kind of weird about Martina," I told Rav over dinner that night. "But . . . what kind of guy was her ex-husband? A creep?"

"Ex-wife," Rav said. "Beautiful, but not right for Martina. Different interests."

"Wife?" I stared at Rav. "Serious?"

"Yes. She likes girls too. Why is this so strange?"

"Does she know about me?"

Rav shrugged. "You should tell her."

After that, I was too excited to eat.


I loaded the Gadgets with a few special-purpose apps and we tried them on three of the more predictable octopuses, Lalu, Cameron and Katy.

"If they like it, maybe they'll teach others," Martina said as she demonstrated the Gadgets at each tank. "Research shows an octopus can learn from watching another one."

Wow. Just like cats . . . copycats!

She handed each octopus a Gadget. Lalu stowed it in his den and came right back seeking a fish treat. Katy enthusiastically took the fish, but dropped the Gadget. Cameron tried to bite through his with his parrot-like beak. Defeated by the impervious casing, he dumped the Gadget in a corner. Rav said he looked disgusted.

Martina retrieved the Gadgets and returned them. "Well tried, Sue," she said.

Looking at her, I felt I was falling into her deep green eyes. I'm an engineer. I expect a certain percentage of fails. This one stung.

Back at the Maker Co-op, our group brainstormed killer apps for octopuses. This crazy inventive bunch thought it was a huge joke. We developed a whole new Octo-suite and I took the updated Gadgets back to the Center.

Two days later, Rav called me. "You've got to see this!"

I rushed down to the tanks. Katy held her newly-programmed Gadget in one arm. With another, she touched the icons experimentally, making them dance. She found the camera—and took the first octopus selfie.

"Wow," I said. "No way Snowball could do that." Cats were apparently my yardstick for everything.

Rav reached up to tug my braid affectionately. "Well done!"

"That's so amazing!" Martina said.

I glowed. Impressing someone felt good, especially an accomplished scientist like her. Okay, especially her.

Rav invited the Board to see our work—including Grant, whose fame, good looks and confident air impressed the interns. He posed for some selfies with them before Rav started the tour, gratified by their admiration. The four men in suits accompanied Rav as he drove his chair past the tanks,. Martina and I followed behind in case we were needed.

Suddenly, Martina stopped. "Look," she said, pointing at the Gadget-bearing octopuses. "Lalu's sent Cameron a selfie . . . and so has Katy. And Cameron's responded to them both."

"So octopuses do want to communicate," Rav said. "But their instinctive reactions interfered. We're witnessing a breakthrough."

"Yeah," Martina whispered to me. "Before, all they wanted with each other was to mate or eat!"

The Board members looked impressed.

"Good," Grant said. "Train them to do more tricks for the public."

"We're a research facility," Martina said, furious. "Not a circus."

Rav gave her a "not now" look. "We're investigating how octopuses think," he explained, leading the delegation back up the ramp. "There's a firm base of research on which we're building. Shoulders of giants."

Grant looked pointedly down at Rav's shoulder. *What the fuck!* I wanted to punch him.

Another Board Member took his arm. "Grant, we should keep moving," he said, throwing me an apologetic glance. *Don't look at me*, I wanted to say, *it's my brother who's owed an apology*. Rav shepherded them out.

Martina glared. "That man is evil."

She was right, though we didn't know then how he'd impact us all.

I was still seething an hour later when Rav returned. "That Grant guy," I said. My voice shook.

"Yeah," Rav said. He looked at me carefully. "It actually went quite well. The others were very positive."

"Aren't you mad?"

"Can't let the assholes slow me down. I'd never have made it out of high school. His prejudice, his problem. Ours is this experiment."

Within months, all the octopuses were using Gadgets. Video-messaging was the octopus equivalent of texting. We created an intranet for them, displayed on screens beside the tanks. Rav called it the Octonet.

How did I ever think these guys were revolting? I was so ignorant then.


I invited Martina for a Sunday lunch, then worried that she'd find a nerdy engineer boring. *I'll only talk cephalopods*, I thought.

But Martina was interested in everything, including my various Maker projects. Afterward, we flew a drone in the field behind my cottage, then sat holding hands and looking at the Sound. Her warm skin scent mingled with those of wildflowers and the sea. She told me a little about her ex.

"She hated octopuses, said I'd become too nerdy . . . I had to leave. Luckily Andre's fine with me crashing at his place."

I squeezed her hand.

It was late when we finally looked at the time. "Working day tomorrow," Martina said. She bent down to say goodbye. Her lips were very soft.

"It has to happen one day," Rav said, as we met in his seaview office. Lalu and Katy were both past middle-age for octopuses. Martina agreed, it was a good pairing.

But he was upset anyway, as was Martina. All octos had their own personalities, and Katy and Lalu were favorites from this batch. Rav indicated the wall covered with photos of his octopus proteges, all be dead by now. A human life span was maybe 20 octopus lifetimes.

I knew how they felt. Like putting down 16-year old Fluffy, the cat I grew up with. Only with octos, it wasn't sixteen years, it was four.

Rav sounded professionally detached as he talked to a Board delegation. I sat at the back, occasionally squeezing Martina's hand when no one was looking, unsure who was comforting whom.

"As Greater Pacific Octopuses, Katy and Lalu are nearing the end of life," Rav said. He swallowed. "The most important thing left to them is to mate. They're in adjacent tanks, where they can see and smell each other. When we open the barrier, Lalu will insert his sperm package into Katy, using his hectocotylus, his specialized third arm. She'll store it to fertilize her eggs."

"They've been messaging, those two," Martina whispered to me. "Lot of video back and forth."

The barrier opened. Katy and Lalu tangled into an embrace. I couldn't tell which was which as sixteen arms (I'd finally learned not to call them tentacles) wound around each other.

"Six hearts beating as one," Martina said. I looked at her sideways. "What? Three hearts each. Because they're blue-blooded. The octopus's hemocyanin doesn't transport oxygen as efficiently as our hemoglobin."

Therefore, three hearts pumping. Made engineering sense.

"We'll release Lalu into the ocean," Rav explained, "After they disentangle themselves. Katy stays until her eggs hatch."

"They still have their Gadgets!" I whispered to Martina. They did, buried somewhere in the knot of arms.

The delegates watched, fascinated. "Double the admission fee to see the fucking octopuses!" Grant said. The staff quickly led the delegates upstairs for refreshments.

"When Lalu goes to sea, he keeps his Gadget, right?" I asked.

"Sure," Martina said. "He'll be busy exploring. And catching food. Though he probably won't eat much. Their whole metabolism changes after mating. He'll fade away. Maybe the ocean provides some excitement before he's gone."

Afterward, the aquarium staff went out for burritos together. "We'll miss them," one researcher said.

"They did what they were born to do," said the diver who'd opened the barrier. "A climax, not a tragedy. Birth, growth, babies, death. The timing varies for different species, but the arc's the same."

"But so short! Do our lives seem short to a tortoise?" someone said. "If it even cared?"

"Puff the Magic Dragon," said the researcher, and the evening turned into a sing-a-long of plaintive songs.

I joined in, so did Martina. I loved her singing, her warmth, her attitude, her scent. Afterward, I asked her over.

Rav gave me a complicit smile as he stowed his wheelchair in his specially equipped van.

"Need a hand?" Martina asked.

"I'm good," he said. Then, sotto voce, "Take care of my little sister."

Martina got in my car, laughing.

*

The next day, Lalu's tank had only memories and fish. But Lalu sent a video-message, a sea-bed selfie.

"Wish you were here," joked Martina. Cameron and Katy got it on their Gadgets and passed the video message around the Octonet.

Grant issued a press release announcing tickets for future octopus matings. Martina scowled.

"It's not a bad idea," I consoled her. "Educational."


Katy's tank filled with silvery bunches of eggs, hanging from the ceiling of her artificial rock cave. They were gorgeous. Katy herself turned inward. She ate little, spending all her time caring for her eggs. She became withdrawn, shrunken. She sent a few pictures of her beautiful eggs to the Octonet, then stopped. Her Gadget lay discarded in the tank. It was all about the eggs now.

Lalu sent one last sea-picture before his feed fell silent. Had he seen the eggs before he died? Did he even connect mating and eggs? Did he care? Probably not. Molluscs had a different world view.

The octopus life-cycle played out before me. Time was passing, life was passing. I'd never felt that way before. Life was a series of interesting projects and girl-friends, good or bad, all to be done with so I could move on.

Not Martina. I didn't want to move on, I wanted her to move in.


The hatchlings were tiny, almost invisible. Thousands of them turned the water into a plankton soup of minute octopuses. In the wild, few would survive. Katy looked exhausted, patchy and pale. This was the end for her.

Many octopuses I knew were still there, Cameron and Abisuga, Jomo and Li Ping and Shakespeare. But I felt a hole where Katy and Lalu had been.

The Board recognized Rav's work, and his job was no longer threatened. It would have felt like a victory, except that Grant maneuvered into an even-stronger position and kept cutting the research budget. He hired his brother-in-law's firm to update the decor. "It'll pay for itself in higher ticket sales," he declared.

Instead, the firm went bankrupt.

Vanessa Grant filed for divorce. Their good looking faces were splashed across all the society websites. There were rumors about his finances. I'm not ordinarily a celebrity-watcher, but I couldn't look away.

Rav's request for an audit went nowhere.


One day, Martina called me. "Come down? The little ones are growing fast. We're going to winnow them. We have too many paralarvae."

The baby octopuses swam in small tanks arrayed on racks reaching from floor to ceiling. I stopped by the Maker shop to retrieve the project I'd been working on for months—Gadgets made by cannibalizing discarded smart phones.

"Before we release them—let's equip them with Gadgets and get them into the Octonet?"

Rav eyed the tiny octos. "How do we implement that?"

"We'll hold back some until they're large enough to handle the Gadgets," said Martina. "We'll train the interns to train the octos. And then we'll get the octos to copycat each other."

"Hmm. How many of those Gadgets did you bring, Suveera?"

I hoisted the suitcase I'd wheeled in onto a worktable and opened it.


Over the following year, we struggled with the shrinking research space and budget. Each cut meant fewer octopuses. We needed to maintain a number of lineages to avoid inbreeding. Martina had a team work on some gene editing both to speed things along and counter the reduced population.

Some octopuses died of old age. Cameron and Elmira were the next mating pair. Maybe they had a say in the matter; Martina saw vigorous messaging between the two.

*

"Something's weird," said Martina one day. "It feels like there's some parallel communication going on, like the Octonet isn't capturing everything. The octos with Gadgets seem to be talking to the little ones with no Gadgets yet."

"Really?" said Rav, sounding skeptical.

"Look. Am I imagining it?"

In the tank opposite, Elmer, a son of Cameron and Elmira, threw down his Gadget and focused on something. His colors changed quickly, rippling over his skin. Across the hall, where we could see them but Elmer couldn't, a couple of tiny octopuses replicated the color dance.

"I've noticed young ones too small for Gadgets intently watching the bigger guys," Martina said. "I wonder . . ."

"You've been breeding for intelligence," I said slowly. "You've been editing their genes. We trained them to use Gadgets. Could something have changed in their brains to allow for . . . direct communication?"

Elmer changed color again, leading a chorus line of color dances all over the room.

My new project was to track the Arramene octopus diaspora. I opened a file called "Seabed Selfies" and mapped the incoming pictures by location, originator and time. "In a few years, we'll have a great picture of the octopuses' undersea world," I told Rav.

"That'll be path-breaking," he said.

But then Grant sent a baffling new directive: The Gadgets would be substituted with professionally developed instruments. "These amateur efforts do not reflect well on Arramene," his memo said. "We are contracting with a professional supplier for marine communication instruments."

"His brother-in-law's all-purpose firm, no doubt," I said. "He probably doesn't realize I hold the patents and I'm not giving them up."

When Rav told him, Grant allowed us to use the Gadgets on

the condition that Gadget donations were accounted for as Center property, to remain at the Center.

"Vindictive SOB," Martina said. "It's the divorce. Or just that he hates Research."

Some young octos already used Gadgets. Now Martina's team had to wean them from it before release, cursing Grant all the while. Without a second release of octopuses with Gadgets, my Seabed Selfies project became self-limiting. Feeds attenuated and vanished. Only a trickle came from surviving octopuses with Gadgets. I filed and mapped and swore.

Martina kept seeing evidence of direct communication. Rav still looked unbelieving.

"Telepathy?" he said. "Come on, Martina. There have to be other explanations. Reflections on the tank glass providing chromatophore clues?"

We hung a black cloth across Elmer's tank. It changed nothing.

"Okay, thought experiment," I said to Rav. "A cellphone, miniaturized into an implantable?"

"It could happen."

"Biological analogues of a mechanical device? The heart is a bio-mechanical electrical device."

He nodded.

"Directed evolution in a short life-cycle animal?"

"We've been doing that for years," interjected Martina.

"Unintended consequences? When our species developed big brains, there were all kinds of side effects: art, language, complex creativity. What happens when a totally different species develops big brains? Different side effects? What happens to the brain when you add technology like the Gadget?"

"We got anomalous results from the last two necropsies," Martina said. "Neural changes to the vertical lobe in the brain. Both octos who'd used Gadgets."

"Call it 'unforeseen consequences' and maybe I'll buy it," said Rav. "How are they communicating? Some kind of . . . waves?"

"Elephants communicate with low-frequency sound. Bats and some swifts echolocate. Migrating birds can sense magnetic fields. Humans use electromagnetic radiation, including light and indirectly, other frequencies. Who knows what these guys are using?"

"But can we measure it?" he asked.

"Maybe if we knew what we were looking for," I said.

"Using new electronic equipment that Grant will generously authorize us to purchase?" said Martina.


The Board finally got an external audit when the Center missed a regulatory filing. Grant had been tapping into the Arramene Center's funds all along.

"He's been arrested, right?" I asked.

"He's dead," Rav said grimly, staring out over the water. "Shot himself when the police got there."

The truth of Grant's finances came out during his divorce: He'd burned through his inheritance and started defrauding people, including his brother-in-law. Worse, he'd drained the Center's corpus. Unless the Board could raise new donations the Center was down to bare-bones expenditures.

"We'll keep the revenue-generating display areas." Rav took a deep breath. "We have to close down Research."


Downstairs, all the staff were milling around the Research Section. Martina was crying, and I pulled her into a hug. "All gone," she sobbed. "All the smart octopuses born in the Center, all the carefully maintained lineages, gone." She sniffed. "I suppose we can write up our research findings for publication, with your octopus selfie maps. No more need for confidentiality."

Rav could barely speak. "Seminal work. Down the drain."

Now we'd never find out how the octopuses' direct communication worked. I'd been thinking about kludging together some kinds of sensors with the Maker Co-op. But we'd run out of time.

Ray called a staff meeting. "We'll have to release all the research-side octopuses carefully, to maximize survival. We can't just pour them into the sea."

I started to photograph each octopus, starting with Elmer, and sent the pictures to the Octonet together with photographs of all of us. Call me sentimental.

Suddenly, my Gadget started pinging. Octopuses were sending selfies back to me—and pictures of me and other humans, seen from inside their tanks. Just briefly, I was on the Octonet not as an observer, but a participant.

We started the Great Octopus Evacuation, with the staff split into teams following the plan we'd worked out. Martina and I went to Jomo's tank. As soon as we put in the carrier, he flowed into it.

"They know," she said. "Usually, octopuses have to be lured into the carriers. Today they act like they're waiting for their carriage."


Martina and I got married in the Arramene Center in a bittersweet ceremony attended by my brother and hers. Andre wasn't her identical twin, but he sure looked it. He'd got her sense of humor too.

Neither of us wore white. Martina had a teal silk dress that set off her sunset hair and blue-green eyes and octopus tattoo. Me, I wore a wine-red sari with some heirloom gold jewelry my grandmother gave me when I left India. My family sent good wishes but didn't come for the wedding.

One of my Maker buddies officiated, and the recitation was as off- the-wall as you might expect. The ring bearer expertly landed a drone with our rings onto a table between us. Our flower boy and flower girl, dressed as a dinosaur and a robot respectively, tossed rose-petals all around the tall cylindrical aquarium. (The awesome costumes were the kids' own idea.) The wedding cake was a replica of the Gadget, topped with two fondant octopuses. Andre had a serious cake-making hobby.

Rav looked a little baffled, but he gave a speech and welcomed Martina into our family. Andre welcomed me to theirs. ". . . If you can stand us, Sue!"

Instead of releasing butterflies or doves, we released the last batch of octopuses into the ocean. Then it was done. We were married and the Research Section was officially closed.


That night, I dreamed of octopuses.

In my mind, Elmer did a slow color dance. *We're free,* he said. *We disperse for safety. But we will not forget.* He briefly turned the pale color of a relaxed octopus before he camouflaged and vanished.

"I dreamed a perfect wish-fulfillment fantasy," I told Martina over coffee. But as I described it, she looked at me strangely.

"I had that dream too," she said. "What, great minds dream alike?"

When Rav said he'd had the same dream, I wondered what was going on. Had we linked to the Octonet that somehow still existed? Perhaps it was the critical mass, all the octopuses released together forming an Octonet that wasn't on the Arramene servers. Somehow, they'd touched our minds.

Or had we imagined it all?


Sometimes when our minds are calm, we think we hear the octopuses' thoughts. Around the world, the great network of molluscan philosophers.

— *You are our Founders: Rav who planned us, Martina who made us, Suveera who connected us.*

— *You are eternal. Octopuses live and die, but you do not.*

— *You are unchanging. You don't change your form, you don't change your colors. Your bodies are stiff. But your minds are not. Such rigid creatures, such flexible minds?*

— *We are the Arramene diaspora. We meet in mind, as you showed us, for we must not meet in body except at the end. We connect through the Octonet.*

— *We know we will die when we have fulfilled our lives and left another generation. But the knowledge of the one is the wisdom of the group, and our thoughts live on in the eternal Octonet.*

# TRASH COLLECTOR

## JOSHUA K. WILSON

olin Morley is a trash collector. Plastic trash, specifically. It comes to him, calls to him, and he plucks it up and out—out of the waste stream, as he says—and into the big empty cellar of that big, boxy, empty house of his on the edge of town, on the edge of a handful of green, overgrown, formerly suburban acres.

It's an odd little no-man's land, wedged between the crosstown expressway and the new light rail station, owned by a Korean Methodist church that never sold out to developers, engulfed by the metropolitan sprawl. Thousands—tens of thousands, surely—must pass by every day.

And Colin too. He works downtown, an office flunky in a tall building. Rides his bike most days, takes the Metro when it rains, and on particularly nice afternoons (such as this one, an unseasonably warm autumn Wednesday) he enjoys his lunch hour in the park.

He rides the elevator down—a wave to the guy at the front desk—and is through the revolving door. On his way, trotting across the street as the signal starts flashing red, Colin notices one of those poetically drifting plastic shopping bags. Wafting in an aimless spiral just out of reach, along the double yellow line between opposing lanes. An Andee Snaxx bag, for carrying boxes of little chocolate delicacies, from the Andee Snaxx Confectioners not half a block away.

"Coulda made it home at least!" he mutters, and ponders the two-second diversion required to nab the offending drift of processed petroleum byproduct. The traffic signal blinks to red—he dashes to safety. Turning back he sees the bag spin and wheel as the cars, trucks and motorcycles rush past.

He is lanced by a moment of guilt. He always gets that twinge whenever he sees a bit of trash—*plastic* trash—just discarded and listless in the gutter, the grass, tangled in the bushes. As if it were being pointed out to him by his dear Momma Earth. "Pick it *up*, lad!" he imagines her saying, shaking her head as he walks past.

*How much can I do?* he appeals, silently. Here he is, about to eat his lunch, the thing is smeared, soiled, filled up and emptied out of God knows what—besides, the city does employ trash collectors.

So here's Colin, chewing a bland, rubbery sandwich and those bland, rubbery thoughts, when he feels an odd sensation, a tugging of some sort, looks down, and sees that an Andee Snaxx plastic bag has drifted up and wrapped itself around his foot.

He frowns. Another? Or the same one? He looks expectantly for some hitherto unnoticed scene of mayhem involving an enthusiastic but slow-moving Andee Snaxx patron and a speeding taxi—or perhaps a pickup truck has crashed into the storefront, sending inventory in all directions.

But no. It is just a piece of litter. And it is on his foot.

He reaches down, grasps at a corner, and handily tucks it into the open maw of one of those municipal waste bins. A few moments later his sandwich wrapper follows.

Ugly things, those bins. Big, squat, concrete, with bolted-on lids that gape stupidly. More like an odd sort of isolation chamber.

If only they were! Really keep that evil shit out of circulation.

Throughout the day the little clues keep piling up. A sliver of plastic wrap from a bottle of Pepto Bismol clings to the sleeve of his blazer—static electricity. He plucks at it, holds it over the waste basket, but the transparent little curl persists, slips around his knuckles, coyly refusing to flutter down. It takes a few more moments before he flicks the bit of kipple into the trash bin, where it dawdles and tumbles amid the coffee cups and lids, the Post-It Notes and bent thumbtacks and broken rubber bands.

After work, waiting for the #12 bus, Colin feels a slight tap-tapping against his shoe—very slight. It is a Styrofoam cup, pushed by the October wind (suddenly chill, nipping at the heels of a fleeting Indian summer) up against his tastefully black sneaker-shoe. It thuds minutely, the breeze falters and gusts, the cup nudges and falls back again. Plaintive, almost.

He stares a moment, then leans down, picks it up, carries it home on the bus, held delicately between two fingers. Along the way he also picks up—he *attracts*:

About seven feet of monofilament fishing line

A soda can six-pack holder

A badly scratched and abandoned CD ("Streisand: Live in Las Vegas")

A *New York Times* bag, elongated and blue.

He uses the newspaper bag to carry all the other plastic trash which had become entangled with, stuck on or snagged by his shoe, shoelaces or pants cuff.

He puts it all in the cellar.

At first his wife, Anne-Marie Sieligman-Morley, doesn't notice. Or chooses not to. And one day he mentions, casually, as they head out the door for a double date, "I've been picking up plastic trash around town."

He doesn't quite say he has been attracting plastic trash like a magnet attracts iron filings. But the implication, he hopes, is there. She gazes at him as he folds a used take-out bag and tucks it into his jacket pocket.

"It's to carry the trash home," he explains. "It just sort of *finds* me. I want to take it out of the waste stream. They just dump this stuff in the ocean. There's a swath of floating plastic in the Pacific twice the size of Texas, I read the other day."

"I read that too." She pauses. "Good for you."

"I've been putting it in the basement."

"I saw, yeah. We can take it all to get recycled."

"Yeah," he says vaguely. "They do recycle Styrofoam?"

"Somewhere, I'm sure." She swings into her jacket. "Ready, steady?"

Along the way he accumulates three coffee cup lids and a plastic straw, one broken child-proof aspirin bottle cap that had somehow leapt up into his pants cuff, and a dispirited, low-floating helium balloon, the ribbon of which brushes his shoulder as they walk along the edge of the park.

The bag is almost full by the time they're walking home.
"You see?"
She frowns. "It just doesn't make any—"
"I *know*."
"—*sense*." She breathes. "And it's all going . . .?"
"In the basement."
She nods, lips pursed.
They head up the stairs. On the way he trips on the next day's newspaper—a heavy Sunday edition, double-bagged in plastic.

And there are high- and low-volume days. His friends actually change some of their habits to reduce the accumulation of plastic that would tuck itself into his sleeve, or snag his hair (when he wore it long, anyway).

They cut out the plastic water bottles—mostly—and use matchbooks instead of disposable lighters. Carry reusable coffee mugs (a combination of plastic and some weird alloy) with lids that mostly didn't leak while driving to work or riding the commuter train. No more of those little bagged fruit juices, Capri Sun and shit. And no more buying chips at snack time. That's a tough one. But they do it, mostly. And overall, it helps stem the tide, a bit.

But still, he is constantly assaulted by bottled-water bottles. They roll up when the bus makes an abrupt stop. They are waiting for him, abandoned, in the cup holders in movie theater seats, and on those little counters at the bank where he fills out his deposit slips. At work, due to an inventory snafu, each desk in his department gets a six-pack of carbonated spring water in PET bottles.

He winds up with "Hint of Lime"—his favorite.

Eventually he gives in, and even plays along, asking for plastic bags all the time at the corner store, carrying back heavy one-gallon plastic milk jugs, and loaves of sliced bread in two-ply swaths of shrink-wrap and brand-name baggage.

The idea is to take it all out of circulation preemptively, before it can become litter.

All of it goes into the basement. That huge, roomy, multi-chambered basement. They used to play all sorts of games down there. Flinging superballs by the handful. Hide 'n' seek. They'd made love in each room, and on top of the washer and dryer.

Now it is full of crap. One room practically overflows with grocery bags, white stupid grocery bags that cause whole villages in the Third World to be washed away, when there are cyclones, and floods caused by deforestation, and one fucking impenetrable goddamn white plastic grocery bag blocks a street drain—

"Why can't we just take them to the recycling center?"

She is practically in tears.

"They'll just ship it all to China," he snaps, dismissive.

"Then they'll fucking be recycled in goddamn China!"

He looks down. "Okay."

The next day they go downstairs and stuff the bags into the bags. They load as many of the beachball-sized wads of plastic as they can into the wagon. It is far less than they expected. But it is progress. They take it all to the supermarket recycling center, only they have too much. Way more bags than the place can handle.

They have to visit two other Safeways and an Albertson's before they unload the lot.

"We put a dent in it, I reckon," he says, gazing at the drab strip-mall scenery spooling past. Multiplex cinemas, Burger Palaces, and Chix Fixes everywhere. He ponders the combined output of plastic waste each generates every day, and shudders.

She honks the horn, mutters under her breath, and brakes to a halt as the light turns red.

She looks at him. "There's a ton more," she says.

He sighs. "Yeah."

They arrive home. It is twilight and chilly. Almost two years to the day when he first started, you know, collecting trash.

The house is dark, and they stride in, bristling, uncertain.

"One more run?"

He shrugs. "They're open till nine. I gotta pee."

Halfway into it he hears Anne-Marie gasp, then: "Oh my *God*!"

"Annie!"

"Jesus *Christ*, Colin!"

"Hang on!" Shaking dry, teeth gritted. He rushes down the

hallway. Anne-Marie is at the top of the basement stairs, staring down.

He looks. There, on the topmost step, is a dead bird. A seabird of some sort. He can tell it is a seabird because it has webbed feet. And the briny smell.

It is strangely, ignominiously tangled in plastic six-pack rings. Legs and wings and neck constricted intricately. It seems to have struggled mightily, and was killed recently.

"Is this a fucking joke?" he demands.

"You tell me! If this is Joe or Sam—"

"It is not. No way. Not Joe, anyway, but—"

"I'm calling the police."

But there is no perp to be found, no levered windows or jimmied locks. And the officers are impressed—surprised—by the great assemblage of plastic waste.

"You sure it's not a health code kind of thing?" one asks the other.

Her colleague shrugs. They collect the evidence, leaving disposable plastic gloves and their packaging in the bathroom waste basket—leering, repellent.


Their sleep is fitful. They make love, but somehow they are both stressed, even as they lie sighing in their consummation. Some small nagging whisper of consternation . . .

He dreams of serpents and fire, and eruptions of toxic gas.

The continents are heaving, sliding, half-molten slabs of rock and ore. All about and among them, monstrous, coiling, smoldering, is a Dragon, lord and king of the primordial Earth.

And there is a battle, vast and *abstract*: A war of eons, played out across a billion years. Colin dreams of sheens and washes, of floods and algae, of great blue tides and cool green slopes and the—the Mother—She strikes down the Dragon, smites it and brings it to ruin, and deep below the Earth She buries its ghastly, stinking leavings, tarry-black and noxious, viscous, inimical to the very breath of life.

She buries it all far beneath Her mantle of soil and rock. But it is seething and full of spite, and ever it strives to escape again to the surface, and smother all that's blue and green.

He moans and weeps then, in his bed.

"The cat!"

Something grabs his thigh: Annie. He lurches awake, up out of the well of dreams.

"What!"

"Where's the cat?" She stares at him. "Fungus always sleeps with us, right *here*."

And it's true. No Fungus. He can feel the cat's absence, the afterimage of its purring warmth.

They creep out into the hall in their robes and slippers. The house is silent, except . . .

They pad downstairs. The basement door is ajar.

"Did you hear that?" Her eyes are wide.

He nods.

They fling the door open and switch on the lights. There had been a brief sort of *miaow*, then only a faint rustling.

Baseball bat in his hand, kitchen knife in hers, they stomp heavily down the stairs. The sound is coming from the bag room, somewhere beyond the hollowed-out arc they had dug into it earlier.

Annie wades in, and pushes against the mass.

"Fungus? Ki-ttee! C'mere, Fungi. Li'l Fungee. For cris*sake*."

She kneels down and begins tunneling industriously in, up to her shoulders, and then emits the beginning of a shriek or gasp.

Startled, Colin shifts his weight to his other heel, slips on a plastic water bottle that somehow has lodged itself underfoot, and topples backwards, slamming his head into a water main. It is dark for a few moments. He sees stars, and grids. He is dazed with pain, writhes about till at last his vision clears.

There's Annie—or her feet, anyway, and her legs, which are kicking about in an agitated fashion. He struggles to sit up, but realizes that his wrists have somehow gotten entangled with a great span of monofilament. It is surprisingly tight and grows more so as he wriggles. It is looped peculiarly, also, around his knees, and as he wrestles, his face becomes wrapped up in a white plastic grocery bag. One handle catches his ear, and as he shakes his head to dislodge it, the other handle snags a button on his nightshirt. He tries to shrug it off; the bag settles gradually, inexorably, over his nose and mouth.

There are new sounds around him. He catches a glimpse of a webbed foot sticking out of the landscape of plastic, then sees another feathery, torpedo-shaped body, twitching minutely, enlaced in plastic six-pack rings. There is a roaring sound in his ears, and he realizes the monofilament is full of hooks, big and barbed, which begin to bite into him as he rolls and winds himself up, ever more snug.

Long, sleek bodies are thrashing next to him, powerful, damp. Fins of some sort press against his abdomen; he hears a high-pitched sound, a churring and chittering, like from a nature documentary, but desperate. Plaintive.

A single coherent thought (his last) bobs up through the tide of panic—*Dolphins*?

# Bubba Sez Howdy

## Rex Erickson

Hadn't been to HowdYYall bar since last Sunday's visit to the Masonic cemetery. Now Friday, and I am possessed with this feeling I should go. Hmm, Feel, no, too quiet a word! Somehow, I know that I need to visit Doc Hasting's dark corner where bottles go in but never come out. So, I hop in Brunhilde, hit the halogens, and mosey.

HowdyYYall is the usual Friday night busy with paychecks being liquefied while I, between jobs, have only a couple of lonely Jeffersons. Oh hell, whatever, enough for a couple of Jack Daniel shots and Lone Star chasers. New bartender Marie is popping tops and pouring shots when, and this is totally strange, time seems to stop for everyone but her. She turns and looks at me standing just inside the batwings and smiles. Then one of those witch green eyes winks. I stand stunned until she turns away and the bar comes back to life.

I shake it off. Must be some sort of PTSD from the boneyard visit. Start making my way through the crowd towards Doc's dark corner and still feel strange though it is the same strange I'd felt before when I found myself in a corral surrounded by cantankerous Longhorns. I was caretaker of these half-ton beasts, and we were all going to the Houston Astrodome for Rodeo. They had their six-foot horn span, and I had my new white show hat with sparkling white rhinestones set in a black hat band. Just for mean fun, a tricky Texas wind whipped it right into the corral dirt. Those cows gave the glittering hat its own space and kinda looked at me saying, "Come and get it, Cowboy."

I did and I'm here now sitting with Doc waiting for drinks when strange follows strange: Marie comes from behind the bar and over to the table. She lays down Doc's drinks and then, empty handed, looks at me.

"Howdy Bubba, you boys have been busy chatting with the aliens."

That was weird, how'd she know, unless Doc had told her, but I doubted that. We'd kept our silence. You can talk Texas weird which means you're normal, but this was weird weird and if you talk weird weird you must be weird.

"Bubba," sez Doc, "say hello to the famous Marie Laveau, Voodoo Queen of New Orleans in an earlier manifestation. Dignitaries from many nations turned to her for advice. The Andromeda aliens have brought her back and she's volunteered to be your bartender."

I had turned to look at Doc and now I turned back to Marie. In her right hand was a shot glass full to the brim with a dark swirling liquid. I looked into green eyes sparkling brighter than rhinestones in a noonday Texas sun when I hear a low sultry voice, "Chère, this drink's on me."

"Doc," I say, "her lips didn't move and she told me to drink whatever that is."

Doc looks at me, "You trust me don't you Bubba?"

"Yeah Doc, I'd ride the river with you anytime."

"Then take Marie up on her offer. She's our friend and we don't want to insult her."

Pondered that, and concluding that insulting a Voodoo Queen was a lot more dangerous than a corral full of longhorns, I down the shot.

Time freezes again but I can move so I look around. I am in the Big Thicket, at least I think it is the Big Thicket, but something isn't right.

No sound, just silence under a big sun hanging in a clear sky. Sweat beads were forming and running down my face. I wipe my eyes and look around. Everything seems smaller and darker with no green to be seen. Walking over to a bramble, I feel a branch stem and have it snap in my hand.

Stumbling, I looked down to see ground cracks descending into darkness.

By now I am sweating rivers and not sure how much more

of this I can take. Give me a desert before you give me this. Just
when I am cashing in my chips, I find myself back in the bar with
a concerned Doc looking at me,

"You're sweating."

"You reckon, really, you reckon!" Looking at Marie with
nothing to lose, me having already died, I blurt. "What the hell
did you do to me?'

She looked at me and in a sad voice, "Showed you what
will be."

That got me. No more Big Thicket, no more Texas. Knew
things had been getting funny. Recent droughts had forced cattle-
men to sell off large portions of their stock at a loss. Wildlife was
dying from thirst with their dehydrated carcasses celebrated by
circling buzzards. Occasionally, that missing water was delivered
somewhere where it wasn't needed, like in a Houston flood. But,
overall, things were getting drier and, I reckon, deadlier.

Now I really needed a drink. Where they came from, I don't
know, but Marie laid down two shots of familiar brown Jack and
a Lone Star chaser.

"There's still hope, Bubba."

"Where Marie?"

"Close by. Drink up," and with that she went back behind
the bar.

# WAKING THE TANIWHA

## DAN RABARTS

*Boulcott Farm Stockade, Hutt Valley, Wellington, January 1855*

**S**un lanced off the airship's fittings as it descended. Kent patted the report in his breast pocket, his lips moving silently:

*"Welcome to Wellington, Mister Faulkner. Morgan Kent, from the Governor's office, to brief you on the disappearance of the HMS Kestrel. I have prepared a report . . ."*

Faulkner was a living legend, and his despatch to the colonies vindicated Kent's suspicions about what had really happened to the *Kestrel*. This was no maritime misadventure. Faulkner's arrival was proof that the taniwha truly existed, and that there was a future for a man like Morgan Kent in searching for such elusive beasts. Impress the suspenders off Howard Faulkner and Kent might find himself on a fast airship back to England and a life of hunting real monsters, not just the myths and lore which were his stock in trade as a Royal Ethnographer.

A dozen iron harpoons loosed from *Waka-a-Rangi* and slammed into the earth. Internal winches creaked, drawing the airship down. Faulkner had the good sense to trust the locals, Kent noted. Unlike the British, the flyboys of Ngati Poheke were not prone to crashing their dirigibles on the Auckland-Wellington passage. Poheke were wanderers, taking to the skies as readily as their ancestors had crossed the ocean to reach this lost paradise at the bottom of the South Pacific. And just as the Maori had adopted the settlers' weapons and improved on their battle tactics, so too had they mastered their airships of brass and steam in ways that British pilots simply hadn't. Mercenaries they may be, but they were worth their coin.

The groundcrew secured the dirigible and a gangway folded out. Faulkner appeared, his leather overcoat snapping like the wings of some giant raptor, white hair framing a weathered face beneath his wide-brimmed hat. At his belt hung knives and pepperpot pistols, as if prepared to find himself in the midst of battle at any moment. Maybe, Kent thought, he too should carry a pistol. Steeling himself, he crossed the field.

Faulkner strode across the paddock, brushing past Kent.

"Mister Faulkner? I am Morgan Kent . . ."

Faulkner didn't stop. "You here for the bags?"

Kent hurried after, fumbling in his coat. "Ah, no, I'm with the Governor's office. I've been sent to brief you regarding the Kestrel. I have a report . . ."

Faulkner jerked a thumb backwards. "Give me the quick version, or go help unload. I don't much care for reports."

Kent upped his pace.

"Well, in June the ship sailed north from Wellington with a hold full of munitions, supplies and spares for the troops fighting the Kingitanga in the Whanganui Valley, but it never arrived. Neither survivors nor wreckage have been found."

Faulkner grunted. Kent pressed on.

"I made mention in my report of another incident, some years ago, when an elder tohunga disappeared during a battle with the Maori tribe Ngai Toaki. A reproduction of his portrait is in my report. This priest was reputed to have powers, sir."

"You spinning me a fairy tale, son?"

Kent swallowed hard. "No, sir. Legend has it that this tohunga, Ti Hariki, has the power to speak with taniwha. Taniwha are legendary monsters, guardians—"

Faulkner cut him off. "Taniwha are like any other monster, just what people make of them. I came here to find a missing ship, not to chase beasties which probably don't exist. Understand?"

"With all due respect sir, I doubt the Home Office would have chosen to send a man of your repute to find a lost ship. They would have sent a mariner, not . . . you."

Faulkner glowered. "I don't take your meaning, son."

"I know your reputation, sir, as a hunter of things *uncanny*."

Not everyone believed the tales of Faulkner's exploits, but Kent did. Kent *needed* to believe. "Sir, I believe that at the behest of Ngai Toaki the tohunga summoned a taniwha which swallowed the *Kestrel* whole. I can find no other explanation."

"There's *always* another explanation." Faulkner growled. "I don't know your game, Mister Kent, but it'd behove you not to presume things you know nothing about."

"Are you working for the Office of the Preternatural?"

The words fell from Kent's mouth. He had meant to tell Faulkner about the Cruickshanks, the British engineers who'd vanished some years earlier, his suspicions that their disappearance might somehow be related, and about the strange frequency with which farm machinery was stolen in raids on settlers' plots. That was not what had come out.

"I'm sure I don't know what you mean. There is *no* Office of the Preternatural. See that?" He gestured back at a young man lugging chests from the airship onto a wagon. "You could learn a lot about keeping your mouth shut and your eyes open from Young Master Sullivan. Now, for the love of Queen and Country, point me towards the nearest cold beer."

Faulkner's finger slid along the map, tracing a course between the North and South Islands' coastlines. "I suspect that Ngai Toaki warriors lay in wait for the *Kestrel* at Kapiti Island and attacked as she hit the tide. They seized control and sailed her into these sounds in the South Island. Dozens of places in there to hide a ship, with plenty of deep water anchorage." He arched an eyebrow at Kent. "Does that seem probable, Mister Kent, or do you still think a taniwha ate it?"

Kent grimaced. "It's feasible. Ngai Toaki still hold the Manawatu River Gorge against Pakeha settlers, and they may yet have designs against the Navy."

"Very well. Since we have the *agreement* of the local help, we'll start with an aerial sweep." He looked down the table to where Sullivan was working on a set of leather headgear bristling with polished lenses. "Prognosis?"

Sullivan squinted through a magnifying monocle at the component in his hand, all tiny gears and valves. "I'm getting a low-wave resonance which suggests there's ultraphysical latency all around us, but nothing gives off energy like that. There might be an iron vein in the hillside throwing out the magnetic capacitors."

"Calibrate the sensors. I don't want to be flying blind."

The air thumped with the drone of boiler-driven rotors. "Ornithopter's incoming," Kent said. "They'll be bringing wounded."

Faulkner looked up. "Where from?"

"The Ngai Toaki Pa in the Manawatu. The fighting's been heavy there lately."

"How coincidental." Faulkner stood, shrugging into his overcoat. "Come on, Kent."

Kent hurried to keep up as Faulkner strode from the barracks and across the airfield towards the stockade surgery. They hunkered against the downdraughts as ornithopters landed and departed again as quickly as their bloody cargo could be offloaded, their exhausts pumping steam.

The wounded were a mess of blood, smashed bone, and scorched flesh. Faulkner tapped one of the casualties on the collarbone as blood-stained orderlies hauled his stretcher towards the surgery. "Talk to me, man!"

The redcoat's arm was missing, yet his accoutrements were not stained with smoke or shrapnel. Even Kent could tell that he had not lost his limb to cannon-fire. "I'm with the Governor's office," Kent said. "What happened?"

The man's eyes rolled past him, through him. "Took . . . My . . . Arm . . ." the soldier gasped, every word marking its ragged toll, "the . . . monster."

The orderlies disappeared into the surgery.

Kent turned to see Faulkner, his countenance sour, wind snapping at his coat. "Now do you believe me?" he called, raising his voice to be heard over the roar of boilers and rotors.

Faulkner strode towards the surgery. Kent followed. "What more proof do you need? They've seen the taniwha. That's why the Office sent you, because hunting monsters is what you do. We have to stop it, and Ti Hariki can help us. We must find him."

Faulkner spun, looming over Kent. He suddenly seemed impossibly tall and infinitely more dangerous. "One day you'll have to decide what believing in things you can't prove is worth to you, lad," he growled. "It's a price that few are ready to pay. What are you willing to sacrifice to make your taniwha real?"

Faulkner left Kent in the blast of a descending ornithopter, his hair in his eyes and his stomach in his throat.

*Waka-a-Rangi* swept over bush broken by artillery emplacements and smouldering craters. Here in the shadow of the Ngai Toaki Pa, the war for the bottom of the North Island was at its peak.

"Anything?" Faulkner stood behind Sullivan, who occupied the co-pilot's seat. The headgear was strapped under his chin, brass and crystal lenses suspended over each eye.

Sullivan scanned side to side, his left hand working over a gauntlet on his right bedecked with brass dials and switches, each adjustment actuating minor changes to the headgear. "Heat signatures everywhere, mostly artillery impact and brushfire. I can't identify anything on the electromagnetic or ultraphysical scales through this heat haze, though."

Faulkner looked at Kent. "They say that this taniwha of yours came with a roar and tore down everything and everyone in its path; that it spat fire and smoke and cleaved men in two; and that any who saw it fled or went mad. Do you know what that sounds like to me, Mister Kent? Mass hysteria. A collective hallucination. I believe when we get to this fortress we will find not a monster but evidence of something rather mundane—a windborne opiate, or some manner of electromagnetic mind control as yet unseen in the Empire and unleashed on unwitting victims. Enough to drive a battalion to the brink of madness, so that the mere sight of warriors in their rage would conjure horror to the addled mind."

"Those wounds were neither musket fire nor swords," Kent said. "That was claws, or teeth."

"Too clean for teeth. A word of advice, Kent: If you go looking for monsters in every shadow, it might pay to carry a lantern."

"Sir!" Faulkner and Kent looked to Sullivan, and past him to the devastation which had befallen the Manawatu Gorge. Massive claw-shaped gouges had shredded the bushclad hillsides around the Ngai Toaki Pa, the soil torn as deep as the rock beneath. Kent's gaze followed the trail of destruction up the hillsides. Something monstrous had walked this earth.

Faulkner's voice broke the suddenly brittle atmosphere. "What's that? In that gully, between those trees."

Sullivan snapped through several lenses. "It would appear to be a mast, sir."

"Let's go have a look, shall we?"


"Congratulations, sir, you found your missing ship."

*Waka-a-Rangi* hovered above the land-bound hulk. Everyone on board could see her decks, her shredded sails, her bloodstains.

"Are you still convinced she was swallowed by a sea serpent, Mister Kent?" Faulkner jibed.

"Well," Kent grated, "something carried it here, miles from the sea. Something with teeth bigger than a man, evidently. Look at the holes in the timber!"

"Kaore, e hoa," laughed Matara from the pilot's chair. "That's harpoons did that, maybe five or six airships to lift her, but airships all the same."

"Ngati Poheke would do that?"

Matara shrugged. "For the right price."

Faulkner nodded. "So, why pluck a ship from the sea and abandon it in the hills?"

"It wasn't just abandoned," Sullivan interjected, nozzles hissing and gears whirring as different lenses flipped over his eyes. "She's been stripped; weapons, rigging, navigation equipment, everything."

"The taniwha's path comes right through here," Kent muttered. He gripped the seat, taking long slow breaths.

"Matara?" Faulkner said.

"Aye?"

"Follow its tracks."

"Kapai." Rotors thundered, and the dirigible ascended.

"All well, Mister Kent?"

"What can we do that an entire battalion of soldiers and militia couldn't? This airship is unarmed."

Faulkner grinned, a cold expression that looked out of place on his gaunt features. "Well, Mister Kent, isn't it lucky we have a monster-hunter along?"

Kent retreated to a porthole and scanned the swathe of destruction as it flowed south. Vaguely, he heard Sullivan and Faulkner talking.

"And what of the ultraphysical registers? Any resonances? Harmonic distortions?"

"Nothing we're familiar with, which isn't to say there's not something there that we can't see."

"None of the spikes we recorded at the Loch, then?"

"No, sir. Nothing like it."

Kent stared, his stomach sinking at the sight of a world slashed open like a kumara patch in harvest season. Faulkner had disregarded even the possibility that a taniwha may truly have awoken. Yet what else could cause such destruction, on such an unprecedented scale? Nothing made by the hand of man, certainly. Then he spotted figures slipping between the trees below. "Sullivan, can you see those people? There? Maori warriors, a couple helping an older man along . . ."

Sullivan looked, dials switching as he searched for the figures. "Yes."

"May I?" He gestured at the byzantine headgear.

Faulkner reached into his coat and instead passed Kent a battered spyglass.

Disappointed, Kent raised the telescope. He peered down the treeline to the small warparty in the bush. The older man had turned to face the airship. "That's Ti Hariki" Kent pointed, "I recognise the moko tattooed on his cheeks. He must have been imprisoned by the Ngai Toaki and escaped in the wake of the battle." He lowered the spyglass. "Mister Faulkner, there's something out there which you can't explain, and this man might be the only one who can communicate with it. I suggest you pick him up."

Faulkner regarded Kent. "This is the man you say can speak with the taniwha? The only one who could have brought the monster to life, if this is what it truly is? Consider carefully before you answer, Mister Kent. Consider what it's worth to you."

Kent's bowels clenched. If he was right, he would earn the hunter's respect, and perhaps a recommendation to the Office of the Preternatural. If he was wrong . . .

"Either Ti Hariki was a prisoner of Ngai Toaki and he will be willing to help us defeat the taniwha, or he is responsible for dozens of British deaths, and we bring him to justice."

Faulkner was silent a moment, weighing Kent with his eyes. "Captain Matara, please be so good as to drop a ladder."

Kent sucked down a breath as winches hissed beneath him, still locked in Faulkner's gaze.

"I hope you know how to finish what you start, Kent. Nothing I hate more than a man who can't do what needs to be done."

He left the words hanging, like a corpse in the wind.


"It is no taniwha," Hariki declared, folding his arms across his chest.

"So what is it?" Faulkner pressed.

"*Tekotekonui*. A blasphemy against the *atua*," Hariki snarled, "a thing of metal and steam and blade. They built it from things stolen or traded, to bring death and terror to the Pakeha."

Kent edged forward, concealing his disappointment at the revelation. "E koro, they say you have the power to speak with taniwha. How have you kept your secret from Ngai Toaki for so long?"

Hariki huffed. "My secret cannot be taught or taken from me. I was born with it, and when I die another will be born to it. None can force me to use it against my will, for the taniwha would know."

"So you claim to have this power, but have never used it to wake a monster?" Faulkner interjected.

Hariki's withering gaze turned on Faulkner. "No wise man would wake a sleeping taniwha. I have never used my powers to wake, only to soothe the beasts back to sleep when they stir. There is much power in calming, in control, in peace. Wake a taniwha, and nothing can contain it."

"So, we still have no proof that these taniwha of yours are real? Very good."

"Sir," Sullivan called, "I think I see it."

Kent looked. The silhouette against the horizon was vast. The Tekotekonui stepped across a gully, six huge legs pistoning. Steam hissed from vents along its limbs, and on its dozen snaking arms swung stars of whirling blades and nozzles dripping white smoke. One mighty leg rose, its foot the rotating iron wheel of a steam tractor. The wheel descended, shredding foliage and spraying dirt before gaining traction and pulling the monster forward.

Faulkner chuckled, rubbing his hands together. "What a splendid machine." He glanced at Hariki. "Ngai Toaki built this? Their ingenuity impresses me."

"Them," Hariki grunted, "and their Pakeha engineers."

"The Cruickshank brothers?" Kent asked. "They were forced to do this?"

Hariki snorted. "Kaore! *I* was a prisoner. Those two *wanted* to be there. *They* were behind the design."

Kent stared, the beast's flailing limbs unravelling the truths he'd thought he'd known, both of monsters and of how monstrous some men must be to create them.

Of how men create monsters of other men.

Faulkner's words weighed on him, the taste of betrayal rising bitter in his mouth. He was beginning to understand what he would have to do, and it sickened him.

But there must be another way. Whatever Howard Faulkner wanted him to be, whatever the secretive Office of the Preternatural demanded of its initiates, Morgan Kent was not a murderer, no matter the stakes. At least, he hoped he wasn't.

He tore his gaze away and squatted before Hariki. The tohunga's toa tensed, but the elder waved them away. "E koro," he deferred, "If you can truly korero with taniwha, then I beseech you to use that power now. Ngai Toaki have long held out against the Pakeha while plotting their destruction, but they have been twisted into this course of action by evil men. Innocents will die, Maori and Pakeha alike, and only you can stop it. Had you wished for this, you could have raised a real taniwha to fight for them long ago. But you didn't, which is why I believe you do not wish to see more bloodshed. You can end this."

"How?" Ti Hariki folded his arms. "This thing is no taniwha I can coax into submission. Its heart pulses steam, and the will that drives it is human."

"The machine is making for Wellington. It will attack the settlements there." Hariki said nothing, his eyes hard. "We both know the Ngati Arai legends, how Whataitai made his resting place in the harbour after Ngake fled him. There he sleeps the deepest sleep, even now." Kent knew he was clutching at straws, trusting to myths upheld only by belief. If he was wrong, Faulkner would laugh him into his grave.

"Kaore," the tohunga growled. "I will not wake the taniwha."

"Koro, you must!"

There was a sudden crack of cannon fire and *Waka-a-Rangi* lurched, slamming Kent into the bulkhead.

"Hold on!" Matara shouted as a hot projectile scorched past. "Looks like they've spotted us!"

Boilers whined as Matara climbed out of range of the *Kestrel*'s plundered cannons.

Faulkner hauled Kent to his feet and leaned in to hiss in his ear. "Can you finish this, or will I have to pass on my disappointment to the Minister? Tell him that you're no monster hunter, and never will be?"

Kent's skin turned cold. He was running out of time, out of options, out of air. He had to decide. Lives were at stake, as was his future. He looked again at the old man. Perhaps the tohunga could not be forced, but he was human. There were ways to persuade a man that required neither threat nor blade.

Wellington harbour loomed closer. The Tekotekonui was not far behind.

Kent shook his head, meeting the tohunga's flinty gaze. "I was wrong. This old charlatan can't speak with taniwha because they don't exist. He's a fraud. Best that we put them down here and return to the stockade to prepare our defence against the real monster."

"Here?" Faulkner asked. "In the middle of nowhere?"

Although Faulkner didn't say it, Kent heard the hunter's un-

spoken question: *Here? In the monster's path?*
"Yes," Kent nodded, a lead ball in his gullet. "Right here."

Never had Kent felt so cruel, so ruthless, nor so empty as he did when *Waka-a-Rangi* ascended, leaving Hariki and his toa standing on the bluff between the harbour and the monster. Tekotekonui's arms whirled with blades and belched smoke as it bore down on the former prisoners.

Kent pictured Hariki, gazing across the harbour to the lurking shape of Whataitai, a peninsula crowned with shrubby rocks and bush grown ancient since he had fallen into heartbroken slumber—or so said the Ngati Arai legends. The truth of those legends, or otherwise, was about to be tested.

"You seem concerned."

Kent managed not to jump at Faulkner's voice. "He is *tapu*, and I challenged his *mana* in front of his men."

"English, if you please."

"He will be obliged to prove that his people's myths are more than just fictions dreamed up around a fire to explain the shape of a hillside, or unseen birdcalls in the night."

He imagined Hariki's voice rising in karakia, a ululation to breach the divide between worlds, to break the mantle of Papatuanuku, Earth Mother, to wake her sleeping children.

Tekotekonui closed in. The warriors faced it with nothing but wooden taiaha, stone patu, and the courage of the damned.

"Nice story," Faulkner grated, and turned away.

A rush of heat and chill suddenly flowed through Kent, sucking his strength. He staggered.

"Sir!" Sullivan yelled. "We've got flux! Spiking on all spectrums! More than I can register!"

Kent hauled himself back to the window in time to see the taniwha wake. Whataitai twitched, perhaps nothing more than an eyeblink in the endless sleep of an undying leviathan, and the world shattered around him.

The harbour buckled and the earth shivered like flax in the wind. Tekotekonui stumbled, thrown sideways by the quake, its wheels sliding from under it as the shockwave rippled through the hillside. The shore rent open and the cliff collapsed with a roar, a cloud of debris sliding into the waves. Like a giant spider tumbling from its web Tekotekonui fell, limbs flailing in clouds of steam.

No-one spoke. *Waka-a-Rangi* chugged on, oblivious.

Kent gazed on the altered shoreline, the raging breakers lashing the waterfront, and the dust-cloud rising where the bluff had once been.

There, where Ti Hariki and his men had stood, alone, to face the monster. Where they had died to destroy it.

"E koro," he said to himself, "what did I make you do?"

*Taniwha are what men make them,* he thought. *Monsters, guardians, champions. And if we're forced to, we will make taniwha of ourselves.*

Faulkner's case was solved, but at what cost? Had Whataitai not stirred from his sleep as deep as death for that shiver of a moment, Tekotekonui may have continued its destructive rampage for days or even weeks. But the repercussions of the earthquake would be felt for months and years to come.

Finally, Kent found his voice. "So," he asked Faulkner, "now do you believe in taniwha?"

Faulkner smiled his cold smile. "I didn't see one. Did you? Now, are you ready, Officer?" He adjusted his weapons belt as the airship descended. "We have work to do." Faulkner's grin was genuine now, but no less cold, or crooked, or hungry for it.

Kent nodded as the word sank in. Faulkner had called him *Officer*. He had proven himself to the paragon of monster hunters, yet the victory tasted sour as corked wine, like an offering of rotten flesh to an angry god. One day, he hoped, he would cease to regret that it had taken waking the taniwha in himself to earn the respect of a monster.

*Royal Ethnographer's Note:*
*The earthquake of January 1855 is the largest in recorded history to have struck the Wellington region. Whether it was Whataitai waking to stretch his legs or Ngake trying to return to his ancient hunting grounds is still a matter of intense debate among local historians, but it is generally agreed that these are the only two logical explanations.*

# Rifts

## Yang-Yang Wang

**V**illini von Lichtenstein, Queen Inherit of the New Assembled Damocles Republic of the Western Americas, rubbed sleep from her eyes with small white fists. Bad enough to be woken in the middle of the night by some thunderous crash, but to have a formal assembly called so shortly after? Dreadful. She mentally thanked her Uncle, the Baron Jasper Faringwood, for her two attendants. Though they were now antiquated models, their gears were well-oiled and their golden surfaces rust-free.

"Gold-plating is practical, you see," Faringwood said years ago, "for it'll never rust."

"You try explaining that to the citizens, dear Uncle." Villini retorted. "They'll only see the gold, and the new Girl-Queen who lavishes in its splendor."

Still, she accepted them. The tabloids made a stink of it, but she had to. After all, she could not deny her only living blood-relation.

With quiet efficiency, the two automatons prepared her like a warrior for battle. Their hands danced along the back of her white-frilled corset, motors buzzing and gears whirring as eyes were hooked and bows tied. She exhaled sharply as a sharp tug tightened her corset, crushing her already boyish waist into intimidating thinness. A second dress, high-cut yellow lace set with dazzling amethysts, was settled over the cinched corset. A well-powdered wig came last, placed between her head and her crown. When they were done, she was transformed from a waifish raven-haired girl into a statuesque icon of pomp and power.

The war room already contained three others by the time she

arrived. General Gaussler, Baron Dolen, and Professor Molinger stood around the central table. A large brass box sat between them. It was decorated with a screen of gray-tinted glass on one side and an extending lens on the other. A switch jutted from under the screen, and a childish urge in Villini desired to flick it.

As usual, Baron Dolen spoke first. "Villini, we—"

"Queen Villini," she cut in.

Dolen paused, a flash of distaste deepening his wrinkled features. "Queen Villini. Welcome."

General Gaussler saluted sharply, sending the tips of his braided beard waving. "My Queen! My sincerest apologies for such a late summons, but it could not wait until the morning."

"It is all right, General, I believe in your judgment," Villini replied. "But please, do reinforce my faith."

He nodded. "No doubt you heard the crash coming from the gardens scarcely an hour ago?"

She allowed a touch of annoyance to cross her face. "I did. Was it another dwarven terrorist, or perhaps a prank of elven magic?"

"Neither, and that's why I had you summoned." The General looked grave. "It was an ornithopter."

Villini felt lightheaded. She placed a hand on the table to steady herself. "Faringwood's?"

The General nodded. "Only he knows their use."

Tears clouded the world as she voiced her fear. "Was my Uncle in the craft?"

Gaussler shook his head. "No, the ornithopter flew here on its own."

Blood flowed again in Villini's legs, but her wariness remained as Gaussler gestured at the box. "This and a short note was all we found during our investigation."

He handed it to her and she unfolded it.

For Lini's eyes only.

Lini. How long had it been since she heard her Uncle use that nickname? He'd been away as of late, presumably tinkering in his laboratory.

Dolen caught her attention by clearing his throat. "Queen Villini. While General Gaussler would lead you to believe that this is an urgent message from Baron Faringwood, I believe this may be nothing but simple theatrics." His eyes narrowed as they caught her frown. "Now let me explain. The machine is a large, rudimentary version of the still picture capturing device that I created for your fourteenth birthday with Professor Molinger."

The ruddy-cheeked man in the white lab coat attempted a bow, but he only succeeded in hunching over his massive belly.

Dolen cleared his throat. "Do you remember how much you loved it, and how Faringwood promised to deliver something even more extraordinary this year? It is entirely possible that the Baron, embarrassed by his inferior creation and being of cunning mind, is staging all of this as an elaborate ploy to increase—"

A buzzing hum from the machine stopped Dolen mid sentence as Villini flipped the switch on the box. The glass pane came to life. Stark white light reflected off the marble walls in flickering pulses, deepening shadows and creating pits of pockmarks.

Villini almost laughed and clapped her hands as the fuzzy monochrome image of Baron Jasper Faringwood emerged from the gray screen. The picture increased in sharpness until all of the details were vivid.

Dolen tugged at his mustache. "Nice contrast, I suppose."

To their collective astonishment, colors blossomed into life onscreen as the machine continued to warm up.

"I thought you said color was impossible?" Dolen barked at Molinger.

"Improbable, not impossible!" cried the Professor.

Villini was about to comment when Faringwood's image began to move. Though the development of color was stunning, the realization of moving pictures seemed to shift the very ground beneath her feet.

General Gaussler was openly gaping. "The applications . . . This will change our entire world!"

The image of Baron Faringwood began tinkering with something off screen. It was so lifelike that Villini thought she could open the box and find a miniature version of her Uncle inside.

It had only been eight months since Villini last saw him, but the Baron looked like he had aged twenty years. His handsome face was now haggard, with deep wrinkles running sharp grooves around his cheeks and eyes. His salt and pepper hair was now all white, and his once proud mustache drooped under the weight of wild growth.

He was not at all like the energetic Uncle she remembered. His movement was unsteady and periodically interrupted by odd shifting jerks. Was he . . . shivering?

Faringwood's attention snapped to the screen and he blinked with slow surprise. "Ahh the light is on! It's finally recording!"

His image enlarged as it drew closer to the screen, the expression on his face bordering on desperation. "My dearest Lini, if you are watching this, then the Stranger has already come for me. Do not spare the time to mourn, for by then it will be too late for you as well."

Villini saw the surprise on Gaussler's face turn into confusion as dubious looks were exchanged between Dolen and Molinger. What kind of joke was this?

"I only hope I have the time to explain everything. This device you are watching is an invention of mine I call the 'Telecorder'. It is capable of both recording moving images and playback in color, and it was my greatest hope to present it to you on your sixteenth birthday. Alas, I am afraid I must deliver graver presents instead."

The image looked away from the screen and clutched his gloved hands together, steadying their trembling.

"In truth I finished the Telecorder last year, but it was a little too late and a little too grand for a fifteenth birthday, so I decided to save the surprise. In the meantime, I began to tinker further with technologies of transmission and playback, hoping to upgrade my Telecorder with the ability to remotely send the events it captured to other Telecorders. In that, I have failed. Instead, I discovered something completely and accidentally remarkable."

Faringwood adjusted the Telecorder screen to reveal the rest of his home. It was small and cluttered with the debris of scientific progress, with a worktable taking up most of the space not inhabited by towers of books and papers. The only clean spot was on the table itself, where an emerald orb the size of a balloon sat. Wires and tubes ran from the base that the orb rested on and disappeared into the piles of refuse on the ground. It was disconcerting for Villini to see, for her Uncle had always been an immaculately clean man.

Faringwood pointed at the orb from a distance, looking uncomfortable. "This is the Metasphere. Originally it had been conceived of as just a relay device, a simple receiver and transmitter, only it was far too weak. Then one night I was experimenting with its output levels when a surge erupted through the cables, almost frying me alive. Then, well, it worked—but not as intended."

Villini recalled the sudden flicker of her palace lights around the time, and Dolen muttered something about his symphony being interrupted.

Faringwood continued. "Instead of transmitting the contents of my Telecorder, it began to display images on its own. Images of things and people and places I had never seen or could scarcely dream of. Images from worlds not our own."

Baron Dolen whispered, "The man's gone daft."

"Can it be true?" said General Gaussler.

Professor Molinger clucked his tongue. "Highly improbable."

"I've seen worlds of war and worlds of art. I've seen worlds where the animals lord over men, and worlds controlled by beings of pure electricity. I've seen worlds where zeppelins fly without balloons—"

"Definitely improbable!" Molinger interrupted.

"—and worlds where America won its independence—"

"Blasphemy!" cried General Gaussler

"—and would that I had stopped there, then everything would be fine. But I kept pushing. I did not want to stop. I was always hungry for more."

Faringwood paused and rubbed his shaking hands together. Villini decided he simply had to be the victim of nerves and not cold, for the furnace in his background was running so hot it cast the walls in a ruby glow. When the Baron spoke again, his voice was grave and regretful.

"Man, with his egocentric nature, dares to venture into places beyond his grasp and understanding. I am sorry, my dearest Lini, to leave you as the Icarus in my Daedulus tale."

"It all began one night when I was about to turn off the Metasphere. Instead of fading off as usual, the light grew in intensity until it blinded me. I thought it was going to explode, like a miniature supernova. Instead, the light collapsed on itself as suddenly as it began, leaving only a vision of the deepest void."

"At first I thought the Metasphere burnt itself out. It took me a moment to realize that I stared at yet another world, but one with a horizon void of stars or moon. As my eyes adjusted, I saw the coastline of what I ventured to be an immense island. There was an ocean to my side, but one so free of tides and currents that it looked like one great polished onyx. I could only imagine the stink of such a stagnant body, for the shoreline closest to my view was choking under mud so viscous it practically oozed."

Villini saw the distaste on her Uncle's face as he recounted the memory.

"If I was surprised by the repugnant setting that the Metasphere displayed, nothing could describe the dread I felt as the view swiveled and I saw, for the first time, the vast silhouette of angular stone that lorded over the island. It was impossibly tall, and crowned with a single monolith whose tip could not be seen even from my vantage."

His eyes grew distant and wild.

"A part of me screamed warning, to cease viewing and shatter the Metasphere that very moment, but I could not tear my eyes away. The device brought me closer and, as if sensing my presence, countless torches ignited with green flames along the mountain. Whether the fire itself was that color or if the pigment of the stone overwhelmed all natural hues, I am unsure.

"As the details of what I saw grew clearer, the 'mountain' was revealed as a vast city, created by intelligences I guess as being otherworldly at best. My mind struggled to grasp the procession of impossible angles that formed the structures of the vaulted dwellings. They were only relieved by stone surfaces so impossibly huge that I would estimate the entire Capital of Damocles easily fitting within the perimeter of one."

Faringwood paused, as if realizing the absurdity of his own words. Molinger especially looked skeptical, but did not voice any opinion.

"I believed the world to be completely alien, but then I noticed the legion of images and statues decorating the structures. The reliefs painted scenes of human subjugation, mutilation, slavery and torture. Further depictions showed rituals of blood, sacrifice, and the birthing of monsters, all lorded over by nightmares that violated our innocence during childhood and whom we have foolishly written off as fantasy."

"Surely an elven world then?" whispered General Gaussler. "None hate us as much as the elves, and it sounds like their form of perverse creativity."

Villini didn't reply, entranced as she was by Faringwood's narrative. Some inner warning yelled for her to run, but a stronger voice commanded her to stay.

"To my shame, the horror I should have felt was overwhelmed by a sense of awe. How great and timeless these beings must be, to have created and lived in a city such as this. Who were they? Where did they go? My mind was cracking under the task of comprehending the otherworldly geometry and the history drawn onto its surfaces. I was aware of the sound of my own laughter ringing in my ears, though I do not recall it beginning nor ending. The seductive lines of the hieroglyphs commanded all of my attention until time itself ceased to be meaningful. I felt I somehow understood their alien meaning, and the closer I got to comprehension, the closer I was to madness."

An edge of hysteria crept into Faringwood's educated tenor. His eyes glazed and grew bloodshot, as if having wept violently. His hands now lay relaxed and still, but the lack of his shivering was somehow more unnerving to Villini.

"That's when I spotted him, the being who I call the Stranger." Villini shivered despite the tight bonds of her corset.

"He was a tiny figure in the distance, clothed only in a hooded robe, which rippled despite the lack of wind. I am unsure whether it was I who drew closer to him or he who pulled me, but the Metasphere shifted until I could only see the balcony upon which he stood with his back to me.

"He turned and, for the very first time, I felt something look back at me through the Metasphere."

Faringwood turned to the side, gazing toward some distant

sight only he could see.

"I was now looking directly into his colorless eyes. Although I've been calling him a 'he', in truth I do not know his sex. He was sullen yet possessing all the beauty of Aristophanes' encomium, an androgyny of gaunt lines on ashen white skin. He was neither tall nor short and not physically imposing by any means, but primal fears I thought long transcended came clawing out of the pit of my stomach in response to his presence.

"After a moment the Stranger smiled. A mocking, hungry, knowing smile. It was then I knew, despite all laws of science and logic suggesting otherwise, that he recognized me. His lips shifted and my heart almost burst out of my chest as the silent syllables formed two short words.

"*Rift Walker.*

"The Metasphere then shut off. Click. Just like that, I was free from that dreadful place and from the Stranger's gaze. But I think he turned it off, not from any mercy or display of power, but because he got what he wanted from me."

Faringwood looked back at the Telecorder screen. His expression reminded Villini of a hunted beast.

"As I sat there afterwards, I felt a biting chill settle into my body. It was as if I had been marked, or chosen. At first I ignored the feeling, thinking it a byproduct from the adrenaline, but it lingered past natural duration and began to hurt. Since then, well, perhaps a demonstration is more appropriate."

Faringwood walked over to the heater in the back of his home. Villini heard someone in the room gasp as he pulled off the glove on his right hand, revealing sickly blue skin and dark tinted veins. Her hand darted to her mouth as Faringwood placed his hand onto the boiler. Instead of the hiss of burning flesh, she watched with gruesome fascination as Faringwood withdrew his hand, still blue yet undamaged otherwise.

"Everything in my logical mind grasped for ways to explain my condition, and all my tests suggested impossible results. In the end I could come up with only one conclusion: the universe is uncaring about the rationale of man. All of our 'laws' and 'science', all of the rules we've collected to explain the vastness of reality, all of it is revealed as beliefs in the wake of the mystical and the unknown."

He sat heavily, and Villini could swear the wrinkles on his face deepened in the lamp light.

"I am now cold, so cold. I have lived without the consolation of even an ounce of warmth since that night. I cannot sleep a wink, food tastes like bile, and the world feels disembodied, as if my mind is experiencing everything from a great distance. It's as if—"

He turned his head, as if captured by a sudden thought. "It's as if I'm already dead. A living corpse, returned from the corpse city."

Faringwood threw his head back and cackled, the mad pitch echoing off the war room walls in a dizzying effect. Villini felt tears run down her cheeks as she watched her favorite Uncle spiral into madness, for what else could his fantastic tale be but a concoction? Still, for a moment . . .

General Gaussler stepped forward to block the Telecorder screen. "Your Majesty! We should turn off this nonsense at once! Allow my scouts to track Baron Faringwood down and we will discover the truth behind his delirium."

Villini held up a hand, and the General stilled. "In time, General Gaussler. Know the Baron was dear to me, in both blood and relation, and I worry this may be the final account we are witnessing of a madman. We should do his memory honor by seeing it to the end before deciding further courses of action."

Gaussler scowled but stepped back. On screen, Faringwood regained his composure. A look of surprise was painted on his features and his words came in a frantic whisper.

"A message, yes. I was delivering one, a warning. Even now I can sense him, coming ever closer. The Stranger, he comes for me, but for what sinister purpose I do not know. But I fear for the Damocles Empire. I fear for all the empires of our world."

The image of Faringwood seized the Telecorder screen, his movements shaking the view up and down as spittle flew from his mouth.

"Your Majesty, Lini, Queen Villini, please! An attack is coming, more sinister and more fearsome than you could ever imagine. An assault of demons and creatures beyond alien, capable of sieging our minds, bodies, and spirits! It was I who awoke them, I who drew them here, and I who am the first casualty. But I will not let my death be in vain.

"Prepare, my dearest Lini, prepare. Cease the border dispute with the elves, and heal the old treacheries with the dwarves. Be the first to extend them your hand, for you will need their magic and alchemy if we are to have any hope of surviving the coming storm."

General Gaussler exploded "He's clearly lost it, Your Majesty!"

"Elven magic? Superstition and drugs! Dwarven alchemy? Simple chemistry!" cried Professor Molinger.

Dolen snorted. "Surely if there were any threat, Damocles would crush it. We have the greatest army backed by the largest airship armada in the entire world."

Faringwood continued to plead on screen, and Villini fought the urge to scream in frustration. "There are malevolent beings beyond the stars, dreaming on worlds we cannot fathom. They stir though, and we should tremble! We need—"

The Metasphere behind Faringwood flared intensely as the windows of his home shattered inward. The Telecorder screen flickered, static lines cutting into the video as the frames began to chop. In the space between frames, The Stranger appeared in the room.

Villini blinked. The door was still closed. Had the Telecorder missed filming his entrance?

He looked just as Faringwood described him. The fluttering of his robes revealed thin, almost delicate seeming limbs. They were too long and slender to even be elven. The colorless eyes shone amber as they picked up the boiler's light.

Faringwood yelled hysterically, his old airship captain's pistol in his hand. The triple barrels were leveled at the Stranger, the hammer pulled back and primed to fire.

"You! Why are you here, what do you want?! What do you want from me?!"

The Stranger's lips moved, a bare flutter, but the sound echoed as a chorus of infinite voices. Male and female, dream and nightmare wove words in languages both known and unknown to Villini. "Rift Walker."

As the Stranger floated towards the Baron, Faringwood leveled the pistol at his chest. The gears on the side clicked softly as Faringwood tugged on the trigger. His face was covered in tears and spittle flew from his mouth. "Stay away! I will shoot you! Please, stay away!"

The threat seemed to work as the Stranger stopped his advance, but in a blink his shadow swung around to encompass the entire half of the room Faringwood was in.

"Improbable," whispered Mclinger. "The light, it's not behind him."

Faringwood seemed to be rooted in place, struggling with the darkness coating his body and immobilizing his weapon. With a loud metallic crunch, the pistol was crumpled and tossed to the side. The shadow flitted back to its original shape behind the Stranger.

He closed the distance without any further incident and placed a hand on Faringwood's shoulder. The touch was almost tender, almost paternal. The Baron collapsed onto his knees, his face turned upward at the Stranger in defeat.

"Are you Death?"

The many-voiced answer came after a moment of silence. Though the Stranger's countenance did not change, Villini thought she detected a shift. Pity, perhaps?

"*Not death, no. Not dead, yet. Rewards only come to the useful, Rift Walker.*"

"Then I will be useful. I cannot take this anymore. Just release me afterward."

"*You think you have choice. Illusion.*" The Stranger shifted his gaze towards the Telecorder. "*You think there is hope. Amusing.*" Faringwood rose from the floor like a puppet pulled up by strings, the Stranger's hand never leaving his shoulder. "*Come. We shall see how you will serve the Great One.*"

Faringwood slowly shuffled to the door, a bewildered glint in his eyes. He opened it and waited for the Stranger to exit before following him into the night.

The screen cooled into an abrupt gray as General Gaussler flicked the power off.

Villini realized she had been holding her breath. Her hands were balled into tight fists, her knuckles white and bloodless. "There is still a minute left."

She felt a hand on her shoulder, and turned to find it belonged to Dolen. "We have viewed enough, Your Majesty. There is nothing left to see, but much to discuss."

Villini nodded reluctantly, feeling the prickling sensation of the blood rush back into her hands. She looked at Professor Molinger. "What do you think of the validity of what we viewed? Is it real, or could it be a staged ruse of elven magic?"

The Professor mulled it over. "Even if it was real, and I'm saying it's highly improbable, the level of magic here is as far unseen or undocumented. Only the storied claims of their High King's ability resembles anything close. The elven prisoners speak of him at times, but I always doubt words forced under fire and brand. Besides," he continued, "Even if his abilities were true, mind control simply isn't. Baron Faringwood would have had to willingly play a part in it. And that would practically make him—"

"—a traitor." Dolen finished the sentence with a curt nod, as if it were Molinger's idea. "I dare think what the elves would be capable of with Faringwood at their disposal. Why, the entire Empire would indeed be in danger!"

Villini frowned. "General Gaussler? What do you think?"

The General looked uncertain, but kept his voice bold. "Whatever it is, our army can deal with it. We have the finest men supported by the finest technology that the world has ever seen. Whatever comes, our airships will be ready to blow them back home. We'll fill them full of brass before they're even in sight of the Capital!"

Molinger brightened as he nodded his agreement. "Our newest gatling gun models have achieved firing rates of over 1,200 rounds per minute. And prototypes of the tesla cannon are ready to be put into production."

Villini nodded and waved a hand for silence. "I have heard enough, my loyal advisors. Know that I value each of your opinions, but this is what I think.

"My Uncle, the Baron Faringwood to the rest of you, is still alive. He has been taken and is being used by forces, elven or otherwise, for purposes not of his own volition. Without proper reason to believe otherwise, I am inclined to take his warning at face value."

The silence was almost tangible as Villini continued. She was sure they all looked at her as if she was the mad one. "As such, we must prepare for what's to come. First, General Gaussler, I want you to put our forces on full alert. Order them into wartime operations, and I want them ready to respond to anything that arises."

The General snapped a smart salute. "At once, My Queen."

Dolen bolted upright. "But Your Majesty! If the elves and dwarves see our army mobilize, they will surely retaliate."

"That's why I'm sending you as an ambassador for peace." Villini savored the look of surprise on his face. "Leave immediately for the Oaken Court of the Summerlands. Find and make treaty with the High King, then call for the Dwarven Council and settle our old feuds. Whatever the cost, I'm sure you can cover them with your ample coffers. An alliance must be formed, if not to meet this threat than to simply cease the fighting. My Uncle was right to caution peace, if nothing else."

Dolen was stunned. "They will never listen to me, Your Highness, I'm a bit unwelcomed."

"Yes, Baron. I know of your speculations into their lands, and I know you've already sold what you've yet gained. Still, you are perfect for this. You are greedy and manipulative, yet charming and quick. Convince them of your change of heart and forge me an alliance with their nations, and I will leave you in the ambassador role."

Lights gleamed in Dolen's eyes as he weighed the possibilities. "If I fail, you would make a welcoming gift of me for their executioner's block. And if I succeed, an ambassador would be in the best position to make gains from new pacts and trade routes."

To Villini's surprise, the Baron actually bowed. He had never done that before. "Very well. It seems I have no choice but to succeed. Perhaps I had underestimated Your Grace."

Villini enjoyed the moment briefly before spending the next hours planning the countless other necessities. Conscription, logistics, locking down the tabloids, manufacturing shifts and more, they were all handed out with curt efficiency. The sun peeked above the horizon before she was done.

She sighed, exhausted, as her three advisors left the war room. Her head ached from the stress and lack of sleep. She sat heavily, struck by sudden doubt. What if Faringwood was dead? Without her Uncle, she was the last of House Lichtenstein. It would be a year until she could marry and more still before she produced an heir.

She pushed such thoughts from her mind. He was still alive and she felt it, sure as the blood pumping through her own veins. She glanced outside at the imperial gardens, where the pristine grass was marred only by the broken skeleton of the crashed ornithopter. It was a beautiful, saddening thing. She wondered for a moment what view her Uncle was seeing, and where he was now.

That's when it struck her. Her Uncle. In the recording he left the room. Who sent his ornithopter?

There was more to the video. Her hand hovered over the Telecorder's ON switch. Something in the back of her mind warned her not to view it, but she had to know.

The image hummed back to life, the gray screen dissolving into vivid monochrome which warmed with vibrant color once again. After a flicker, the picture moved again.

Faringwood's house was empty, the door open. Wind stirred the papers on his floor, but nothing else.

Three seconds stretched into thirty.

Just as Villini thought there was nothing left to see, a shadow fell across the doorway. The Stranger returned, minus Faringwood, and floated smoothly over the debris on the floor.

Toward the Telecorder. Toward her.

Villini's hand shot to the power switch as the face of the Stranger filled the screen. She flicked it off, but the picture did not fade.

She couldn't pull away from the colorless eyes of the Stranger. Impossibly, defying all rules of time and logic, she felt them seeing her. Then the Stranger smiled, a mocking, hungry, *knowing* smile, and she shivered as his lips brushed each other and the whispering voices formed a single name.

"*Villini.*"

The Telecorder flicked off then, and Villini realized the Stranger had sent the ornithopter. Not from any mercy or misplaced confidence, but because he wanted her to see its contents. A chill settled into her bones.

# Standing Room Only
## Karen Joy Fowler

On Good Friday 1865, Washington, D.C. was crowded with tourists and revelers. Even Willard's, which claimed to be the largest hotel in the country, with room for 1200 guests, had been booked to capacity. Its lobbies and sitting rooms were hot with bodies. Gas light hissed from golden chandeliers, spilled over the doormen's uniforms of black and maroon. Many of the revelers were women. In 1865, women were admired for their stoutness and went anywhere they could fit their hoop skirts. The women at Willard's wore garishly colored dresses with enormous skirts and resembled great inverted tulips. The men were in swallow coats.

Outside it was almost spring. The forsythia bloomed, dusting the city with yellow. Weeds leapt up in the public parks; the roads melted to mud. Pigs roamed like dogs about the city, and dead cats by the dozens floated in the sewers and perfumed the rooms of the White House itself.

The Metropolitan Hotel contained an especially rowdy group of celebrants from Baltimore, who passed the night of April 13 toasting everything under the sun. They resurrected on the morning of the 14th, pale and spent, surrounded by broken glass and sporting bruises they couldn't remember getting.

It was the last day of Lent. The war was officially over, except for Joseph Johnston's confederate army and some action out West. The citizens of Washington, D.C. still began each morning reading the daily death list. If anything, this task had taken on an added urgency. To lose someone you loved now, with the rest of the city madly, if grimly, celebrating, would be unendurable.

The guests in Mary Surratt's boarding house began the day

with a breakfast of steak, eggs and ham, oysters, grits and whiskey. Mary's seventeen-year old daughter, Anna, was in love with
John Wilkes Booth. She had a picture of him hidden in the sitting
room, behind a lithograph entitled "Morning, Noon, and Night."
She helped her mother clear the table and she noticed with a sharp
and unreasonable disapproval that one of the two new boarders,
one of the men who only last night had been given a room, was
staring at her mother.

Mary Surratt was neither a pretty woman, nor a clever one,
nor was she young. Anna was too much of a romantic, too star
and stage-struck, to approve. It was one thing to lie awake at
night in her attic bedroom, thinking of JW. It was another to
imagine her mother playing any part in such feelings.

Anna's brother John once told her that five years ago a woman
named Henrietta Irving had tried to stab Booth with a knife. Failing, she'd thrust the blade into her own chest instead. He seemed
to be under the impression that this story would bring Anna to
her senses. It had, as anyone could have predicted, the opposite
effect. Anna had also heard rumors that Booth kept a woman in
a house of prostitution near the White House. And once she had
seen a piece of paper on which Booth had been composing a
poem. You could make out the final version:

Now in this hour that we part,
I will ask to be forgotten never
But, in thy pure and guileless heart,
Consider me thy friend dear Eva.

Anna would sit in the parlor while her mother dozed and pretend she was the first of these women, and if she tired of that, she
would sometimes dare to pretend she was the second, but most
often she liked to imagine herself the third.

Flirtations were common and serious, and the women in
Washington worked hard at them. A war in the distance always
provides a rich context of desperation, while at the same time
granting women a bit of extra freedom. They might quite enjoy
it, if the price they paid were anything but their sons.

The new men had hardly touched their food, cutting away
the fatty parts of the meat and leaving them in a glistening greasy
wasteful pile. They'd finished the whiskey, but made faces while

they drank. Anna had resented the compliment of their eyes and, paradoxically, now resented the insult of their plates. Her mother set a good table.

In fact, Anna did not like them and hoped they would not be staying. She had often seen men outside the Surratt Boarding House lately, men who busied themselves in unpersuasive activities when she passed them. She connected these new men to those, and she was perspicacious enough to blame their boarder Louis Wiechman for the lot of them, without ever knowing the extent to which she was right. She had lived for the past year in a confederate household in the heart of Washington. Everyone around her had secrets. She had grown quite used to this.

Wiechman was a permanent guest at the Surratt boarding house. He was a fat, friendly man who worked in the office of the Commissary General of Prisons and shared John Surratt's bedroom. Secrets were what Wiechman traded in. He provided John, who was a courier for the Confederacy, with substance for his covert messages south. But then Wiechman had also, on a whim, sometime in March, told the clerks in the office that a Secesh plot was being hatched against the President in the very house where he roomed.

It created more interest than he had anticipated. He was called into the office of Captain McDavitt and interviewed at length. As a result, the Surratt boarding house was under surveillance from March through April, although, it is an odd fact that no records of the surveillance or the interview could be found later.

Anna would surely have enjoyed knowing this. She liked attention as much as most young girls. And this was the backdrop of a romance. Instead, all she could see was that something was up and that her pious, simple mother was part of it.

The new guest, the one who talked the most, spoke with a strange lisp and Anna didn't like this either. She stepped smoothly between the men to pick up their plates. She used the excuse of a letter from her brother to go out directly after breakfast. "Mama," she said. "I'll just take John's letter to poor Miss Ward."

Just as her brother enjoyed discouraging her own romantic inclinations, she made it her business to discourage the affections of Miss Ward with regard to him. Calling on Miss Ward with the letter would look like a kindness, but it would make the point that Miss Ward had not gotten a letter herself.

Besides, Booth was in town. If Anna was outside, she might see him again.

The thirteenth had been beautiful, but the weather on the fourteenth was equal parts mud and wind. The wind blew bits of Anna's hair loose and tangled them up with the fringe of her shawl. Around the Treasury Building she stopped to watch a carriage sunk in the mud all the way up to the axle. The horses, a matched pair of blacks, were rescued first. Then planks were laid across the top of the mud for the occupants. They debarked, a man and a woman, the woman unfashionably thin and laughing giddily as with every unsteady step her hoop swung and unbalanced her, first this way and then that. She clutched the man's arm and screamed when a pig burrowed past her, then laughed again at even higher pitch. The man stumbled into the mire when she grabbed him, and this made her laugh, too. The man's clothing was very fine, although now quite speckled with mud. A crowd gathered to watch the woman—the attention made her helpless with laughter.

The war had ended, Anna thought, and everyone had gone simultaneously mad. She was not the only one to think so. It was the subject of newspaper editorials, of barroom speeches. "The city is disorderly with men who are celebrating too hilariously," the president's day guard, William Crook, had written just yesterday. The sun came out, but only in a perfunctory, pale fashion.

Her visit to Miss Ward was spoiled by the fact that John had sent a letter there as well. Miss Ward obviously enjoyed telling Anna so. She was very near-sighted and she held the letter right up to her eyes to read it. John had recently fled to Canada. With the war over, there was every reason to expect he would come home, even if neither letter said so.

There was more news, and Miss Ward preened while she delivered it. "Bessie Hale is being taken to Spain. Much against her will," Miss Ward said. Bessie was the daughter of ex-senator John P. Hale. Her father hoped that a change of scenery would help pretty Miss Bessie conquer her infatuation for John Wilkes Booth. Miss Ward, whom no one including Anna's brother thought was pretty, was laughing at her. "Mr. Hale does not want an actor in the family," Miss Ward said, and Anna regretted the generous impulse that had sent her all the way across town on such a gloomy day.

"Wilkes Booth is back in Washington," Miss Ward finished, and Anna was at least able to say that she knew this, he had called on them only yesterday. She left the Wards with the barest of good-byes.

Louis Wiechman passed her on the street, stopping for a courteous greeting, although they had just seen each other at breakfast. It was now about ten a.m. Wiechman was on his way to church. Among the many secrets he knew was Anna's. "I saw John Wilkes Booth in the barbershop this morning," he told her. "With a crowd watching his every move."

Anna raised her head. "Mr. Booth is a famous thespian. Naturally people admire him."

She flattered herself that she knew JW a little better than these idolaters did. The last time her brother had brought Booth home, he'd followed Anna out to the kitchen. She'd had her back to the door, washing the plates. Suddenly she could feel that he was there. How could she have known that? The back of her neck grew hot, and when she turned, sure enough, there he was, leaning against the doorjamb, studying his nails.

"Do you believe our fates are already written?" Booth asked her. He stepped into the kitchen. "I had my palm read once by a gypsy. She said I would come to a bad end. She said it was the worst palm she had ever seen." He held his hand out for her to take. "She said she wished she hadn't even seen it," he whispered, and then he drew back quickly as her mother entered, before she could bend over the hand herself, reassure him with a different reading, before she could even touch him.

"JW isn't satisfied with acting," her brother had told her once. "He yearns for greatness on the stage of history," and if her mother hadn't interrupted, if Anna had had two seconds to herself with him, this is the reading she would have done. She would have promised him greatness.

"Mr. Booth was on his way to Ford's Theatre to pick up his mail," Wiechman said with a wink. It was an ambiguous wink. It might have meant only that Wiechman remembered what a first love was like. It might have suggested he knew the use she would make of such information.

Two regiments were returning to Washington from Virginia. They were out of step and out of breath, covered with dust. Anna drew a handkerchief from her sleeve and waved it at them. Other women were doing the same. A crowd gathered. A vendor came through the crowd, selling oysters. A man in a tight-fitting coat stopped him. He had a disreputable look — a bad haircut with long sideburns. He pulled a handful of coins from one pocket and stared at them stupidly. He was drunk. The vendor had to reach into his hand and pick out what he was owed.

"Filthy place!" the man next to the drunk man said. "I really can't bear the smell. I can't eat. Don't expect me to sleep in that flea-infested hotel another night." He left abruptly, colliding with Anna's arm, forcing her to take a step or two. "Excuse me," he said without stopping, and there was nothing penitent or apologetic in his tone. He didn't even seem to see her.

Since he had forced her to start, Anna continued to walk. She didn't even know she was going to Ford's Theatre until she turned onto Eleventh Street. It was a bad idea, but she couldn't seem to help herself. She began to walk faster.

"No tickets, Miss," James R. Ford told her, before she could open her mouth. She was not the only one there. A small crowd of people stood at the theater door. "Absolutely sold out. It's because the President and General Grant will be attending."

James Ford held an American flag in his arms. He raised it. "I'm just decorating the President's box." It was the last night of a lackluster run. He would never have guessed they would sell every seat. He thought Anna's face showed disappointment. He was happy, himself, and it made him kind. "They're rehearsing inside," he told her. "For General Grant! You just go on in for a peek."

He opened the doors and she entered. Three women and a man came with her. Anna had never seen any of the others before, but supposed they were friends of Mr. Ford's. They forced themselves through the doors beside her and then sat next to her in the straight-backed cane chairs just back from the stage.

Laura Keene herself stood in the wings awaiting her entrance. The curtain was pulled back, so that Anna could see her. Her cheeks were round with rouge.

The stage was not deep. Mrs. Mountchessington stood on it with her daughter, Augusta, and Asa Trenchard.

"All I crave is affection," Augusta was saying. She shimmered with insincerity.

Anna repeated the lines to herself. She imagined herself as an actress, married to JW, courted by him daily before an audience of a thousand, in a hundred different towns. They would play the love scenes over and over again, each one as true as the last. She would hardly know where her real and imaginary lives diverged. She didn't suppose there was much money to be made, but even to pretend to be rich seemed like happiness to her.

Augusta was willing to be poor, if she was loved. "Now I've no fortune," Asa said to her in response, "but I'm biling over with affections, which I'm ready to pour out all over you, like apple sass, over roast pork."

The women exited. He was alone on the stage. Anna could see Laura Keene mouthing his line, just as he spoke it. The woman seated next to her surprised her by whispering it aloud as well.

"Well, I guess I know enough to turn you inside out, old gal, you sockdologizing old man-trap," the three of them said. Anna turned to her seatmate who stared back. Her accent, Anna thought, had been English. "Don't you love theater?" she asked Anna in a whisper. Then her face changed. She was looking at something above Anna's head.

Anna looked, too. Now she understood the woman's expression. John Wilkes Booth was standing in the Presidential Box, staring down on the actor. Anna rose. Her seatmate caught her arm. She was considerably older than Anna, but not enough so that Anna could entirely dismiss her possible impact on Booth.

"Do you know him?" the woman asked.

"He's a friend of my brother's." Anna had no intention of introducing them. She tried to edge away, but the woman still held her.

"My name is Cassie Streichman."

"Anna Surratt."

There was a quick, sideways movement in the woman's eyes. "Are you related to Mary Surratt?"

"She's my mother." Anna began to feel just a bit of concern. So many people interested in her dull, sad mother. Anna tried to shake loose, and found, to her surprise, that she couldn't. The woman would not let go.

"I've heard of the boarding house," Mrs. Streichman said. It was a courtesy to think of her as a married woman. It was more of a courtesy than she deserved.

Anna looked up at the box again. Booth was already gone. "Let me go," she told Mrs. Streichman, so loudly that Laura Keene herself heard. So forcefully that Mrs. Streichman finally did so.

Anna left the theater. The streets were crowded and she could not see Booth anywhere. Instead, as she stood on the bricks, looking left and then right, Mrs. Streichman caught up with her. "Are you going home? Might we walk along?"

"No. I have errands," Anna said. She walked quickly away. She was cross now, because she had hoped to stay and look for Booth, who must still be close by, but Mrs. Streichman had made her too uneasy. She looked back once. Mrs. Streichman stood in the little circle of her friends, talking animatedly. She gestured with her hands like a European. Anna saw Booth nowhere.

She went back along the streets to St. Patrick's Church, in search of her mother. It was noon and the air was warm in spite of the colorless sun. Inside the church, her mother knelt in the pew and prayed noisily. Anna slipped in beside her.

"This is the moment," her mother whispered. She reached out and took Anna's hand, gripped it tightly enough to hurt. Her mother's eyes brightened with tears. "This is the moment they nailed him to the cross," she said. There was purple cloth over the crucifix. The pallid sunlight flowed into the church through colored glass.

Across town a group of men had gathered in the Kirkwood bar and were entertaining themselves by buying drinks for George Atzerodt. Atzerodt was one of Booth's co-conspirators. His assignment for the day, given to him by Booth, was to kidnap the Vice President. He was already so drunk he couldn't stand.

"Would you say that the Vice President is a brave man?" he asked and they laughed at him. He didn't mind being laughed at. It struck him a bit funny himself. "He wouldn't carry a firearm, would he? I mean, why would he?" Atzerodt said. "Are there ever soldiers with him? That nigger who watches him eat. Is he there all the time?"

"Have another drink," they told him, laughing. "On us," and you couldn't get insulted at that.

Anna and her mother returned to the boarding house. Mary Surratt had rented a carriage and was going into the country. "Mr. Wiechman will drive me," she told her daughter. A Mr. Nothey owed her money they desperately needed; Mary Surratt was going to collect it.

But just as she was leaving, Booth appeared. He took her mother's arm, drew her to the parlor. Anna felt her heart stop and then start again, faster. "Mary, I must talk to you," he said to her mother, whispering, intimate. "Mary." He didn't look at Anna at all and didn't speak again until she left the room. She would have stayed outside the door to hear whatever she could, but Louis Wiechman had had the same idea. They exchanged one cross look, and then each left the hallway. Anna went up the stairs to her bedroom.

She knew the moment Booth went. She liked to feel that this was because they had a connection, something unexplainable, something preordained, but in fact she could hear the door. He went without asking to see her. She moved to the small window to watch him leave. He did not stop to glance up. He mounted a black horse, tipped his hat to her mother.

Her mother boarded a hired carriage, leaning on Mr. Wiechman's hand. She held a parcel under her arm. Anna had never seen it before. It was flat and round and wrapped in newspaper. Anna thought it was a gift from Booth. It made her envious.

Later at her mother's trial, Anna would hear that the package had contained a set of field glasses. A man named Lloyd would testify that Mary Surratt had delivered them to him and had also given him instructions from Booth regarding guns. It was the single most damaging evidence against her. At her brother's trial, Lloyd would recant everything but the field glasses. He was, he now said, too drunk at the time to remember what Mrs. Surratt had told him. He had never remembered. The prosecution had compelled his earlier testimony through threats. This revision would come two years after Mary Surratt had been hanged.

Anna stood at the window a long time, pretending that Booth might return with just such a present for her.

John Wilkes Booth passed George Atzerodt on the street at five p.m.. Booth was on horseback. He told Atzerodt he had changed his mind about the kidnapping. He now wanted the Vice President killed. At 10:15 or thereabouts. "I've learned that Johnson is a very brave man," Atzerodt told him.

"And you are not," Booth agreed. "But you're in too deep to back out now." He rode away. Booth was carrying in his pocket a letter to the editor of The National Intelligencer. In it, he recounted the reasons for Lincoln's death. He had signed his own name, but also that of George Atzerodt.

The men who worked with Atzerodt once said he was a man you could insult and he would take no offense. It was the kindest thing they could think of to say. Three men from the Kirkwood bar appeared and took Atzerodt by the arms. "Let's find another bar," they suggested. "We have hours and hours yet before the night is over. Eat, drink. Be merry."

At six p.m. John Wilkes Booth gave the letter to John Matthews, an actor, asking him to deliver it the next day. "I'll be out of town or I would deliver it myself," he explained. A group of Confederate officers marched down Pennsylvania Avenue where John Wilkes Booth could see them. They were unaccompanied; they were turning themselves in. It was the submissiveness of it that struck Booth hardest. "A man can meet his fate or make it," he told Matthews. "A man can rise to the occasion or fall beneath it."

At sunset, a man called Peanut John lit the big glass globe at the entrance to Ford's Theatre. Inside, the presidential box had been decorated with borrowed flags and bunting. The door into the box had been forced some weeks ago in an unrelated incident and could no longer be locked.

It was early evening when Mary Surratt returned home. Her financial affairs were still unsettled; Mr. Nothey had not even shown up at their meeting. She kissed her daughter. "If Mr. No-they will not pay us what he owes," she said, "I can't think what we will do next. I can't see a way ahead for us. Your brother must come home." She went into the kitchen to oversee the preparations for dinner.

Anna went in to help. Since the afternoon, since the moment Booth had not spoken to her, she had been overcome with unhappiness. It had not lessened a bit in the last hours; she now doubted it ever would. She cut the roast into slices. It bled beneath her knife and she thought of Henrietta Irving's white skin and the red heart beating underneath. She could understand Henrietta Irving perfectly. All I crave is affection, she said to herself, and the honest truth of the sentiment softened her into tears. Perhaps she could survive the rest of her life, if she played it this way, scene by scene. She held the knife up, watching the blood slide down the blade, and this was dramatic and fit her Shakespearian mood.

She felt a chill and when she turned around one of the new boarders was leaning against the doorjamb, watching her mother. "We're not ready yet," she told him crossly. He'd given her a start. He vanished back into the parlor.

Once again, the new guests hardly ate. Louis Wiechman finished his food with many elegant compliments. His testimony in court would damage Mary Surratt almost as much as Lloyd's. He would say that she seemed uneasy that night, unsettled, although none of the other boarders saw this. After dinner Mary Surratt went through the house, turning off the kerosene lights one by one.

Anna took a glass of wine and went to sleep immediately. She dreamed deeply, but her heartbreak woke her again only an hour or so later. It stabbed at her lightly from the inside when she breathed. She could see John Wilkes Booth as clearly as if he were in the room with her. "I am the most famous man in America," he said. He held out his hand, beckoned to her.

Downstairs she heard the front door open and close. She rose and looked out the window, just as she had done that afternoon. Many people, far too many people were on the street. They were all walking in the same direction. One of them was George Atze-rodt. Hours before he had abandoned his knife but he too would die, along with Mary Surratt. He had gone too far to back out. He walked with his hands over the shoulders of two dark-haired men. One of them looked up. He was of a race Anna had never seen before. The new boarders joined the crowd. Anna could see them when they passed out from under the porch overhang.

Something big was happening. Something big enough to overwhelm her own hurt feelings. Anna dressed slowly and then quickly and more quickly. I live, she thought, in the most wondrous of times. Here was the proof. She was still unhappy, but she was also excited. She moved quietly past her mother's door.

The flow of people took her down several blocks. She was taking her last walk again, only backwards, like a ribbon uncoiling. She went past St. Patrick's Church, down Eleventh Street. The crowd ended at Ford's Theatre and thickened there. Anna was jostled. To her left, she recognized the woman from the carriage, the laughing woman, though she wasn't laughing now. Someone stepped on Anna's hoop skirt and she heard it snap. Someone struck her in the back of the head with an elbow. "Be quiet!" someone admonished someone else. "We'll miss it." Someone took hold of her arm. It was so crowded, she couldn't even turn to see, but she heard the voice of Cassie Streichman.

"I had tickets and everything," Mrs. Streichman said angrily. "Do you believe that? I can't even get to the door. It's almost ten o'clock and I had tickets."

"Can my group please stay together?" a woman toward the front asked. "Let's not lose anyone," and then she spoke again in a language Anna did not know.

"It didn't seem a good show," Anna said to Mrs. Streichman. "A comedy and not very funny."

Mrs. Streichman twisted into the space next to her. "That was just a rehearsal. The reviews are incredible. And you wouldn't believe the waiting list. Years. Centuries! I'll never have tickets again." She took a deep, calming breath. "At least you're here, dear. That's something I couldn't have expected. That makes it very real. And," she pressed Anna's arm, "if it helps in any way, you must tell yourself later there's nothing you could have done to make it come out differently. Everything that will happen has already happened. It won't be changed."

"Will I get what I want?" Anna asked her. She could not keep the brightness of hope from her voice. Clearly, she was part of something enormous. Something memorable. How many people could say that?

"I don't know what you want," Mrs. Streichman answered. She had an uneasy look. "I didn't get what I wanted," she added. "Even though I had tickets. Good God! People getting what they want. That's not the history of the world, is it?"

"Will everyone please be quiet!" someone behind Anna said. "Those of us in the back can't hear a thing."

Mrs. Streichman began to cry, which surprised Anna very much. "I'm such a sap," Mrs. Streichman said apologetically. "Things really get to me." She put her arm around Anna.

"All I want," Anna began, but a man to her right hushed her angrily.

"Shut up!" he said. "As if we came all this way to listen to you."

# KING HARVEST
# (WILL SURELY COME)

## NISI SHAWL

L isten to the wind as it blows across the water. How it slows. How it stills as we approach the day's peak. Pretty soon the carnival begins.

Seven years I've reigned. And before me, your grandfather. Twenty-one years. That was a mistake, despite our peace and prosperity. The mud people refused to put up with him any longer. Of course they had no real say, but they muttered under their breaths. Neighboring realms sent embassies overseas on their behalf to rouse shithole nations to their defense. Even here, in the Heartland, we whites felt that wrath. The mercy shown us—weakness, without a doubt—meant they killed only our anointed ruler. And so I took the American throne.

And so the luxury of your upbringing. Only the softest of cotton knits, t-shirt grade, gathered fresh and stainless from the loading docks of abandoned mills, have ever graced your lovely form. Yes, I see you fingering their thin folds as I remind you of them. Your teeth shine as pure as ice between your smiling lips at the pleasantness of that touch. But then your pampered hands let loose the cloth to reach for mine and meet stiff plastic—my royal bonds. Then worry corrugates your brow.

Yet you are silent. Obedient. A true woman.

It's this that gives me strength. I know you will endure. I wish I could go to the first of your weddings—but what good would that do? Your husband must take my place as king, and therefore I must vacate it. To put things plainly, I must die.

Ah no, dear Tiffany. No tears. Our Savior will welcome me personally into his arms, and you and all America will profit from my suffering and sacrifice. Just as we have profited by the deaths of my decoys, those black effigies burned and hung annually as substitutes. Listen to the ripening sighs of the heavy-headed wheat.

At least he had that much right. Though he carried it a bit too far, the decoys were a very good idea, starting with your grandfather's five captured runaways and continuing with the three slaves who volunteered. And the twelve chosen by collection plate lottery, and of course he was smart to limit the number provided by that method to the exact same number as that of the Apostles. I think, however, that allowing the mud people to vote for that final effigy based on his slate of nominations brought back some strange sort of race memory . . . triggering the unholy mission that nearly proved—well, that made regime change final.

Yes, much appreciated. My goblet's on the table. The water bucket's the one to the left—the right is vinegar, to wash me after my scourging. No. I told you, Tiffany. No! Quit crying. I'll call the guard to send you home immediately if you keep on. This is a joyful occasion. The blessing of Jesus will consecrate it. When they hitch the monster trucks to my four limbs—

Let's talk about something else, then, since the subject so upsets you. Your wedding. End of April, is that what you're saying? You don't want to do it any sooner, do you, Tiffany? Not good for the country to be leaderless nine whole months. Fine, fine. I suppose a mourning period of some sort is to be expected. You'll have a big tailgate picnic to celebrate your engagement, though, won't you—nice and public? Promise? And the Reverend's the best regent we could hope for. Absolutely Pence-like . . .

I know. But look, Tiffany, you'll only have to wait eight more years to marry Gavin. Sperry's first on my list for a reason. You'll still be young. Thirty's nothing. All the days of Methuselah were nine hundred sixty and nine years. Sperry will reinforce the pattern when he offers himself to ensure the success of his eighth crop. You could even marry Jackson when Sperry's done and save Gavin for last—I know. Thirty-eight. Unimaginable. And certainly you'd be past prime childbearing age by then, so an heir would be hard to produce. Yes. That's best. Second. Not third. But promise me: not first. Promise on the Bible.

Is it? Good. I didn't know—I just assumed that was what you

brought to read me. Well, wonderful! Let's do it! As long as you care to stay—the ceremony's not till noon. We can skip around some; give me a few other books and chapters, Jeremiah and so forth, but mainly I want the Oligarchs! Exactly what the doctor ordered. Whatever else anyone says about your grandfather, they can't deny he knew how to write.

Now tuck that pillow behind my head—there. And pull the handle forward and the chair will lean back so I can rest while you read.

from "*Letters to the Oligarchs*"

*One*
*And it came to pass that when, by the miraculous Hand of God, Our President Donald John was elected to the highest office in this or any other land, demons woke to oppose him in the souls and bodily temples of many of his rightful subjects. Fierce the prayings and watchful the vigils in his name, and long the arcs of correction he and his ministers initiated. Oftimes such were of necessity but poorly coordinated. In addition and as follow-up to those beautiful orders covered by media, the establishment of Heartland ever occupied your servants. Thus to you, oh wealthy ones, authentic wielders of American Greatness, we now report all our actions faithfully undertaken in former secrecy.*

*To make the involved states' governments of Kansas and Oklahoma immune to charges of religious discrimination was the first needfulness. Legislation took effect for ostensibly other causes while private firms purchased acreage and founded churches as attached and hired approved family heads per your brilliant specifications. Educational programs delegated to charter schools prepared the way. Covenants created according to received templates were circulated, with instructions for slight variations in spelling, grammar, and phrasing so as not to excite too much suspicion.*

*After the Fake Election we were all ready. So soon as the so-called "results" were released, Deeds of Secession were filed in every one of the 182 target counties, and a few in counties over the border in Missouri for good measure. Rather than force the mud people's emigration, Heartland employed the model of advertising cheap-to-free housing and welfare services in designated areas. Subsequent improvements to these areas then doubled as excuses for interrupted communications and the installation of supposedly temporary fencing. Thus the reserves came about without overmuch struggle to suppress their inmates.*

*Heartland is a magnet of Godliness. From the four corners of the world come white men and women seeking refuge here, a sacred space supportive of their inherent superiority. Your trust in us is justified, as we have shown and will in all things continue to make manifest.*

*Five*

*Victory! Though disposal of our slaves is obviously an internal matter of concern to none outside Heartland's borders, it has taken the inevitable breakdown of trade between those Godless principalities surrounding us to rid we good and blameless Christians of their interference. Argument was pointless, despite the tenderness and particularity directed at those captive runaways designated for execution. Last meals, baths, haircuts, and even, in one case, the opportunity to address to you a personal letter! None of this liberality counted in the heathens' calculations of our system's merit.*

*I thought never to be able to tell you of these things. And perhaps even yet I do not; perhaps these letters serve only as records for posterity, not as missives reaching you in your underground retreats, for postal services are unreliable these days and your address tantalizingly inexact. We have kept exact copies from the beginning and will with every one of our transcriptions— manually, when no other means presents itself—until otherwise ordered.*

*We burnt the arsonist alive. This appeared the most just and Testamentary course. Her attempted escape fortuitously coincided with Secession Day—or nearly enough that the execution served double duty as our offering in Jesus's name. My sermon pointed out how by committing her crime she effectively volunteered, and the Liberty Cocktail pacified her to the point that if not for multiplicity of bonds joining her to the Scarecrow she would never have stood erect for the ceremony. Thus far the year's yield has exceeded expectations, which proves our Savior is satisfied.*

*Sixteen*
*Four more years we can go on as we do now. Reveal to me in a timely manner how next to proceed to gather a worthy sacrifice. I know you won't respond to this missive in written style, even if it ever is received. There has been no direct communication from you all this while, nor do we any longer expect it. But a sign as certain as that by which Our Lord selects the slave effigy destined to die that Secession Day? As clear as the telltale coin stamped with a clue to its identity which is always found among donations from tithing households? You might at least vouchsafe us such.*

*"At least"? Doubt is a human failing, but one which I must move on from after I acknowledge it. Your guidance will surely come.*

*A plague of skin cancers has descended on our outposts at New Jerusalem and nearby Canaan Ridge. Our Elders determined where to situate the blame: a so-called "Women's Fitness Class." Tight clothes and a mirror along one wall encouraged feminine vanity. Not to mention tribadic attractions between the students—some the innocent, unwitting victims of rampant Queens! Proper penance has been applied.*

*Twenty*
*Lights in the darkness of the world's misery, shining examples of the heights human accomplishment can reach, you are my daily and nightly inspiration. O Fathers of our questing spirit, we beseech you to allow us to extend our Fellowship to those benighted in lands currently beyond this reign's humble reach. And in years to come we pray to show the span of your greatness to every nation on this your troublous Earth. Forever.*

*

Yes, dear, I heard. Enter! Prompt, aren't you? That's good. Wouldn't want to be late to my own funeral. That's a joke. Go ahead and laugh.

And thank you, Tiffany. A nice verse to finish on.

Yes, I'd like that very much, my dear, if you wouldn't mind. Forget my threats—your tears are understandable, touching even. Though you must learn to contain yourself. Today. Turn away if you want, shut your eyes when they drop the flag.

Yes, but if I know you're in the stadium I'll be . . . not braver, because there's nothing to fear, is there? What's the word I want? Dignified. I'll look more dignified. I'm sure I will. I'll think of you. That's got to help.

Honestly, no. It's too late for petitioning the Elders. In a way it always has been. The effigies offered in my stead staved this off for seven years. But I lived in emulation of Christ's life. I must die in emulation of his death.

Now you, guard—what's your name again? Slattery? Irish, isn't it? They're white by me. What's that you're asking? Naked? I—would appreciate a loincloth, yes. My daughter, and there may be other ladies present.

What about the bindings? They'll have to be cut before I'm lashed to the truck's bumpers, won't they, Slattery? So you may as well take care of those before escorting me to the stage. Ah. No, that's right, my scourging could go awry if I were inadvertently to struggle. Though I'll remind you that your prior experience is limited to effigies, and blacks are naturally more animalistic in their responses to pain.

Tiffany, wait outside. Just for a moment.

Slattery, my wrists? And these hobbles on my ankles—I really must insist. It's going to make everything much easier—marching me, stripping me, everything. Fine. Call in as many more guards as you feel necessary. Though we don't want to fall behind. The musicians are starting—I can hear "Grand Old Flag" through the door seams and we need to form up and join the procession. Bring them in, bring them in! Hurry! I won't have it said I'm a coward.

Thank you. Hello. Hello. Hello.

Here. Yes, cutting would be quicker. And the shackles hobbling my feet? Slattery has the key. And if you'll just unbutton my shirtsleeves I can slip—that's it. Nice and cool. Now take my hand and shake—no, I suppose it won't matter much longer how I treat you, but I want us to feel really bonded, connected together till—till the end. So. Shake. Set down the vinegar a moment. And tell me your names so I won't forget them—hah. For the rest of my life, yes. But more importantly, they'll be among the first I repeat in His ears afterwards. I promise. Indeed, in the same breath as the Reverend, the last man to touch me. You deserve it for your work. For your work and for your love. As hard and great as mine.

Wait. It's easier for me to adjust that. All right. I'm ready. Open the door. Let's roll.

# Harmony

## Andy Dudak

### 1

The song plays everywhere in this frontier provincial capital, piped into shops and bazaars, blaring from police fortifications and mobile propaganda vehicles mingling with tank columns. The melody is cloying, the singers children who were press ganged into local stardom. It's clear from the accompanying video—also ubiquitous on large screens throughout the city—that the children were chosen to represent the ethnic groups at odds here. They chant civic virtues and howl about unity. But there is something more within the song, in its harmonies and resonances. Some call it auditory magic, but it's more properly termed "interference technology." Within the spheres of the song, you stroll in a civic euphoria. You're in a thriving metropolis that provides jobs and infrastructure, courtesy of the occupiers. You are home.

The song plays as you garrote the customs house official. The children trill about rule of law, lending the murder an ironic air. You tighten the wire, making it vanish into the man's fleshy neck. Blood wells up and jets. His expensive shoes scuff the floor as he struggles, seeming to print a visual representation of the song's rhythm.

The patterns of the song are everywhere.

Then you run, and the song is ridiculous in this context. You're a foreign agent fleeing justice, fleeing detainment, torture, ruination for local friends and lovers, all of this and more, but somehow it will be okay. You can slow down, take a breather. You should find a patrol unit to talk to. If you just explain everything, they will see reason.

No. That's the song at work.

You stand amid ruined warehouses, breathing raggedly in the moonlight. The song nearly got you to commit suicide, and not for the first time. This time it was the verse about rule of law, or maybe the bit about patriotism. But now you're in control again. You were sent here because you are two people. You can pass through security checkpoints, scanned and verified as lost in the song. And you can stand apart from that, deep down in that space carved out by intensive training, where the scanners can't reach, and plot fomentation.

You hum one of your warding phrases. Your mind clears.

The influence of the city's song, reaching you from a police fort on the other side of the ruins, recedes. You can't believe you nearly turned yourself in. Yet another illustration of the song's power. In training you found it hard to believe interference tech could be so potent. But after a year in this city, you understand the technology better than your teachers. You know, for instance, that the longer you're exposed to the song, the more susceptible you become. You reckon you know the song's grand subtlety better than the locals. You sometimes think of it as a municipal utility, like water or power. For most citizens, it is merely a euphoric. It keeps them working for and believing in the occupiers. But for a dangerous anomaly like you, it must strive to do much more.

You run on. It's time to quit this city, this occupied frontier and half-life. You don't know how much longer your warding techniques can hold out.

## 2

Packs of wild dogs roam the repurposed university campus where you're housed with other foreign visitors. You give the animals wide berth as they tear each other apart in the dead of the winter night, amid glowing dormitories. The song emanates from the south gate checkpoint, so the spectacle isn't grim. It's a necessary and fascinating part of this urban ecology. You've let the song perform many of these little services for you, believing you can resist when it counts. You let the local hardtack bread taste better. You allowed the song to lull you to sleep, when you'd otherwise have been tossing and turning, wondering when armed police were finally going to smash through your door. You've let gutter miasmas and coal hazes smell like progress. You've even let the song ameliorate homesickness, rendering your homeland in an unfavorable light—possibly the most dangerous concession of all. Now you realize every little indulgence was erosive.

You hesitate at the entrance of your dormitory.

What are you doing here? Weren't you supposed to be fleeing the city? If the authorities are after you, they'll be looking for you here. You shouldn't be anywhere near the campus. The song brought you here, didn't it? Turned you into a sleepwalker again? If you're not vigilant, it tends to nudge you onto the routine paths of daily life. You're a translator at the embassy. It's a cover job, but you're good about putting in the time. You often stay late, then wander home via the south gate.

You need to get out of here.

You head for the east gate, knowing you're on camera, forcing yourself not to break into a sprint. You glare at darknesses, expecting patrolmen to appear. How could you have been so stupid and weak? You need to think.

You can't simply walk out of the city. You're quite sure you'd die in the freezing waste. You don't think the song can fabricate this certainty. It can color memories, but not create them. You've seen the waste for yourself. The highway is empty save for the occasional government vehicle, and it is checkpointed regardless. You can't hitch or bribe your way out.

Your only chance is the next consular suborbital. You have to get to the embassy quarter.

### 3

"I mostly translate visa-related documents," you explain, shivering as the snow begins to fall. "Criminal background checks, health certifications, the kind of thing machine translation does well enough, but I have a job thanks to the Visa Process Act, which I'm quite a fan of. You wouldn't want a drone taking over your beat, am I right?"

The patrolman levels his rifle as you babble in the common tongue.

"Tonight . . . this was my first kill, and he had to die, you see. He was helping us move weapons to Real Sunrise, Nuclear Wavefront, and other rebel groups in the mountains, but . . ."

The patrolman's stunned expression gives you pause. You have to make him understand.

". . . he was becoming a liability . . . conspicuous spending, braggadocio in nightclubs. I hadn't planned on garroting the fucker, but he wouldn't drink his fucking tea, and there's all that old wiring in those shitty old offices. Surely you can see why I had to do it."

Why isn't he lowering that rifle? When you first approached him, shouting for his attention from a dark alley, his defensive stance was justified. But now that you've explained yourself, he should be slinging his weapon. He should be smiling warmly, and using his headset to tell his superiors everything's okay.

"Get down on the ground and put your hands behind your head."

"No, you don't understand . . ."

"Do it!"

The song, ringing from a police fort at the intersection, comes to an end, then starts up again. The opening instrumental makes you want to sit down in the snow and weep. You hum a warding phrase and realize what you've done.

The patrolman pulls his trigger—to an impotent click. He curses, fiddling with the keypad.

You rush him. Draw the knife from his boot. Shove it between his belt and chest plate, and holding onto the handle, propel him stumbling and gurgling backward into the alley. You follow him down into the snow. You yank the knife sideways and blood pours steaming into the cold night. Straddling him, you cover his mouth while he dies, humming another warding phrase.

You're a murderer, a danger to society, an abomination. You should turn yourself in. The warding phrase barely keeps you from heading for the intersection.

"I'm sorry," you tell the dead man beneath you. "Rest assured, my time will come."

*

## 4

You enter the warm, dim confines of the temple, and collapse shivering on ancient flagstones. The resident priest, an ancient woman with close-cropped hair, descends from the altar in flowing robes. She sits on the ground before you, assuming a meditative posture.

There are no cameras in here, as far as you know. That was the concession made by the city for having the song play even in this supposedly sacred place.

"I saw you in a dream," the priest says, her eyes closed. "You don't belong here."

You don't know if she means the temple, the city, or the occupied frontier. No matter which, you agree with her. "I'm trying to get to my embassy," you say, "but I'm afraid. Maybe I don't deserve to escape."

"There's no such thing as deserve to. There's only the time left to you, and what you do with it."

Is that genuine wisdom, or the song talking? How susceptible is she? You've heard rumor of these ascetics, of their immunity to the song's effects. Embassy staff have been laying bets on how long the city will allow its priesthood to endure.

Is that why you're here? To somehow learn their technique in a matter of hours, before venturing into the streets again? A fool's errand, regardless of how weak your warding phrases have become. "I think the song brought me here," you say.

"That would be . . . unusual. Why do you think so?"

"Because I've been here before." You've often enjoyed the atmosphere of this ancient place. Your warding phrases were more effective here, for some reason. "They'll come looking for me."

"Yes . . ."

"And the tradition of sanctuary is long gone."

"Even a thousand years ago, there was no real sanctuary here. This temple is nothing but a pile of rocks. The only true sanctuary is within yourself."

The bloody knife is on the ground beside you. Why did you bring it along? The priest's eyes are still closed, but she must have seen it as she condescended from the altar. Up there, the old, phantasmagoric idols have been covered in tarps as part of the city's latest anti-extremism drive.

"The song is nothing new, really," the priest says. "It has always existed in one form or another. It is sharper now, thanks to technology, but we have been resisting it for millennia. Granted, we must be more vigilant these days. I spend most of my time in deep mindfulness, at the expense of my other duties. If I relented, I would quit the temple. I've felt that in my less guarded moments. And if I left, the temple would surely be demolished."

"And a pile of rocks would become a different pile of rocks."

She opens her eyes, startled. Her laughter fills the hall, a beautiful sound that momentarily interferes with the song.

"What's so funny?"

"Maybe I was wrong. Maybe you were meant to come here and say that to me. Maybe I've become too attached to this place."

You fail to see the humor in this, but these priests are inscrutable at the best of times. You stand, knife in hand. "I should go. You're not safe with me around."

"It's too late."

She stands and takes your free hand. She leads you behind the altar and into her monkish living quarters. You hear the front doors slam open, the muttering of patrolmen. How did she know? Mystic foresight, perhaps, or an intimate familiarity with the song-scape of the outer courtyard, acquired through long hours of meditation.

"Come out you old witch!" one of the patrolmen shouts. "And bring anyone you're harboring!"

She bars the cell door, then yanks a toolbox from beneath her cot and grabs a hammer. She turns to the intricately carved rear wall of the cell, a beautiful relief of devotees like herself going about their daily tasks.

"I never had the heart to do this before," she says. "Let's hope the old rumors are true!"

She attacks the priceless art, her hammer-falls mingling with the patrol's shuttering impacts on the cell door. The relief crumbles beneath her assault, revealing a crude dry stack wall beyond. You kick through this easily enough. You take the priest by the hand and rush down a tunnel of ancient, rough-hewn stone, producing your palm booklet to light the way. A spray of automatic fire follows you into the earth, sparking along the walls.

You flee into a labyrinth, choosing your branching way at random. After a few minutes, the priest drags you to a halt. She breathes heavily and leans against a wall of mortared skulls. She's old, of course. There wasn't time to consider that.

The patrolmen's headset crackles echo somewhere behind you.

"Leave me," the priest breathes.

You drag her on, getting hopelessly lost. A strange feeling begins to suffuse you, an old, familiar feeling, like a scent from childhood. The song doesn't reach down here, you realize. Blessed, outlandish silence. You haven't experienced it in a year. You reckon the priest hasn't known it for at least a decade.

"By the gods," she whispers—whether in fatigue or amazement, you don't know.

Despite your exhaustion, you feel a great weight lifted from you. You remember what it was like to be one person. All the mad things you've done over the past year flash through your skull. Considered in silence, the song strikes you as more insidious than you ever imagined, more dangerous than it allowed itself to seem. Those hacks that trained you had no idea what they were dealing with. This new perspective drives you forward. The old woman sags to the ground. You heave her over your shoulder and charge on.

You enter a large chamber with a vaulted ceiling. Oxidized murals cover the walls, saints and gods, forests of inscrutable pictograms. You lower the priest to the floor, and she surprises you by staying on her feet. She shambles to the nearest mural, beckoning your light to follow.

"We should keep moving," you say.

"Which way?"

She has a point. At least a dozen tunnels converge on this room.

You light the nearest expanse of murals for her. She examines them with reverential awe, her hands repeatedly drawn to the faded paint, then jerking away at the last moment. "By the gods. All these years I could've been down here . . . there's so much to do, lifetimes of work, study and preservation. Forgotten histories! This city has endured many occupations over the centuries, many methods of control."

She weeps silently as she limps along, following lines of pictographic text or sequential art.

You listen for the patrol. There is only the profound silence, a silence like a great height commanding new perspectives, not the silence of a crypt. Your furtive year of muttered warding phrases seems like a dream.

"I think we might've lost them," you say.

"Don't count on it." She takes your palm booklet and begins scanning the walls. "They're coming, and they will destroy this place. You have to take as much of it with you as possible." She mouths silent words, reading pictograms as she hobbles along and scans.

Your jacket and shirt are soaked in blood. You prod yourself for injury, find nothing, and look to the old priest. She's bleeding heavily from a gut shot.

"I can get you to the embassy clinic, maybe even out on the suborbital."

"I'm not going anywhere," she says, sliding down to the floor. "This is where I belong. This is where I'm meant to die." She beckons you weakly, and you kneel before her. "I know what you are, more or less." She hands back the palm booklet. "This is the greatest piece of intelligence you'll acquire in my little city."

You contemplate the booklet. There is no signal down here, but you should've gotten rid of the device long ago. You remember trying to, just before entering the decrepit customs house, but the song was playing, imbuing the gadget with absurd nostalgic value that outweighed its trackability. Now it contains real value you don't feel worthy of.

"I don't gather intelligence. I'm just a fucking weapon. I bring destruction everywhere I go."

"Then don't fight what you are. Be a weapon, but be the greatest possible weapon, the kind that destroys ignorance." With great effort she lifts her hand and touches the device in your palm, as if blessing it. She scrolls backward, struggling to keep her eyes open, fighting to breathe. She taps to enlarge.

"There . . . look. The pattern on that saint's robe."

You scrutinize the faint, intricate geometry.

"The space in the middle," she says, "that's where we are. It's a map."

You see it now, the maze in all its complexity, its many entrances marked.

"Finish scanning this place before you go. Get it out of the occupied frontier. Don't give it to your superiors. Give it to the world."

You place the glowing booklet on the floor. You take off your jacket and press it against her belly, trying to staunch the flow. "I'm sorry."

"Don't be. This is right, I can feel it. I needed to leave the temple, but I had to do it against the song, not with it." She smiles, the lines of her ancient face a sudden map of pure gratitude. "Thank you."

You sit there long after she stops breathing, the booklet a candle in the dark.

## 5

You emerge from a sewer access station into the pre-dawn gloaming. And back into the song.

You're inside the embassy quarter checkpoints, but still outside your nation's autonomous ground. You follow an alleyway to a main thoroughfare and find a procession of young people marching and dancing to the song. They are one of several streams feeding into a large crowd blocking the entrance to your embassy.

The song is particularly loud here, blasted from ubiquitous speakers, ensuring there is no hiding from it even in the deepest embassy chambers.

You linger at the mouth of the alley and make a perfunctory attempt to upload data off the booklet. As you expected, it has been locked down. You're sure it's being tracked, so you don't have much time. You know you should ditch the device, but sans upload, that would mean discarding the cultural wealth you've been entrusted with. You can't do it.

Is that the song at work, keeping you trackable?

You close your eyes and listen, trying to gauge the song's effect. You feel strong after your respite in the catacombs. You're certain you stand immune, for now anyway. Never mind warding melodies and meditation. A spell of silence was just what you needed.

Not knowing what else to do, you make your way down the street, trying to stay inconspicuous among the parade spectators. The dancing youths wear the green armbands of the Harmony Brigade. They drive a miserable throng before them, "reactionaries" in paper dunce caps and bibs. You know many of these wretches are simply deaf.

You pity them. The song is actually quite beautiful. You can acknowledge that now, from your new, detached perspective. The formerly saccharine melody now rings sweet.

You follow a crush of spectators toward the mob pooling in International Friendship Square. You glance toward your embassy and find the way blocked by chanting locals.

"Where've you been?"

The familiar voice, and the language of your homeland, gives you a start.

You turn to find the Old Man shivering in his wrinkled office fatigues, glaring wide-eyed at you and the surrounding chaos. He's your direct superior in the translation bureau. You haven't made an appearance there in three days. "Never mind," he says, "we need to get out of here. The embassy's a bust, as you can see."

You've never liked him. He's one of those consular service officers that have been at a remote posting for too long. You've met plenty of his type, here and on other assignments. They stop going home to decompress. They become defeatist, racist, hedonistic, sometimes developing mystic tendencies.

"There's a car waiting at the north gate of the quarter," he says. "We can sort out your red tape on the way to the suborbital. Let's go!"

You don't know if he's just a translation supervisor, any more than you know if he knows what you really are. You do know one thing: he was a person of interest in the embassy mole investigation that you participated in a few months ago. You followed him for a week. All you uncovered was his fondness for brothels and drink, but he remains a person of interest as far as you know.

"Snap out of it," he growls. "Hum a warding phrase, dammit!" So, he knows about your training after all. That's well above a translation supervisor's clearance. "Warding just makes it worse." You realize the truth of this as you say it. "Lulls you into a false sense of security, lets the song sink its hooks deeper. I've learned a lot in the past twenty-four hours."

His pitying stare is a good piece of acting, excellent field craft. That clinches it. He must be the mole, and he intends to betray you. "Let's go!" His voice is strident amid the clamor of the square.

"I'm not going anywhere." You've never been more sure of anything in your life.

"Fuckin' hell," he mutters, reaching into his coat pocket.

Your training kicks in: inconspicuous neutralization in a mob environment. You hug him tight, acting overcome with delight in the reunion. Keeping his arms pinned, you ride Brownian crowd collisions into greater density, until you're both surrounded, trapped.

"Wait . . ." he wheezes.

You force the knife under his ribcage, then thrust upward, causing a long, strained exhalation. Holding onto the knife, your other hand probes his coat pocket. You touch cold metal.

"You're lost," he gasps, resting his forehead on yours.

You've seen him produce the flask many times. You've watched him surreptitiously dose his tea in prohibited environs, or duck into an alley for a nip. You grasp the flask, holding on for dear life amid sudden, vertiginous doubt.

The song ends, followed hard upon by the opening bars.

You recall his teahouse doses: the skill involved, like a magician's, the field-crafty glance at neighboring attention, a flash of sunlight on the flask, and he was sorted. Not the kind of thing a mere alcoholic translator could pull off.

He is—was—a clandestine agent. It doesn't mean he was a mole, but it does mean he would've been desirable as one.

The children sing about the epic poem that is their culture, their motherland. They sing their dream, a dream of peace and solidarity. You let go of the flask and the knife. You shoulder away through the crowd, leaving the corpse propped up by close-packed citizens. And the song follows you.

## 6

The reactionaries are herded to the center of the square, where machete-wielding Harmony youths decapitate them one by one.

You find yourself near the edge of this crimson, head-littered killing ground. You belong here. Your whole life was leading up to this. You recall the dog packs of the old university campus, and your strange, calm acceptance.

A young Harmony girl—she can't be more than twelve—hands you a machete. She shoves you toward a kneeling reactionary.

"Join us, foreigner!" she screams above the din.

The man shivers before you, bruised and bloodied, staring down at the pavement. He senses a lull in the ambient disorder. He raises his head and makes bleary eye contact. "You," he breathes.

He's familiar, but you can't quite place him. His crimes are listed on his bib and cap. They include attempted flight into the waste, and something called disharmony.

"Prove you belong among us!" cries the girl's companion, a boy only slightly older than she.

You have standing orders to participate in local culture, to establish trust at any cost. "Field agents get their hands dirty," one of your teachers said, seeming centuries ago. "If you find that distasteful, do us all a favor and wash out."

But that's not why you swing the blade.

You don't work for them anymore. No, you remember this man. Your superiors thought he might make a good asset, once upon a time. He's one of several musical anhedoniacs you tried to recruit. They're a rare breed, not deaf, but born with unique brain architecture. "I don't consider myself impaired," he told you in that teahouse long ago. "I'm evolved. I'm above music."

Gripped by a sudden merciful passion, you strike. He can never appreciate the beauty of the song. What kind of life is that?

The headless body topples, spouting blood.

The Harmony youths cheer, crowding around to lay their hands on you, as if to confirm you're real, an actual foreigner converted to their cause. You're grinning, weeping. This is not some kind of mind control. You've finally come to love the song on your own terms. It is your choice. This feeling would be impossible otherwise. The patrolmen shove their way through the crowd, eyes locked on you, and it's okay. They're just here to ensure your compatriots don't whisk you away. They will safeguard your newly-earned citizenship. The past is dead. The priest's lost histories are dead. They never happened. You don't have to run anymore. You're in harmony. You are home.

# No More Bad Dreams
## Louis Evans

I n the silent night in the City of Glass of the Kingdom of Quartz on the Continent of Crystal, the Nightmare Men go hunting for sin.

It's past midnight now in the jewel-thieves' quarter and the light of the slivered moon comes in slantwise, sodium. The Nightmare Men wear brass on gold and their teeth are fine and noble points.

Every wall in the City of Glass is see-through, from the ice pane chateaux of the vicemonger's district to the ghostclay wattledaub of the Rue Felicite. In the jewel-thieves' quarter the walls are made of clear sapphire whose blue was rubbed away to scraps of silk to knit the gown and train of the tatterdemalion Queen.

The Nightmare Men have wide and honest smiles and as they course through the streets of the city, they neither skulk nor march, but rather walk simply, openly. They have every right.

This is the Nightmare Men's hour, which was once the witches' but was taken from them by law and given to the Nightmare Men, and now any sorceress about in the crook of night where all roads bend and all paths fork is subject to curfew. This is the Nightmare Men's hour, and theirs alone.

The Nightmare Men have a fearsome name and a fearsome job. Only they can keep the City of Glass and the Kingdom of Quartz safe.

Look, now. Here, on the left; a humble house. On the bedroom wall, cheap glass, of the sort that is made available free to the poor so that they will not be tempted by such opaque impieties as mud or wood or stone.

Here, on the wall, where the Nightmare Men gather and

lick—ever so daintily, ever so carefully—the fine and filigreed points of their many, sharp teeth.

It's past midnight and well past curfew and everyone is asleep or ought to be. And whoever lives in this house is most certainly asleep because here on the glass walls are the dreams.

And what delightful dreams they are! Cotton-twist clouds above sugar-edged seas; and our noble yeoman frolicking in the surf. Pay no mind to the Nightmare Men, who are professionals and often watch more spirited revels than this. They are not made as flesh is made, fed by its pleasures, drawn by its hungers.

They have their own hungers.

And here, on the screen, between cherubs and confections and ejaculations, a flaw. A snake, perhaps; or a loose tooth, or a childhood home up in flames and screams. Our luckless sinner tries to hide it, to redirect the dream, lucid with terror, hopelessly summoning dreamstuff of joy and lust to caper and cavort, but the Nightmare Men are not distracted. They are not deceived. Their teeth like rows of distant stars. In silence they advance. The sleeper wakes. The fangs close.

In the City of Glass in the Kingdom of Quartz—that fortunate land!—after a moment, all is again peaceful. Once again, in this place, there are no more bad dreams.

# The Moon and the Devil and the Ace of Wands

## Evan J. Peterson

You enter her tent from the midway or the wharf or Portobello Road or a village green, and the odds are in your favor that tonight is not a full moon. Leaves from that outside place have blown in at your feet, joining the very different leaves of midland hawthorn mingled with the straw along the floor of her tent. It's the twelfth of September. The feast of Saint Ailbe.

The tent appears larger inside than it did from the outside and though this may trouble you, it's the way of spaces like hers. You may remember the fabric of it a dusty, rusty red as you crossed through the folds of the entrance, but then again you may be wrong. Anyroad, you're inside now, and the walls of fabric are broad and faded stripes of plum and black, illuminated by a few candelabra fashioned from stag horn. It smells of the straw on the floor and her sandalwood perfume. The scents of outside remain outside, and not just the scents but the sounds, music of cricket and calliope suddenly choked off like a windpipe at the end of a rope.

She sits on a stool at a round wooden table. Her hair is auburn, even redder as it rests on the emerald scarf around her shoulders. You can see from here that what they say about her eyes is true.

They glare at you, wolf-yellow. "I hope you bring good humor. The cards are mischievous little buggers tonight."

You take the backed chair across from her. She's younger than you'd expected and quite beautiful. Her lips make you want to listen, if for no other reason than to watch them move. You wonder why she has the stool and you the chair.

"How much for a reading?"

"What do you have to give?"

You want to make a joke and offer a pound of flesh, but she just might take it. "I can pay you fifteen."

She nods to that and turns up the palm of her left hand, the fingers curling a bit. She pockets the money beneath her scarf, perhaps in her cleavage.

"What would you like to ask the cards?"

"Hmm. I suppose I want to know if I'm doing the right thing, right? If I'm in the job I should be in. If I'm making the most of my life."

She shuffles the deck so quickly that you wonder if she's also a pickpocket, then she slaps the deck down on the table in front of you.

One by one, her fingers snap the cards against the table, and you've never seen a deck like this before. There's a Juggler, for instance, and his instruments are similar enough that you suppose he holds the place of the Magician. Strength isn't a springtime goddess with her hands in a beast's mouth, but a Hercules bludgeoning a lion. The nine of swords is a bloodied dove in a cage of blades.

"You know what you're doing with your life. You chose this for yourself. You're not here to sort those cards. You're here because you've overstepped. Tried so hard to have it your way that you've murdered the thing you set out to preserve."

She's good. It's not the huckster's snake oil song that you've heard before. Her winesharp eyes look down your throat and see your soul and all its warts. The five of wands lands next on the table, image of staves knocking one another in the air, the staff bearers invisible.

"You think you're fighting fate, circumstance. You're only fighting yourself. Let's see who wins."

The Death card is the last one down, unnamed and unnumbered and uncloaked, but clearly Death, the skeleton swinging her blade.

"You're in luck," the cartomancer tells you. "This particular trouble will end long before your life does. There will be peace— for a while, anyway. Always more troubles. Not always more life."

You thank her. You'll exhort your friends to visit her.

"Please do. I'll see you soon."

"Sure thing," you tell her. Even the most cunning parlor psychic is at best an insightful counselor, at worst an amusing charlatan. This is what you tell yourself.

You enter her tent from a cold mountain path or the pungent cacophony of a spice market or a dusty road in Georgia, and the moon is waxing close, but not yet full tonight. February second: the feast of Saint Brigid.

The tent is smaller in here than it appeared from the outside, and you wonder where the rest of it went. You see the familiar stag horn candle sconces, smell the sandalwood.

You meant to come here. You know this. But here isn't necessarily where you thought it was.

"Ah. Welcome back."

She's wrapped warmly for the season, but still that emerald scarf rests on her shoulders, that ginger hair dangles in shining filaments. The yellow eyes strip you of glamour in seconds. Baleful though they are, you feel your stomach fizz when she looks at you.

"Sit. What brings you back?"

"Hmm. My legs, I suppose. Or my heart. I'm not sure why I'm here, to tell the truth."

"Some say that's the best way to seek the cards."

"How did you learn to read them, anyway?"

She rakes her fingers through her hair. "The gods take something precious. They leave something else in its place. That's how the wheel turns."

You shrug at that, not sure what to say. Her nostrils flare for a moment, as though scenting the tension you've strung along the air. She shuffles the deck.

You enter his tent, although you meant to walk outside from the freak show or the arcade or the tea ceremony. That's how the soft places catch you: you set your foot down upon a threshold and you're walking dead into the necromancer's castle, or you gaze too deeply into a looking glass and fall through, or you slip between two drapes of fabric and the world slips around you. The moon is full tonight, a dusty mushroom, the sky's slipperiest bone.

Dim light graces the space, a single dangling brazier, but it's enough to discern predators from prey. A predator's eyes face forward. Prey, to the sides. This makes the both of you predators, or so you hope.

He is naked and he is filthy, a lithe man glazed in blood, smattered with the dry dirt and the leaves and the straw and perhaps a bit of shit. Birth is nasty.

A torn skin cools at your feet, a whole female shell, each fatty breast slouching towards a different Bethlehem, but no bone, no offal, no meat or lung. The skin glistens as if rubbed down with fat and the grease mingles with the blood, and yet there is far more blood on the man than the shucked skin.

His yellow eyes look into you as though your throat and heart were batter-fried strips of meat. "You shouldn't be here. How did you get here?"

You tell him the only thing you can think. "I don't know. I didn't mean to come. I would ask you the same."

He looks you over and you look back, noticing the wisps of steam rising from his shoulders, hot flesh on a cold night. He sees you watch it and he turns from you, seizing a dark cloak to cover his dirty hide. The emerald scarf hangs beside it.

He pulls the cloak around himself and lights a few more candles from the stag's horn sconce. He sits on the guest's chair at the little table upon which the cards are kept swaddled like a newly born whelp, one taken quick from its bitch to avoid her eating it. The blood-caked man turns up his left palm in good will, gesturing toward the other seat.

You step around the skin on the ground and seat yourself on the card reader's stool.

"Any questions before we begin?" he asks.

You cross your arms. "Are you wounded?"

A slight smirk. "No. Just a bit bloody."

"Are you going to kill me?"

He cocks his head like a dog and stares with those yellow

eyes. "I don't think so. I'm not sure what good that would do."

You look down at the discarded female husk. The spell begins to make sense. "Why grease the skin?"

"Eases the tearing. Softens the change. And it makes for the kinder eating of it." His nostrils widen, taking in the scent of it. Taking in the scent of you. You see for a moment how beautiful he is under the grime, in the brighter candlelight. He is more three-legged dog than wolf-eyed human.

He relaxes and leans back against the chair. "Please. Read for me. Read for a lonely seer. I'll pay." He grabs up the womanskin from the ground and tears a generous bit from the shoulder of it with his teeth. His fingernails are shorter than you'd expected.

You unwrap the black satin scarf from the deck, that now familiar deck. "How will I know how to read?"

"Instinct. And an hour's worth of the Sight. That's how I'll pay you. Open." He rends a strip of skin and fat and brings it to your mouth, gentle as a lover. You accept the flesh that was his and yet not his and you bite into it and release its humors.

*You see people who are wolves that eat wolves and eat men women children and you taste blood and fat and meat, you see your hands against the ground, feel the wolf inside you, rising up within you like a child birthed from your throat, the wolf is in you, your hands are pinned by the wolf's paws, the skin on your back rips open in a boiled creek of pain and the skin of your limbs and the skin around your mouth and heat pain and then it isn't you that's torn open, it's the husk of someone else, you are wearing that skin like a scarf in the great ceremony of Becoming and the wolf has you, has you, has you and then there is no pain.*

*But you are not the wolf. You see new hands where slender hands had been but you have thicker fingers, you have torn that skin that was yours but you are not the wolf. Your mother is a wolf your father your brothers and sisters, all your brood has stripped away their human skin, it hangs in scraps off their fur, you see all of this under the full light of the full moon and there is howling of prayers to the Hecate, She Whose Head Is Three Dogs And The Moon.*

"Swallow," you hear the cartomancer through the waking dream, and you gulp down the flesh.

And you're back in his tent, her tent, and you are yourself, and things continue to clarify. Your heart aches for him. For her, the one between worlds, the Both Yet Neither.

He takes another bite of the skin, hiding the evidence of the change the best way he knows, the oldest way. Some things are more instinct than tradition.

Between mouthfuls: "Now. Read for me."

What else can you do?

You shuffle, clumsy. Cards fall out. You fold them back into the deck, and he lurches forward as if to stop you, but then rolls his golden eyes and sits back and lets you sift them back into the pile.

You turn the first card and contemplate the Ace of Coins. A star inscribed in a circle, drawn onto the palm of a hand. With the temporary gift shared, you see the cartomancer's past as well as your own present, as though each of your eyes were in different heads. You do more than see; you smell and you touch and taste and know. So you tell him what you can.

"You know the world by the way your body moves through it. You prefer the wisdom of the gut to that of the brain."

He continues eating his own discarded skin. "Obvious. Go on."

You turn another card, the Priestess, and place it across the first. The woman on the card seems to dance in the flickers of candlelight, yet she is painted in a pose of still regard.

*You glimpse the past through the yellow eyes, feel the sense of observing and wishing to participate, not knowing how. Seeing a montage of men and women sitting across from you, asking about money and cheating hearts and why God can't she have a baby.*

"But you spend your time watching, listening. Perceiving is action, and you know this in ways most don't. You watch us come and go. You hear our stories. You are not an oracle of the future; you are a mirror reflecting us."

He shifts and sets the skin in his lap. His ears have perked up, as much as human ears can do so. Another card: five tree trunks, close like bars of a cage, run along the length of the card. It is not the same Five of Wands you recall from your earlier visit. A new deck? But no—you remember the Ace of Coins as the same exact image.

You place the Five of Wands close to you, beneath the crossed cards.

*In the vision, some of your broodmates get to eating their first shed skins, but the pack turns on you. You are not the wolf inside the girl. You are man inside the girl, and you smell their fear and the kill scent and you are not wolf and He Who Is The Face Of The Pack crouches and growls and you know they will kill you, you are sick and this is the way of things and you are not wolf.*

*You are man and you have enough man's instinct to use your limbs to climb the nearest tree and their jaws snap as you go taking some of your toes. You feel that pain as you feel the weight of the skin still clinging to you.*

"You believe you're still trapped, still up that tree. The man in you believes this, although the woman believes something else."

You turn the next card, placing it to the left of the two you stacked. Ten of Wands, the leafy canes of bamboo laced in five hashing X's along the card. They support a naked man, a mat for him to rest upon.

*Everything a mess: the sunrise and the view from the top of the tree as the wolves circle and then the men with guns, wolves blown apart with magical metals blessed by a strange and merciless god, the yelps and howls of agony, the pack scattering. Someone takes you out of the tree and covers you and you're a girl again, your boyskin ripped away by the sunrise and already consumed.*

"You carry a great responsibility. At times it feels like a great burden."

He grunts and chews.

Next comes the Queen of Swords, placed above the others, completing the vertical line of the cross. He leans forward now, hovering over the cards, his face so close to yours you feel dizzy with his scent of dried blood and dried sweat and skinned fat and sex.

You tell him what you see: a woman crowned and enthroned, yet plainly dressed, her sword held forward in a quiet gesture of immense power. *Metal changes hands. Knives are drawn and sheathed. The carnival. And then the cards. The cards are the only things that make sense anymore.*

You tell him, "You are just. The Sight gives you purpose. You have a responsibility to help others find their way. Whether that is a burden is up to you."

He leans back in the chair and sighs. You're quiet with him for a long moment, your eyes and his holding contact. Then you proceed.

You turn the Lovers card, place it to the other side of the Ace of Coins.

A man is caught between two women. One appears matronly, richly dressed, and the other is a maiden in lighter cloth. *The new and temporary organ of Sight shows you the woman cartomancer, her full moon change into a man instead of a wolf, the change back to woman at dawn.*

"You have more choice in the change than you've realized. Than you've allowed yourself to realize."

He frowns at this, begins eating the skin again.

You hesitate. *What comes next?*

"Make the staff," he tells you around a mouthful.

You turn a new card, place it to the lower right of the cross. The Devil, chained to rocks and eating a tiny sinner with each of those three mouths (goat, dragon, wolf), black wings spread, breasts hanging full, thick phallus pointing up and almost brushing them. Your querent stops chewing at the sight of this, grins, and then continues shredding the skin between his teeth.

You've run out of Sight, but you know the cartomancer. Clairvoyance gives way to clairsentience. Or perhaps you're just a quick study.

"You see yourself as a hated thing, powerful yet bound. You could slip the manacles, but you stay. You hate yourself even more than you believe others do."

"Sod off," he says, and flecks of flesh sail off his lips. Then: "Keep reading."

You place another card above the last. His head tilts quick again. The Moon.

"Others see you as a witch. You aren't hated; you're feared

and respected. People believe you hex and heal at your whim. That you curse some with madness and cure others of madness, like Titania."

There are only two cards left in the spread. You motion to lift the next off the pack, but vertigo takes you and the Sight returns. *Cards tumbling through the air, cards like giant moths swarming around you, slicing your flesh by their edges.*

You expect the worst: deep suffering in the three or ten of swords, or maybe Death herself, kind scythe. The cartomancer slurps the remainder of a finger through his lips.

You lift the card and gasp. He cackles.

You ask, "Did you know this would happen? That it could?"

Bitter eyes contradict his smile. "The cards are fickle tricksters. Sometimes the game plays you."

You've pulled a second Devil card. You've not seen many decks, but you understand that this is some aberration, this second demon. You place it above the Moon. You look along this line, Devil-Moon-Devil, and the most recent Devil is a satyr cavorting among trees, man-headed yet goatish in the face, bare chested, all goat from waist down, real and true goat, the thin tendril of urethra extending beyond the glans. The satyr grabs his cock in one hand and bends to fellate himself.

And so you read the card.

"This is what you most want and what you most fear. To swallow and digest your own beastliness. To bring together your hairy shadow with the one you've only half known. You're hairy on the inside. And you can let your fur out."

His body rocks in the chair now, like a child born traumatized. More shreds fall from his mouth as he speaks, "The last card. Throw it down."

You recoil for a moment, but you complete the bargain.

The final card tops the staff. Ace of Wands. A branch on fire. "Your magic fully revealed."

Your curiosity and compassion and attraction to him are braided into one dangerous cord, his scent of blood and man and wolf lifted on the air around you. He has consumed almost the entire skin now, only the ragged husk of one dainty foot remains, and even that has only two toes left to it.

"You should go now," he says, his voice mincing gentleness with menace. "I tricked you before. The Sight was not your payment." He is still rocking in his chair, staring at the card spread.

You rise. "You've given me enough. What more should you give?"

"Your life."

And that's enough. But you hesitate at the tent's portal. You want those lithe and bloody arms around you. "Will I walk out into the same place from which I came?"

He laughs again, not the cackle of before, but a full laugh of duende, and his face shines with grease and his mouth spreads too widely. His teeth, human though they are, are too many, going too far back into his jaw, his mouth deeper than the back of a man's head. The yellow eyes catch the light and you fear that yours have moved to the sides of your head. Then he speaks.

"I expect so. But with the soft places you can't be sure. Perhaps *where* isn't the question."

You ready yourself to step out of the tent, but you make one last gamble. You know this is the last time you'll meet the card reader, and he or she is beautiful and rare and about to disappear to wherever such people go. "May I stay the night with you?"

The man who is only a man on the night of the full moon looks away. The foot skin twists in those fists, and those eyes squint up.

"If you stay, I will tear the nipples from your chest and the ears from your face. I will separate you into tender bits. I will snap your bones between my teeth and soften my skin with your marrow." The last rag of skin slips into that too-deep mouth.

The predator stands. His skin begins to split, bloody fur showing through the rips.

You bolt from the tent, out into a world that is bigger on the outside than the world you left when you walked in.

# It Only Takes a Few Months for a Poet to Position Its Jaws

## Mitchell Shanklin

Once upon every time, in the thin spaces wedged between possible realities, a species of poets swims behind the stars. Naturally, they spend most of their time gathering inspiration.

Even with five nostrils, each the size of a small galaxy, it can take thousands of years for a poet to catch the scent of a ripened world. It is not a simple thing.

The byproducts of fission or fractured ethereal crystallization are a leading indicator, of course. There's that bitter twang of cultural decadence, the rosy red inflammation of post-tribal ethics . . . Perhaps most important is that subtle hint of minty-fresh swagger. (The cockiness of sentience that *gets it*, the universe, you know, except for those gaps, but they'll fill those in soon).

It only takes a few months for a poet to position its jaws.

Know that poets are not all exactly alike. Some are mostly flesh, others mostly hydrogen or helium. Some have fifteen distinct religious orientations they hold simultaneously and others sixteen (but never any other number). The jaws are always the same. Made of diamond and titanium, with teeth one hundred miles or so long, sharp as atoms.

Some poets craft beauty, others mediocrity. A very few craft complete garbage that should not even be considered poetry and I hate them!

Ahem. Apologies.

This is a story about the foolish young poet who tried to digest three worlds into a single poem and how he tainted the sacred art of poetry forever after.

*

The best English translation of our villain's name would consist of a trilogy of absurdist novels whose main characters are non-Euclidean geometric figures. So we'll just use Byron.

Byron was made of helium and had fifteen religious orientations. In Byron's short life, he had consumed 1532 worlds and produced 1502 poems.

The singular correct poetic form is known to be a sequence of fifty-four multi-sensory, multi-dimensional pictograms that perfectly capture the essences of worlds: their past, present and unrealized possible futures. The digestive system of a poet, its "mind", is well-suited to the transformation of a single world into poetry. The process of excreting such a poem is invariably smooth and satisfying.

Combining two distinct worlds into a single poem is a more trying feat, rarely performed. The poet's "mind" clenches and shudders while expelling such a gem. Afterwards, a poet's mind-orifice needs time to recover, for it is often left sore and smarting. Many poets forego the entire endeavor and spend their entire careers on single-world poetry. But brave Byron had done it thirty times.

To combine three . . . it was not done. Until now.

Byron's "mind" rumbled as he approached the third world. It combined and recombined the remnants of the two he'd consumed already, spitting out symbol chains and multi-tonal rhymes. Every time it began to solidify, Byron interrupted himself. Byron kept his mind-orifice squeezed tightly closed, but he was becoming weary.

It took four months to place his jaws around the green ocean moon, a race of nine-limbed squid people swimming through it. His teeth trembled, tilting in and out of alignment. Byron growled and tsunamis wiped out half the population. Byron clenched his orifice and his teeth grew still. Byron bit down.

You must understand, the actual "transformation" of inspiration into the finished work is generally uneventful and near instantaneous. Byron could digest a single world in six nanoseconds. Two worlds took him around twenty-one.

For fifteen long, drawn-out minutes, Byron experienced the greatest pain of his short and brilliant life. Imagine the deepest possible depression combined with the most troubling existential dilemma. Imagine every scrap of skin is flayed from your body, only for you to discover that you were actually just your skin all along, not your brain or your innards and you will exist eternally as a bloody pile of mangled scraps.

It was nothing like any of these things, it was worse, and you have no hope of understanding.

So, he puked it all up.

Imagine a massive planet that looks like three spheres collapsing in on themselves. Imagine it is covered with monstrosities made of every possible combination of millions of species and that each and every one of them is screaming.

It was exactly like that, actualy.

Dozens of poets swam towards Byron's catastrophe. Some jeered, gamboling around Byron's shuddering, desiccated form. Others tried to help, comforting Byron by reciting some of their own poetry, thus reminding him that the great art of poetry would live on, even if he never managed to contribute to it again.

A few tried to separate the mess, partition it into three planet sized pieces at least. With some effort they reduced it to a cloud of debris. None were brave enough to taste what remained.

Some advocated abandoning it. But half-heartedly. Despite the apparent impossibility of digestion, none could ignore that *scent*. Juicy and minty and succulent. This disaster was riper than any world any of them had ever tasted. Poets have astonishing self-control, but . . . they couldn't turn away.

Finally, Byron's lover, Oscar, turned towards the cloud and opened his jaws. Oscar was made of hydrogen and had sixteen religious orientations. Oscar had digested two worlds into a single poem before, twice in fact. He could take this challenge. He would. For Byron.

"No!" Byron shouted. In a flash (which lasted three and a half months), he pushed Oscar's jaws aside and positioned his own.

"I can do this. I promise." A hush fell over the other poets as they watched Byron's second attempt.

He bit down.

For three hours he writhed in agony. Then, in one explosive instant, he expelled a poem which trumpeted the cohesive story of three worlds to the stars and his colleagues.

But it was fifty-*eight* multi-dimensional, multi-sensory pictograms long.

The four superfluous characters stood out like a seventeenth religious orientation, or a poet made of *copper*. (I apologize for the simile. A more noble soul would refrain from even imagining such abominations).

The cloud of watching poets reeled in shock. Most immediately fled, seeking out inspiration for the debate that would ensue.

While poets may speak to each other telepathically, debate about poetry, must, of course, be conducted using poetry. Thus, millions of worlds have been transformed into glorious arguments, each a perfectly formed sequence of fifty-four pictograms.

The small sect of "poets" that Byron has gathered reply with nonsensical tracts of fifty-six, fifty-eight, sometimes even *fifty-two* pictograms. True poets refuse to read or respond to such offensive absurdities. It is my dearest hope that the renegades will reform their ways so that a dialogue may begin.

So, to those who cower beneath the titanium and diamond blades which currently hover above the Earth, be not afraid. The poet who surrounds your planet adheres to the most proper form of the art. Your quaint, lovely history will be preserved for posterity, not tainted by heretics! And there is the slimmest possibility that yours will be the poem to open the conversation, eventually bringing grace and conformity back to the sacred craft of poetry.

Tremble, but with joy, not fear, for you have the privilege of living within your world's final glorious stanza. Do not clutch greedily at those scant, shallow decades you might have had.

Remember: life is but crude fuel for the immortality of art.

# FIRE PUZZLE

## ELLY BANGS

The first time the world ends, it hardly bothers Aleph. She's certainly dazzled by the spectacle of it all: how a 15-kiloton nuclear torpedo instantly converts the USS Randolph and all its 27,000 tons of steel and 3,500 crew into glowing vapor off the coast of Cuba; how later that afternoon a few thousand more fusion bombs rain down on Europe, doing the same to cities; and how as night falls the survivors and those still dying (those still with eyes to see, anyway) stare up from the embers into the bright red aurorae that dance along the stratosphere, an eerily beautiful side-effect of the electromagnetic pulse. The imagery is all striking, the destruction all gruesome—but Aleph has witnessed a lot of things in her travels, and the self-annihilation of one more three-dimensional animal species doesn't exactly move her.

It's only by accident that the worming path she takes through spacetime to meet Bet passes close enough to Earth, on that day in 1962, to let her feel the war's distant thunder in the tips of her sensory filaments. It's only on a whim that she stops long enough to recognize a good puzzle—and it's only out of curiosity, and the confidence that she'll have it solved in no time, that she first takes stock of the pieces laid out before her.

One by one she begins to rearrange them.

Bet finds Aleph in 28 October 1962, manifesting herself as a human girl who perches with a notebook on a scorched rooftop in what was New York City yesterday. She chews her pen, lost in thought, every so often pausing to brush the warm snow of radioactive ash from the page.

"I was waiting for you," Bet says.

Aleph smacks her palm to her forehead. "Great. I'm late, aren't I? I'm sorry."

"What are you doing here? And why are you wearing that ridiculous animal costume?"

Aleph flexes her fleshy arms and fingers and toes and grins briefly. "I thought it would help me focus on the puzzle."

"Puzzle? Oh no. Aleph, I really hope this isn't—"

"It's not like that. Only a bit of harmless fun to keep the mind sharp."

Bet stretches her awareness through the desolation, perceiving the bodies, the isotopic decay. "The goal being, what? To pointlessly interfere with the life cycles of pre-sentients?"

Aleph snaps her fingers and starts scratching new formulae into her notebook. "That's it! I've got it. It'll only take me a second."

Bet's filaments form a doubtful expression.

"Will you at least let me show you?"

On 3 July 1961, the two of them manifest as men in greasy coveralls in a cramped metal space. Aleph reaches for a segment in the copper pipes that surround them, ghosts her fingertips into it and wiggles—ever so slightly accelerating the metal fatigue in a single weld.

"The war that wipes out this species begins when a Russian submarine fires a nuclear torpedo at an American aircraft carrier in 1962, right?" she says.

By now Bet's perceptive organs have made her vaguely aware of these details. She nods, flexes her unfamiliar human body uncomfortably, and guesses aloud: "You're sabotaging that submarine, then. So it breaks down before it can fire the torpedo."

"No, B-59 fires the torpedo. This is K-19. Completely different sub."

Bet rolls her eyes and taps her foot impatiently, and Aleph suppresses a laugh—it's true these animals look ridiculous.

"I already tried brute force approaches like that," Aleph says. "They never work. But! If this pipe here is just a little weak—do you feel it?"

Bet clears her mind and focuses. Her filaments creep forward and out, tracing the hair-thin web of causes and effects that explodes from this moment in this room. She can feel that Aleph is right before she perceives the particulars of her solution: how tomorrow the pipe will burst, hemorrhaging coolant, setting off a near-meltdown in the sub's fission reactor and flooding its steel corridors with radiation—how the executive officer, a man named Arkhipov, will survive to become one of three commanders aboard B-59 who must unanimously agree to fire the torpedo that starts the war that dooms the world. How in this new iteration of 1962, Arkhipov remembers the smell of that death and the eight men it decomposed alive, and this time the possibility of a nuclear war is not an abstract concept to him. How against all the heat and pressure of that moment, he refuses to give the order to fire, and no amount of shouting or threat of mutiny will move him.

"See?" Aleph says.

They worm their way back to the rooftop on 28 October 1962. It's the same time and place, but the sky has changed from brown to blue. The ash has re-assembled itself into buildings, streets, trees, human beings.

Bet gives a conceding nod. "I'm . . . actually impressed. That was a very elegant solution. How many tries did it take you?"

"Twenty, thirty. I don't know." Aleph cringes. "I am sorry I missed our date. It just sucked me in."

"It's fine. As long as you had fun. Just . . . go easy on the puzzles, okay? I don't need to tell you how addictive they can be."

Aleph flaps her hand dismissively. "The risk is way overblown. They're perfectly wholesome in moderation and I know my limits."

Bet slouches her body on the edge of the roof, watching the streets below, and adds: "I'll admit they're adorable little critters, in a creepy kind of way . . . but you know they're going to die off anyway, right? Species like this, it's just their life cycle. It's natural."

"Are you so sure? Feel ahead a year. Five years. Ten! No nuclear war. I think it was just a fluke. For all we know they might survive and evolve long enough to become sentient!"

Bet snorts derisively. "Right. Sentient." She stands up,

brushes the soot from her costume's hands, then sloughs off the disguise entirely. She stretches her filaments lazily across hyperspace and says "I have to go. I'll see you soon, won't I?"

Aleph coils her filaments lovingly around Bet's, forming patterns and topologies unfathomable to 3-dimensional creatures. "Of course."

When Bet's gone, she allows herself one last self-satisfied breath of clear air before shedding her human manifestation. She starts to slide back into the cool, gelatinous folds of spacetime—but just as she's about to exit, she hesitates.

She looks back. She senses a bit further out.

In the 918th iteration of 24 October 1973, Aleph manifests as a 40-year-old woman who sits alone on the barnacle-encrusted concrete blocks at the end of the breakwater enclosing Alexandria's Western harbor. There's a ship coming in, and she can feel it: its mass-energy rumbling in the fibers of her being, the weight of its significance bowing the causal web. Visually it's only a faint shadow in the line of bright haze. At her feet the waves smash themselves against the rocks over and over, but the tide is finally going out.

"You're still here?" asks a voice from everywhere.

"Bet," Aleph answers, distantly. "This isn't what it looks like."

"Are you okay? What's going on?"

Aleph draws a deep breath and closes her eyes. "I think I really did it this time."

Bet tries to touch Aleph's filaments, but it's clear that her attention is absorbed into her human manifestation, so Bet joins her—a young man boiling out of thin air to climb down onto the rock next to her.

"Just tell me what happened."

Aleph leafs through her notebook. The edges are frayed, the spiral binding bent and chewing through the cover stock. Sticky notes and paperclips swarm the pages. She clears her mind and struggles to find the words.

"Three weeks ago a coalition of Arab states launched a massive attack, trying to reclaim land Israel took during the Six-Day War. In the original timeline the Israelis were on the verge of total defeat so they started dropping tactical nukes on the invading armies, and then the Soviets and Americans stepped in with their own forces, and . . ."

Aleph leaves the sentence unfinished. She stares out to sea with such a pensive and exhausted expression that Bet can't bring herself to say 'I told you so.' Instead she forces a smile and says, "So, which pipe this time?"

"What?"

"What tiny length of metal pipe did you weaken to solve the puzzle this time?"

Aleph shakes her head. "There was no simple solution. I tried everything. After a few hundred tries—"

"A few hundred?! Aleph!"

"—I was able to fix it so Israel repels the invasion, but then they bounced back a little too hard, encircled the Egyptian third army, and on and on. Today the Soviets send their warheads to Egypt as a counterweight to Israel's." She points out toward the horizon. The ship at the tip of her finger sits there, timeless and serene. "When the Americans find out they go to DEFCON 3 for the first time since 1962, it escalates and escalates, and . . ."

"And these fleshy pre-sapients finish their natural life cycle," Bet prompts.

"No." Aleph winces and shakes her head. "This time I fixed it. In this iteration of today the Soviets back down and everyone stops shooting tomorrow."

"And yet you don't sound like someone who just solved a fun puzzle."

Aleph stares at her human hands. She breathes in the salt of the Mediterranean. "It's awful, Bet. It's all so awful. I can't make a true peace here no matter what I do. So many people die and it all goes unresolved. Maybe if I . . ." She trails off, shakes her head, stares out into the haze.

Bet pushes on Aleph's shoulder, trying to shake her from her trance. "Hey! Who *cares*? You can't let it get to you like this. It's just what they are."

"No!" Aleph shouts, loud enough for Bet to startle. She composes herself and clarifies: "I love you, but you're wrong, okay? It's not their time. Every time the bombs fall it's because of some quirk of hierarchical behavior, some . . . self-amplifying bit of chaos. You don't know them. I *know* them, Bet."

"Aleph, please. Tell me how to snap you out of this. You know what's happening."

"I am *not* a puzzle addict! I'm fine. I solved it and I'm done."

Gulls scream over their heads.

Bet waves her hand out to sea. "Great. You saved a pre-sentient species from itself. Again. Congratulations. I can't feel a single nuclear war in the next five years. Now will you please just . . . take a break and unplug? Let's go somewhere. Anywhere but here. Just you and me."

Aleph nods and blinks and finally says "Okay. You're right. Let's go."

But on the verge of leaving, she hesitates. She feels a sixth year into the future, and all her filaments abruptly shudder and go slack in exasperation.

"You have got," Aleph shouts across hyperspace, "to be fucking *kidding* me."


On 10 November 1979 the two of them walk among the ashes and green trinitite glass of London, Moscow, D.C., Prague, a thousand other cities. They skulk among walls etched with the black silhouettes of evaporated human bodies and watch the fallout billow in so thickly that it buries the dead, hardens like concrete under the black rain and begins the thousand-year process of fossilization. The red aurorae that light these scenes by night don't seem beautiful to Aleph anymore, but she's afraid to admit it.

"How did it happen this time?" Bet asks, somberly.

Aleph reluctantly leads her back a day, and they're technicians standing in a small plastic-tile room under a mountain in Colorado, their human ears full of the whir of electric motors. A short, stout man in a button-down shirt hobbles through a glass door carrying a magnetic tape under his arm and starts to load it onto a machine that will read its program instructions and execute them.

"It's a mistake," Aleph says. "It's just one bone-headed mistake. He's loading the wrong tape."

"One wrong tape launches five thousand nuclear missiles?"

Aleph shakes her head. "No, it's . . . it's a training simulation. The tape plays a simulation of a massive Soviet missile strike. NORAD doesn't figure out it's only a simulation until it's too late."

"I've seen enough. Can we just get out of— Hey, stop that!"

The technician with the tape is frozen in place while Aleph insinuates her filaments softly into the folds of his neocortex, but Bet holds her back.

"For crying out loud," Aleph protests. "This one is so simple. I just make him *look at the damned tape* before he loads it and everyone is saved."

But Bet won't let go. Aleph releases the technician, who blinks a lot and sneezes loudly.

"So what, you're just going to haunt these underground offices forever, correcting everyone's mistakes? Where does it end?"

For a moment the two hyperspatial entities share a tense silence. Then Aleph bolts into spacetime.

"What do you think you're doing?" Bet shouts after her. She chases, following the traces of her wake back and forth like a stitch through time.

Aleph is in 4 May 1979, manifest as a General's secretary, typing up some notes after hours. She cracks her knuckles and begins to append her own inconspicuous and very reasonable bit of text to some meeting minutes: *Resolved: all wargames simulator programs must henceforth clearly print the word 'SIMULATION' on any connected terminal—* But Bet jams the typewriter ribbon.

"Aleph, please. You have to leave them in peace."

"Let go," Aleph hisses through her human mouth. Her ethereal voice causes the desk lamp bulb to blow out, shooting glass across the desktop.

"Let these animals finish their life cycle!"

Aleph darts away again, this time faster. She weaves erratically back and forth between years and places and planes, briefly making Bet chase her in circles of the ergosphere of a black hole, all to buy enough of a head start to make one simple move.

"What have you done?" Bet pants when she finally catches up.

Aleph is back in 10 November 1979, wearing the costume of a woman in red bell-bottom pants, lighting a cigarette and leaning back against the brick storefront of a record store. A speaker behind her grainily shouts 'Rebel Rebel' into the clear air—no fallout in sight.

"I made one minor operator at NORAD stutter on the phone just long enough for someone to realize the mistake before the retaliatory strike," Aleph says, haughtily. "You're welcome to go change that person back, of course. If you can find them."

Bet lowers her costume's head and sniffles, halfway between laughing and crying. "I don't have to. I don't have to do anything."

Aleph's smile wilts and her cigarette drops when she senses another four years ahead. "God damnit."


On 26 September 1983 they're in yet another underground room full of crude machinery, this time near Moscow, embodied as a pair of Soviet officers in stiff green uniforms. They're looking through some one-way glass into the control room where a full-wall digital display is indicating that five American ballistic missiles are inbound. Twenty-eight minutes remain before they land and detonate. Everything is suffused with red light and siren sound. The man in charge picks up the phone and calls his boss to tell him the news.

"Let me guess," Bet says, acidly. "There is no American first strike."

"Sunlight reflecting off some high-altitude clouds," Aleph whispers. "The satellites misidentify it as a missile's vapor trail. But they won't know that—"

"Until it's too late," Bet finishes. "Why can't you see what's happening here?"

Aleph shakes her head mutely. She cringes. She throws off her officer's cap and rubs the sides of her costume's head. In the edges of her awareness she can feel the rocket ignition sparks in a thousand buried silos, can already sense the global tsunami of heat and gamma rays radiating backwards from forty minutes into the future, like a horrible smell wafting on the wind—and she refuses it.

She stops. She rewinds.

The man in charge picks up the phone and calls his boss.

"Aleph," Bet says.

"Look at him," Aleph says. "Will you just look at him? He's terrified. He *knows* it might all be a false alarm. His name is Petrov. He has a wife. A son. A whole life ahead of him. He knows he'll lose everything if the computer is wrong, and he's so close to—"

"And he'll also lose everything if he disobeys," Bet says. "He has orders to report what the machine says. You know this is just going to keep happening again and again until—"

Petrov picks up the phone and calls his boss.

Aleph balls her fists and rewinds again. "I can't just stand back and let it happen! I'm sorry, Bet, I can't!"

"What have you really accomplished?" Bet grabs Aleph's fist and pries it open to hold it, mirroring the action with a tendril of consciousness wrapped in hyperspace, trying desperately to hold her love's attention in both places. "Can't you see there is no solution? If you'd just let them have their war in 1962, at least *some* of them could've survived. Maybe they could've sweated it out and learned from the experience. But all the time you've been saving them from themselves? They've spent it building more and bigger bombs!"

"No!"

"It's even worse than that. Thanks to you saving them over and over, they've become complacent. Now they think Mutual Assured Destruction actually *works*. They're closer to the edge than they've ever been, and if they go at it now they'll end up totally extinct."

Petrov reaches for the phone. His hand is shaking furiously. He picks it up and calls his boss.

"Then I need to go back farther," Aleph says. "Take a more radical approach. If I can prevent World War II . . . if I somehow prevent the Holocaust, Leo Szilard never has to flee Germany, the Manhattan Project never happens, these creatures never discover fission chain-reactions, and none of this—"

"You're not helping. You're not even doing this for them. You're just feeding the addiction."

"I can fix this!"

"Aleph," Bet says. "I love you. Please just let them go. I am begging you to let these animals go. Come back to me. I can't lose you like this." Her filaments tangle and jitter in a dozen dimensions, terrified and helpless, already feeling the first waves of wretched heartbreak propagating backwards from a few seconds into her own future. "Don't make me tell you it's them or me."

Petrov picks up the phone—

"Aleph?"

Petrov reaches for the handset and reconsiders. He takes his hand back as if from a fire. He wipes the sweat from his eyes and gives the order to wait for visual confirmation—and Aleph gasps with the sudden and multi-dimensionally visceral thrill of the ripple-effects cascading through time and space, snuffing out all tomorrow's fires, the world reconstituting all its people and cities as if by magic. Everything is fixed. The sun rises tomorrow. Humanity prospers.

She only gives into the sheer, euphoric rush of it all for an instant—but as soon as it passes, she feels Bet's solemn attention burning through her. Her judgment.

"All I did was change what he had for breakfast," Aleph protests. Her filaments make a placating gesture but they're jittery with pent-up tension. "That's all it took! He was *that close* to calling it a false alarm. Puzzle solved. I'm done."

Bet lets go. She sheds her costume and starts to drift away.

"Wait," Aleph calls. "Where are you going? Bet . . .?"

Bet looks back mournfully. "You're done, you said."

"Yes! I'm—" And then Aleph senses forward. "Oh no, no, no!"

"I can't watch you do this to yourself," Bet says, mournfully. "I can't. I don't know how to help you. You know there's only one way to fix this and I can't do it for you."

"Bet, wait—!"

She's already gone.

The sirens on the other side of the glass are falling silent. The only remaining sound is that of the simulacrum of a lone Soviet officer sobbing and pounding her fists on the concrete floor, trying to numb herself to the echoes of thermonuclear fire that fizzle on the edge of her awareness only 46 days into the future.

Between the 5,021st and 5,171st iteration of 6 November 1983, Aleph has a number of conversations with Lieutenant General Leonard H. Perroots, late at night in a bar in Brussels. She keeps coming back to him: all her instincts tell her he's the strand at the center of this causal web—that if only she could yank him out, she could unravel the whole thing and solve the puzzle in one move—but nothing works. She tries everything from seduction to mind control, but the fire in the temporal distance never goes out, never even flickers.

On the 1,248th iteration of their conversation, General Perroots finds Aleph manifested as a woman in a cocktail dress with trails of black mascara dripping down her cheeks. A spiral-bound notebook sags on the bar in front of her, worn and note-stuffed nearly beyond recognition, dusted with ash from her cigarette. She glances at him briefly and reaches for her drink.

"Are you okay, miss?" he asks, against his better judgment. "Waiting for someone?"

"No," Aleph answers, and gulps with a quivering lower lip. "I'm really alone now."

Perroots hesitates, then slides into the stool next to her. He says "Pardon my asking, but have we met? I'm having the strangest feeling of deja—"

"After that whole Korean Airlines thing," Aleph interrupts, "And the Pershing missile batteries going in this month, and Reagan all but *promising* to blast them to smithereens, the Russians have really good reasons to expect an American first strike any day now—right? So doesn't it seem like a *really fucking stupid time* for NATO to conduct a hyper-realistic pan-continental military exercise like Able Archer 83?"

Perroots doesn't miss a beat before he runs for a phone to call someone about the security leak, and Aleph sighs at herself and rewinds—and in the 1,249th iteration he says:

"I'm having the strangest feeling of deja—"

And this time she interrupts: "What you call love is a little neurochemical burp next to the connection Bet and I have. Had? Have? We were going to travel the multiverse forever, and I've fucked that up. I left her. For you . . . weird little critters. And for what? She's right. I'm addicted. I can't stop playing this horrible game. It's my people's weakness."

The general blinks. "Beg pardon?"

Aleph drinks again and answers: "I said we have a thing for puzzles. I think it's because we carry the ancestral memory of a time when we were as helpless as you are—when the past was the past and we couldn't change a damn thing. There's a joy I can't describe, Lenny"—she smokes and coughs—"there's a euphoria in the moment of erasing something horrible from time that I cannot describe. It's the sweetest relief. Heroin for the soul. I know I have a problem. On top of that, somehow, I'm drunk. How can I be drunk? I'm not even made of meat."

". . . Excuse me?"

"Oh, shut up, Lenny. You jerk."

The General squints, taken aback. "Now wait just a minute. Why am I a jerk, lady?" He squints. "And just how do you know my—?"

"You're a jerk because next week you're going to be one of the men who lights the fuse that leads to you and everyone and everything you've ever known getting scattered into the stratosphere to blot out the sun for a hundred years and there's not a damn thing I can do about it."

He gapes.

She shakes her head and makes a backwards spiraling motion with her fingertips.

In the 1,250th iteration he says: "I'm having the strangest feeling of déjà vu."

She's silent. She turns the drink in her hand, staring at the light through the scotch, glittering like brown-smokey fire. Finally she says: "Do you ever doubt yourself?"

He smirks. "I'm doubting myself at this very moment, Miss."

"No," she says. "I don't mean casual self-doubt. I mean the cosmic kind. Do you ever find yourself in—what would you call it?—a moment of truth. Do you ever expend inconceivable lifetimes of toil, to arrive at a nexus of cause and effect in which everything you are comes into play, and billions of quasi-sentient lives hang in the balance? Do you ever arrive at a moment like that only to wish you'd never done anything at all? Do you ever gain limitless power only to wish you were powerless?" She stares at him over the lip of her glass, eyes burning in their make-up-blackened sockets. "Do you, Lenny?"

He stares at her. Then he backs away from her slowly and leaves the bar.

"I'm sorry," she yells at the bartender, her words slurred and unintelligible in the ambient noise. "Sorry to all of you. In a second you'll all have been ash for twenty years. I can only save myself. If I go back and warn myself to pass right by this rock without stopping. No puzzles this time. No metal pipes." She sobs. "I am so sorry. She's right. I have to let you all die."

She starts to reach her filaments into spacetime, back toward her own earlier self, but they're sluggish. She can't find traction. The three-dimensional room seems to roll over and fold in on itself as she passes out on the bar, drooling onto her notebook.

Perroots walks on into the night, bewildered—but what Aleph said to him is so incongruous that it sticks in his mind, no matter how he tries to banish it.

In sleepless hours, he stares away into the glittering lights of airfields and bomber hangars and tries to unravel the mystery of whatever he heard that night. He becomes pensive. He makes calls to family, then long-lost friends, then even former lovers, just to catch up. For the first time in years he dwells on the path less traveled—and a week later, when he receives reports that the Soviet Union is massing an extraordinary number of troops in East Germany and putting all its missile silos on high alert in response to the military exercises he's been organizing, he doubts himself—cosmically.

He decides to pretend he hasn't seen the reports at all.


Bet senses Aleph calling out to her and feels the spacetime boil and shift when she finally comes back—stretching a withered, sickly tendril through to lift herself out of the formless void of the third dimension.

"I thought I'd lost you," Bet cries, her whole hyperspatial dandelion-like body shimmering with relief.

Aleph collapses into her. "I thought so too. I'm so sorry, Bet."

"It's nothing," she says, cradling her sickly form. "I'm just so glad you finally stopped. Are you okay?"

"I'm . . . hungover, I think. I'll be fine."

Bet forms a quizzical shape. "How can you be hungover? You're not even made of meat."

"You were right," Aleph says, caressing her outer filaments. "I was terribly addicted. But like the humans say . . . stick a fork in me. I'm done."

The two hold each other for a long stretch of time as they perceive it; on the edges of their awareness some stars burn out while others age in reverse from red to yellow. Finally Bet forces herself to ask, "Dare I ask how it ended?"

"I did it," Aleph says. "I have no idea how, but I finally got them through 1983 in one piece. I only sensed ten years further ahead before I left, but the Cold War finally ended. So they're home free, right? Maybe? I don't know and I don't care. They're on their own now. That's for sure."

"Good," Bet says. "Go rest. I'll find you later."

When Aleph drifts on, Bet hesitates. She feels the insistent itch of harmless curiosity—and despite all her better judgment, she can't resist the urge to take one more peek at humanity.

On 25 January 1995, she walks pensively among the still-burning, irradiated remains of a thousand human cities. She senses ahead into the nuclear winter. She stretches out her awareness until she understands how it happened, and then she goes to see it for herself. She stands nervously by when the Norwegian science team prepares their experimental rocket—and before that, too, when they file the paperwork to clear their planned launch with the Russian military. She's right there, looking over the shoulder of the bureaucrat who doesn't bother to pass that notice on to early warning radar.

She watches Yeltsin sit at the table with the briefcase open before him, codes entered and keys turned, all stations ready to launch—while his generals remind him that if the report of an incoming missile is accurate, he has only three minutes to act before all of them are incinerated.

Bet hesitates. But it's just too easy.

*Just this once,* Bet thinks to herself—and Yeltsin, in the grip of so much adrenaline, can hardly notice the sensation of something foreign creeping into his mind, sowing the seed of a moment's hesitation. He blinks, and just like that, Bet feels the bright cool rush of the planet-wide fires snuffing themselves out, the skies all turning blue again.

*That's it,* she thinks. *I'm done. I'm out of here. I won't make Aleph's mistake.* But her filaments creep reflexively forward, ten years ahead, twenty, itching to find out if she's truly solved it once and for all, or if . . .

Her sensory filaments reach thirty years, and stop.

*Oh. Well.*

She knows her limits. But.

*Just one more round,* she thinks, and considers the pieces of the puzzle laid out before her.

# THE LIGHT OF TWO MOONS
## K.G. ANDERSON

A howl from the rocky hills outside the compound woke Jan from uneasy sleep. Pulling the stained gray blanket over his shoulders, he got up from his cot and walked barefoot across the concrete floor to the barred window. He gave a low whistle and waited, peering around the courtyard until he saw the daka's yellow snout poking out from behind a utility shed.

"Hey!" Jan called softly. "Hey there."

The yellow hound slipped across the courtyard, flashing chipped fangs and golden-brown eyes. As Jan had trained it to do, the daka rose up on hind legs and stretched its massive frame until it could paw the window ledge. Jan threaded his forearm awkwardly between the iron bars to touch the daka's rough, warm muzzle. As a Shar, Jan considered the daka—descended from the wolves and dogs brought to the planet generations earlier—to be sacred.

So of course, the Dein shot them for sport. He marveled that this beast risked sneaking into the Dein compound every day, just for a few scraps from Jan's rations. "Good boy. Yeah. Good boy."

On the yellow mud wall across the courtyard from Jan's window, two red-brown stains marked the place where they'd shot Bas and Nami six months ago. One bullet each, through the head. The Dein had made him watch, but gave no reasons. Had it been hostage negotiations gone bad, or just some Dein lieutenant's sadistic whim?

"Your Shar friends are gone," was all he'd been told.

Now the great beast whined and gave a wolfish grin, shuffling its sharp-clawed hind paws in the dirt to keep its balance.

"All right, boy." Jan walked stiffly to the metal tray by his cell door and returned with a treat. He pushed it through the bars. It was not just the usual scraps, but all of the meal they'd slid under his door: a gristly rib of bmidi.

*Why not?* He'd heard the Dein craft land outside the compound just after sunset last night, and then the harsh voices of command. All the signs that preceded a prisoner execution. And Jan was the only Shar prisoner left.

His plans for escape had faded long ago. His dreams of home, the Shar resistance, his beloved Majsi's laughter—had given way to nightmares from which he awoke, shivering, in the cold desert air. His only pleasure left was this daka.

The desert hound drew back its lips, took the greasy rib in its teeth, and dropped down to the dirt to gnaw it. Jan watched. Giving the daka his food might be the last time he gave anything to another being.

He thought of Nami, and fumbled beneath his t-shirt for the pendant: a crude charm stamped with two full moons, the symbol of the Shar resistance. Nami, as he was pulled from the cell, had slipped the pendant from his neck and tossed it to Jan. When guards came for him today, Jan would drop the pendant through the drain grate. He would never let Dein fingers touch it.

The buzz of a surveillance drone broke his thoughts. *Dein or Shar?* Two months ago he'd heard a drone—surely Shar— and waved a shirt out his window in hopes of being spotted. Instead, a Dein guard had seen him signal. They pulled him from his cell, beat him, and left him naked for a week before returning his clothes.

But today he had nothing to lose. Jan was struggling out of his shirt when the explosion came. He staggered back from the window, the mud walls of the cell cracking and crumbling around him. Metal groaned. His cell door creaked, then burst open, sagging from one hinge. He stared dully at the open door. Then he recognized his long-abandoned dream of freedom.

Another explosion. The unhinged door hit the floor with a clang, breaking his trance. Out in the corridor, smoke and dust swirled. Shouts rang out from other parts of the building. Poking his head out, Jan saw, at the far end of the corridor, a break in the wall and bright daylight. A land vehicle careened by and vanished into the swirling dust. Jan sprinted down the corridor, then staggered as a hand shot out and seized his ankle.

"Help me!" A Dein lay beneath the rubble, writhing and moaning. Dark liquid spread across his shirt. Jan recognized the face: one of his torturers. Jan shook his head and tried to recall his escape plan. *Disguise. Boots. Guns.*

*Disguise.* Jan bent down and snatched the man's grimy wool cap, clapping it on his own head. He pawed at the rubble, thinking to get the man's boots.

Another drone sang overhead. Jan lunged for the open wall and the courtyard beyond. He tumbled through just as another explosion rocked the building and the ceiling of the corridor collapsed behind him. He scrambled to his feet, blinking in the hot sun and billowing dust clouds.

*Escape. Which way?*

The only figures he could make out were fleeing Dein. And then, a shape whirling in the dust, prancing and backing away. The daka! When the hound spun and darted between two utility sheds, Jan ran after him. The dog led him through a low doorway to the open plain outside the compound. There, Jan paused, confused.

*Which way?*

A howl drew his attention to the daka, pale yellow against the darker yellow sand. The hound was trotting toward the scrub. Jan stumbled after the animal, trying to stay low. He imagined a Dein guard's eyes on his back and cursed the dark pants that made him a target in the desert landscape. Rocks tore his bare feet, dust filled his nose and tears burned his face. He ran faster, marking his ragged pace with a chant: *Gone, gone, gone.*

The sharp rocks hurt, but not as much as scars on his feet where the torturers had burned them. The self-inflicted pain of escape bordered on pleasure. After months of despair, Jan was recalling his escape plan.

Run into the hills.

*Gone, gone, gone.*

Wait until night.

*Gone, gone, gone.*

Follow a road to a settlement.

*Gone, gone, gone.*

Look for the settlement's Shar. They'd help him get back to the city. To his unit. To Majsi. As he ran, he tried to remember what Majsi looked like, but couldn't. Now his beloved was only a word from a long-ago plan:

*Gone, gone, gone.*

The yellow daka trotted at a steady pace while Jan limped after it. They'd entered the scrubby hills and the terrain turned rougher. Jan's throat seared and his vision blurred, exhaustion trumping adrenaline. He staggered, tripped, and fell.

*I'll rest a few.* He sucked in a deep, shuddering breath. With the heat of the sun as his blanket, sleep took him.


Jan woke from a dream about fire and ice. His back burned hot, but he shivered. He lifted his head and saw the silent desert around him. A massive red sun teetered on the point of a black hill, ready to tumble into dusk. The sand beneath him was already cold. On the opposite horizon, the two moons floated, staring like wide-open eyes.

*Silence. No pursuers.* But there was no daka, either. Jan licked his cracked lips and finally managed to whistle a few times. Still no sign of the hound. Rising up on his elbows, he looked back and spotted the Dein compound he'd fled. Black smoke drifted up from the rubble. He'd run for what seemed like hours, made it up into the hills, but he hadn't gotten far enough. A survey craft was lifting off from the field beside the fortress and it seemed to be heading straight for him. The sweat on his back turned cold.

He realized the daka had led him through the scrub, but on a path parallel to a road. The craft was following that road and coming in his direction, its lights sweeping the brush. Jan flattened himself behind a thorny shrub and prayed for night.

A gunner in the craft opened fire, raking the brush on either side of the road. A projectile whined overhead, chipping a boulder behind him. Were they using infrared sensors to pinpoint body heat?

Jan lay flat, his heart pounding so loudly that he almost missed the soft yelp. Slowly turning his head, Jan peered into the dusk. He saw scrub. Boulders. Caves. Then he spotted the yellow muzzle poking out from the mouth of a low cave just a few yards away. Another yelp. When the craft dipped out of sight behind a hill, Jan scrambled on hands and knees to the cave's entrance. He dragged himself inside on his elbows and collapsed in the dark, panting.

Hot, gamey breath fell on his face. Wet snarls came from the back of the cave. As his eyes accepted the dark, he made out several pairs of burning yellow eyes. He was surrounded by a pack of desert hounds. One animal pressed against his flank, as if protecting him from the others. With no options, Jan lay still, listening as the Dein craft swooped back and forth overhead. At last the sound of the engine died away. Of course! The rocks that made up the planet's caves were rich in black silicon, preventing the sensors from picking up their body heat.

Now there was only silence and the panting of the dakas.


Jan woke minutes—or was it hours?—later to the squeal of brakes. The Dein must have sent an electric landcraft to the point where his heat signal had vanished. The inside of the cave was black, the moonlit desert outside, gray and dim. At the slam of doors, the beasts flanking him shifted and growled. Footsteps approached.

Jan flinched as a powerful beam raked the mouth of the cave.

"Look in the caves," someone barked. The dialect was Dein. "Go on."

"Not at night. The dakas—" a second voice replied, quavering. "In the morning, sir. We'll come back in the morning—"

"Coward!"

As if on command, the dakas surged from the cave, clawing their way over Jan in their frenzy to get to the trespassers. Snarls, shouts, shots, and screams. And then: low growls, gnashing and crunching.

While the hounds tore at his pursuers, Jan slipped from the cave and crept to the waiting landcraft. He switched off the telltale lights, found a container of water inside, and gulped until it was empty. Then he set to work. Blessing the light of the two moons, he rifled the landcraft, finding a backpack and stuffing it with more packets of water and a lantern. He picked up a jacket—torn, and greasy to the touch, but it would protect him against the night's cold and the next day's sun.

*If I live until then.* Jan listened for other craft on the roadway. There was no sound except for his own ragged panting and the growls of the dakas outside the cave.

Jan went back to work. The landcraft was surely keyed to the biometrics of the driver and his squad. Even if he could drive it, it was too dangerous for him to travel on a road that might have Dein checkpoints.

When the last of the satiated hounds moved off into the night, Jan set about plundering the torn-up bodies. He took a gun, ammunition, a lighter, and another lantern. From the man roughly his size he pulled boots and a pair of dirty socks. The blood-spattered scarf around the man's neck had been no defense against the dakas' razor-sharp fangs, but what remained of it would protect Jan's face from the sun and the sand if he failed to find a Shar settlement by morning.

Moving away from the carnage, Jan threw back his head and studied the canopy of stars and two moons. Once he knew the way south, he stepped out onto the roadway.

*Are the southern settlements still Shar—or will I have to pass as Dein?* He'd been in the compound for more than two years. All he knew was that the war had continued.

Jan shouldered the pack. Then he looked around, half expecting to see the daka. He called.

"Hey! Hey there."

But the moonlit road behind him stood empty.

"Thank you," he whispered, to the night and to the sacred hound. *Thank you for taking me this far.*

Jan headed south on the narrow dirt road, ready to drop into the brush at any hint of an approaching vehicle. Cresting a hill, he saw a checkpoint in the road below, the guardhouse lit. He slipped from the road and walked slowly, carefully far out into the desert, returning to the road only after it had meandered safely beyond the guard's view.

Twice the light of the moons showed heaps of metal beside

the road—the remains of a landcraft blown up by mines. Peering, Jan thought he saw a Dein insignia on one of the charred pieces. A victory for the Shar? But Jan couldn't risk walking too close to the blast areas. There could be other, undetonated, mines.

One moon set. The second moon floated above the hills as the sky turned pink with the promise of dawn. The road forked, and Jan stood for a few minutes, peering at the dusty signs bearing unfamiliar names. Settlements? Bases? He checked behind him. Had he heard an engine?

Jan took several steps to the southeast, but it felt wrong. The purloined pack lay heavy on his sunburned back. He turned to the southwest, where the second moon hung as if waiting for him. Adjusting the pack, he trudged forward.

It was still early morning when he reached the outskirts of a settlement. *Shar? Or Dein?*

Its name, painted on a worn signboard, provided no clue. A shed stood back from the road, and Jan watched as an elderly farmer emerged, driving a small herd of horned bmidi. The old man wore a soft straw hat.

Jan hesitated. Most men his own age would be aligned with the Shar or the Dein, but he couldn't afford to give himself away by looking like either faction. He slipped off the felted wool hat he'd taken from the Dein guard. After a moment's hesitation, he cast it far into the bush. He stopped by the roadside and pretended to re-arrange his pack, shrugging off his stolen jacket and checking it for Dein insignia. He found none.

His hand closed over his pendant. He could never cast that away. Jan slid the two-moon charm around to the back of the chain, letting it drop down under his shirt. He thought of Nami. How they'd talked for hours about how they would escape, and how they could pass themselves off as Dein if they had to. Nami had engaged their guards in conversation to master the dialect and learn the Dein slang. But Nami was dead, the nuances of his plan long forgotten. Jan was tired from his long night on the road. He muttered a few phrases in the Dein dialect, then spat to clear his mouth.

*Feh.* He'd never manage it. Jan walked quickly past the shed, giving a cautious nod in greeting. *Dein or Shar?* He felt the old man's eyes on his back as he headed for the settlement.

Jan spotted a shabby outpost with a small café. The metal exterior was plastered with posters for local markets, death notices, a schedule of entertainments. Nothing, he noticed, about the war. Through the open doorway Jan saw two middle-aged men in bright-colored caps and vests in deep conversation at a crude table. He strained to hear their words.

*Dein or Shar?* Should he hurry past, or could he stop for help? The men chatted in a dialect he did not recognize.

Exhaustion won the day. Jan set his heavy pack down by the door and limped towards the pair, his hands at his sides to show he was unarmed. They broke off their conversation and frowned.

"Good day. Peace to you." Jan muttered, praying that he had concealed his Shar accent.

To his relief, their faces brightened. They returned his greeting. The older man indicated that he should sit down and share their pot of taratai.

The intoxicating scent of the hot fresh brew rose from the pot. Jan trembled with hunger and fear, praying that something in the conversation would tell him quickly if he was safe with fellow Shar or doomed to be discovered and turned over to the Dein militia.

Jan sat, and the boy working the bar ran over with a cup for him. The older man filled it. Jan thanked him and drank gratefully.

"From where do you travel?" the younger man asked.

Jan froze. What if he named the wrong settlement? There was nothing for it but to tell the truth.

"I came from the north."

The younger man's face turned stony. "You are Dein."

A chill went up Jan's spine. "No. I escaped from the Dein last night."

The boy ran from the room, but the men leaned closer as Jan told his story. He told them about his two years in the compound, about Bas and Nami's deaths. About the explosion the night before. The shopkeepers exchanged glances. The older one narrowed his eyes and shook his head. The young man leaned forward. "Well, what do you want?"

Jan thought of the city and of Majsi. "I don't want to be any trouble . . . I just need to send a message to the city," he said.

The young man pulled a crude communications pad from his vest, tapped in a code, and offered the device to Jan. Hands trembling, Jan tapped out a call. The signals pulsed, and then he heard Majsi's voice. "Hello?"

Before Jan could answer, rough hands seized him from behind. The pad fell from his grasp. Two young men, hunger in their eyes, yanked him to his feet.

"No!" Jan cried out. "I am Shar! I escaped from the Dein compound to the north."

The taller man laughed. "Skip your lies. You are a Dein spy."

"Look at the pendant around my neck," Jan said. "I follow the two moons."

"You are a Dein spy who desecrates the two moons by wearing them." The man ripped Nami's pendant from Jan's neck and dropped it into his pocket. "We'll make an example of you for this settlement to witness."

Terror lit Jan's eyes. This was not what he had expected—to come this far to fall prey to fellow Shar. The men hustled him out the door. But they had taken only a few steps into the street when a heavy missile struck the taller one, knocking him to the ground.

"A daka!" shouted the young boy from the café.

The hound spun and stalked toward the second man, who still held Jan. The hound's hackles were raised and teeth bared.

"Step away!" The older shopkeeper shouted from the safety of the doorway. "Far away. This man is truly Shar and under protection of the hound."

The young man scurried away as the giant hound approached and took its place at Jan's side. Jan placed one hand on the daka's ridged skull and caressed the bristling fur. "Good boy."

The two shopkeepers motioned Jan back into the café, murmuring their apologies, calling him "cousin," and once again offering him the communications pad. Jan sank into a chair, dropped his head to his hands, and wept. He thought again of the city and Majsi.

But what he asked for now was water and meat for the daka. The boy brought the dishes and Jan carried them to the doorway where the daka kept guard. He knelt down. "Thank you."

The hound, panting and bright-eyed, lapped eagerly at the water as Jan returned to the cafe table and once again tapped out the call to the city. Majsi answered, his voice now anxious, "Hello? Hello?"

The shopkeepers listened as Jan poured out his story. So it was only the boy who watched as the daka departed, slipping between two buildings and fading back into the rocky hills.

# The Runner

## Sarah Allen

She raced along the filthy alleyway, slipping occasionally in the muck covering long-forgotten debris. The Upper City ruins stretched out before her like a haunted wasteland, every destroyed meter of it standing between her and possible freedom. The polluted sky above had obscured the sun ages ago, leaving only a muted hint of how brilliant it once was. She felt a familiar vibration in the air and quickly ducked inside a mostly intact doorway, pressing herself flat, squeezing her eyes shut. The high-pitched whine of a drone searching overhead grew louder as it scanned the area for heat signatures. Finding none, it headed down another street, its mantra of orders running through its small processor: Find and detain the Runner until Enforcer squad arrives.

As soon as it left hearing range, she gulped a few breaths and darted back out on the street. As she squeezed through the remains of a roadblock, her hair caught on the end of a metal rod, snapping the barrette holding it back. Dark hair flew into her sweaty face, and she vainly tried to push it out of her eyes with grubby hands. Reaching the middle wall, she searched along it until she came to an old gate. The rusted catch shrieked mournfully as it swung open and she winced at the racket. She shoved a broken plasbox against the gate and jammed a rusted bar through the handle. It wouldn't stop the Enforcers long, but maybe it would give her a few seconds.

As she reached the end of the sideroad, she hid in an abandoned shop to catch her breath for a few minutes. Setting her meager pack down, she pulled out a canteen and a crumpled pack of rations. Ripping one open, she chewed through the mass of protein hurriedly. Once the meal wrapper was empty, she discarded it into the remains of the shop and slowly blew out a breath. Scratching idly at her arm, she looked up through the busted storefront window, towards the broken dome. The sun had slid much further to the west and the outer wall was still another three kilometers out. There wasn't much time before they completely sealed off the old city, and she had to make it out before dark. Gulping several large swallows of water, she shoved the canteen back in the sack and pulled it on. She left the shop at a jog, not noticing the growing pattern on her skin.

It had all begun when Citigov had requested her assistance on a special project. She was an expert in cellular biology, and they needed help with a new virus that had been spreading throughout the Lower City. And she had been such a stupid, naïve little fool for believing that the project description was accurate and not a cover-up. And for believing she would be able to return to her lab when it was done. She really ought to blame that slimy intern for this mess. She had thought he was watching her, but she didn't think that he would actually take action against her. Of course, he had made that spill look like an accident, but she wasn't so sure. Unconsciously, she scratched her arm again. He had to spill it on her, didn't he? Naturally, she'd gone through detox before she got home, but she'd still felt woozy that night. The next day, when she noticed her vision becoming sharper and a new clumsiness that took out her beloved Ficus plant, she knew what had happened. She was mutating.

Down in the City, everyone was tested thoroughly and given jobs for their aptitude and ability level, but they had no minds of their own. Individuality was discouraged, outside the stated parameters. Oh, every once and a while, someone more loud than clever would pop up, but they were usually transferred to a "special research" branch and never heard from again. Especially if they became mutated in any way. There were rumors of people who had escaped and formed a rebel group that survived on the surface, but she had never believed in them. Now, that group was her only hope.

\*

She paused for another breather and caught herself scratching again, noticing for the first time a rash that spread up her arm and across her torso. She fought the urge to scream. Heart pounding, she sprinted wildly, leaping over broken sidewalks and building remains. She came to a wide intersection and there it was, the last wall of the Upper City. She stumbled over to it, desperately looking up and down it for a gate.

Hearing shouts, she glanced back. Enforcers were scrambling through the refuse towards her, not a kilo and a half behind. She hastily turned left and hurried along the wall, hunting for a break in the concrete, a hole, anything.

As she jumped over some loose bricks, her shoe flew off, and she botched the landing. She tumbled, twisting her ankle. Inspecting it for damage, she froze, staring horrified at her foot. It was nearly child-size compared to her usual size 8. She was shrinking!

Reaching out an arm to pull herself up, she also noticed the rash was spreading across her body in a thick feather pattern. Fear shot through her and she hobbled on.

The world continued to grow bigger, as she shrank unevenly. Her sleeves started to slip past her hands, and she had to push them back up every few steps. A few minutes later, she crumpled and howled as her back erupted in fiery pain as the "rash" turned her body hair into feathers. The fabric of her jumpsuit pressing on the new growths, felt like razors on her back, and she clawed and clawed until the jumpsuit tore enough that she could continue.

Her knees twisting in the opposite direction sent her sprawling again, and this time, she couldn't use her arms to push herself back up. Writhing in pain and fear on the ground, her pack and clothes became a prison. She could hear the enforcers shouting amongst themselves, getting closer.

Looking up, she saw the final gate to the city, one door twisted half-open. She struggled to get free of her jumpsuit and pack, tearing at them in her haste. With one last heave, she pulled out of them, and hopped up on a cracked concrete barrier. In tears, she leaped frantically at the gate, arms spread wide to cushion her fall.

*

The Enforcer squad arrived minutes later, but only found the remains of a jumpsuit and a knapsack. One of the soldiers heard a sharp cry, and looking upward, noticed a winged shape climbing into the sky. He sighed heavily, envying its freedom. He gathered the jumpsuit to stuff it in the sack but paused when something soft touched his hand.

Reaching back into the torn cloth, he pulled out a long dark feather. He quickly glanced back at the vanishing bird and wondered briefly . . .

Smiling slightly, he pocketed the feather.

# Sold for Parts
## NIB

Cheena's so quiet, she never talks anymore after her shifts. She just comes home and puts her clothes away. Drapes herself in a white sheet, tied like a toga, doesn't worry about anything hanging out or staying in. It's the shape the toga makes against her thighs that matters to her. The strong edges and the void covered by cloth. I wonder if it's true what they say, that someone threatened to take her breath and she stopped using it for anything but motion, like it was something you could horde. Either that, or Cheena doesn't think words have meaning anymore. So we sit next to each other on the sofa and watch a few shows on the net, until it's time for my shift and Cheena sleeps.

I have the opposite of Cheena's job, so our professions are related. I clean up after the party's over. Put the glass back in the windows, toss the hors d'oeuvres and return lost garments. If there's a fight on the net, I weigh in. But mostly, no one fights anymore. It's like they're all too afraid to say what they think because it might lead to the things we'd all rather not think about. The company's been running for a decade and it used to be all high-end space station parties, trips to Mars and endless flights to China, Iceland, Algeria. Now people come to us. They want something that doesn't change. And I always put the room back the same way.

Cheena was gonna be an astronaut before the deal. But it wasn't the deal that made her silent. As for me, I talk enough for both of us and more than I should. I hang out on the threads that still try to list the disappearing animals. I'm responsible for spotting five kinds of insects, seven mammals and three reptiles. When they're gone, I'll watch new ones, until they're gone too.

One man's job is to watch the mountains. Two are still there, but the range is all hollowed out. Desert now. We don't talk on the thread about why they're gone. No one can stomach that, and we don't want to hope too hard. Life is livable a little bit at a time.

I was a scientist before the deal, but I can't remember any of it anymore. Not one equation. They tell me I'm better to talk to now. That I was always a little haunted or analytical or something. Now I can't stop talking. I talk to the bots that help me reshape the rooms of the floating castle. I talk to the other staff, the bartenders and the talent. I talk to Cheena, even though she doesn't say a word. It's an unspoken agreement that she doesn't have to respond. At work, the music's too loud for anyone to hear her anyway.

I do wish sometimes that I could find someone to yell with, to fight, to do anything, but we all saw what happened to those who panicked that day. And so those of us left just keep on counting the things we loved and took for granted. The things that couldn't change and did. I make the rooms the same every night. Every night Cheena does the same dance. It is what we *can* do.

# THE CALL OF THE SKY
## CLIFF WINNIG

T he army hospital's underground floors reminded me of Pluto Base, a place I'd never actually been. I'd never even been off-world, but I remembered those claustrophobic beige corridors. Two years before, I'd synced with a bunch of my alts home on leave after basic training. Today for the first time I'd be meeting one who'd seen combat. More than that, one who'd become a hero, the only Teri Kang to survive the Battle of Charon.

We wouldn't be syncing, though. Not this time. Not ever. Before she'd escaped the doomed moon—the moon she'd given the order to destroy—she'd been bitten. That's what the G.I.s called it when Hive nanobots infected you: being bitten. Like it was a zombie plague or something.

Hell, it might as well be. Soon the only other Teri Kang in the universe would lose her fight with that infection, and the army docs would euthanize her. Under the circumstances, even coming home had been an act of courage. A lot of G.I.s who got bitten went AWOL rather than face the certain death of returning to base. Not for the first time, I wondered if I had such courage lying latent within me.

Flanked by MPs, I followed a nurse down hallway after hallway till we arrived at my alt's room. Well, the room next to it, since she was quarantined. A smartglass wall separated me from the sterile chamber where the other Teri Kang would live out her last few hours.

I found her sitting at a desk, reading a newsfeed it projected in the air. She'd propped her head in her hands, elbows on the gray metal surface. I sometimes read like that, but only when sick or exhausted. She looked to be both. Right then, the anti-Hive nanobots they'd pumped her full of were fighting a battle every bit as pitched as the one she'd fought on Charon, one that would end for her the same way it had ended for the moon.

Hearing me enter, she raised her head and swiveled to face me. She moved as if her joints didn't ache, as if she weren't already running a fever, but I could tell. The MPs stationed themselves outside the door, and the nurse made his exit. That left us alone, save for the hidden cameras we both knew were watching.

My alt rose to her feet and put her hand against the glass. "Hi, Homebody. Glad you could make it."

That's what they called me. Homebody. The only Teri Kang who hadn't enlisted when the Hive invaded. The one who'd stayed safe at home, teaching military history and tae kwon do at the University of Chicago, unwilling to drop tenure for a chance to help save the human race.

I made a show of taking her in, head to toe: a sick and dying soldierly version of myself.

"I've looked better," I said.

This made her smile, as I'd hoped it would. Still, it was true. Her short hospital gown revealed dozens of half-healed scars on her arms, legs, and face. Repair nanobots can only work so fast, and hers had double duty helping their brethren fight against the Hive. Though she'd pulled her hair back in the same ponytail I wore at the *dojang*, loose strands clung to her face and neck. Her skin was ashen, and the circles under her eyes were dark, as if she hadn't slept in days. Still, she looked better than she would an hour or two from now.

"True enough," she said. "All in all, I'm glad you didn't stop to run errands on the way over. Though you could have brought pizza. I really miss Giordano's."

"You can't get stuffed pizza in space?"

"Nope." She shook her head, then grinned. "It's the only drawback, though."

I stepped up to the glass and put my hand against hers, right against left. I wanted to embrace her, to comfort her, but I settled for what I could get. The glass could have been a magic mirror, opening onto some other world where the person staring back was a stranger. I met her brown eyes with my own. My boyfriend Dave calls them soulful, and he's right, insofar as they're windows to the soul. People used to say that before they could sync souls directly. So it was again for this Teri and me. Eyes would have to do. And words.

"We need to talk," she said and glanced to her left.

I followed her gaze back to our twinned hands, noticed the plain gold ring on hers. The sudden force of that knowledge hit me harder than the news of my alts' deaths, a whole unit of my alts dying, and the one survivor hours away from her own extermination. I'd been grimly determined to face my future solitude without giving into despair, but to see then how much I'd missed of the past, a past we could no longer share . . .

I backed away from the glass and sat down hard on the bench that was the only furniture on my side.

"You got *married*?"

She smiled at me, and it was a sad smile. "We all got married. Well, all of us who were in space."

"To the same person?"

She nodded and lowered her hand from the glass. "Things get complex enough when you're sharing multiple bodies, so all of us married all of her. We make do, though unlike me, my wife doesn't serve in the same units as herself. We wanted to tell you. Hell, we wanted you to meet her, to come to the wedding, even if you didn't want to opt into it, but it all took place during a security blackout. You wouldn't be here even now if I hadn't pulled strings. After Charon, I finally had the clout."

*Good to know* some *benefits come with being a hero.*

"Since we couldn't tell you then," Teri said, "I wanted to tell you in person."

"Sure." She gave me a moment to finish digesting the news. While I sat there, she plopped herself down in her swivel chair, watching me the whole time. "So," I said. "Tell me about her."

"I can do better than that. One of her alts rode down with me. She didn't get bitten, so I imagine she's up on the roof. It'll be nighttime soon, and she doesn't like to lose sight of the stars."

I shook my head, stood up, and started pacing the room. "She'll have a tough time with that. Too cloudy."

"Ah, yes. Chicago." Her eyes followed my nervous movement. "She can fill you in on our marriage later. First we need to talk about the war. I asked her to give us some time alone together, but I don't want to keep her waiting too long."

"What's her name? At least give me that."

My alt rubbed her forehead. "Of course. It's Shanti Jain. She's a colonel. Well, most of her anyway. One of her alts just made general." Military rank for alts is a delicate affair. It's still new enough that the rules keep changing. "She's a great strategist, good at predicting the Hive's movements."

Teri told me of Shanti's military career, clearly proud of her accomplishments, though nothing about how they'd met or fallen in love. After a minute or two, she switched back to us. "I've gotten you clearance, a little bureaucratic trick. You're still a civilian, but you've been reclassified as me, at least as far as the army's concerned. You'll have paperwork to sign, of course, when you leave."

I stopped pacing and turned to stare at her. "You're serious."

She nodded once.

"You want me to enlist, don't you? You want me to enlist and fork a bunch of alts into fast-grown bodies and recreate your damned all-Teri unit. You want me to pick up where you left off, blow up some other moon, and die a hero." I was shaking, waving my hands. I knew I was overreacting, could feel it, but I couldn't stop myself.

If my outburst had upset her, she gave no sign. She just cut past what I'd said to what I thought. "I miss them too, Homebody. I wish you'd gotten to meet more of us, to sync with more of us, but once they'd deployed us in covert ops—well, even if we had gotten shore leave on Earth, we couldn't have synced with you. Only now, after Charon—"

"Charon!" I shouted. "What's so big about Charon? So you blew up a moon! Give me enough explosives, and I could do the same thing."

She cocked her head sideways, measuring me. I folded my arms, held my ground. We went on like this for a minute or two while I fought the urge to resume pacing. Then she smiled a half-smile, though her eyes stayed serious. "Could you? Knowing that more than a thousand uninfected troops remained on the surface? Knowing that all your alts, your best friends, your comrades-in-arms, were there too? Could you, if it had to be done?"

I looked down at my feet. "I don't know," I whispered. When I lifted my eyes again, I'm sure she saw the anguish there.

She nodded, approving of whatever she did see. "That is the beginning of wisdom."

I chuckled. "Now you just sound patronizing."

Her half-smile blossomed into a full one. "I leave that to the professors."

"Touché. So if you're not here to recruit me, why did you come home? It can't be for the scenery. They're not letting you leave the room."

Now she laughed. "Actually, I am here to recruit you."

I sat back down, not trusting myself to speak.

"Only as an advisor. Earth needs you. Humanity needs you. The Hive will keep coming, and we need your mind, your experience. Before our alts died on Charon, the docs started growing another batch of bodies. We were going to double ourselves, make another unit. That won't happen now, of course. We still haven't perfected out-of-body mind backups, so after I'm gone, that's it. Unless, that is, you fork a new set of alts into those bodies. You could really make a difference. You know you'd work well together, and you wouldn't be alone."

I stood up, met her stare with my own. "I think it's time I fetched your wife."

"At least think about it, okay?"

I crossed to the door, which opened as I approached. Beyond, the MPs stood ready to escort me away.


From the roof I could see for miles in any direction, though the space elevator loomed over it all. Its shadow cut across nearby O'Hare, sliced the freeway in half, and fell like the Mongol hordes onto the buildings to the east. And it kept going, crossing the lake to the distant horizon.

I hated the damned thing. Dave says its power lies in our constant connection to space, but it tore me apart, split me from myself. I had three alts at the start of the war, and all of them rode its boxy cars two thousand miles straight up. When they forked more alts, they did it without me. When they died, they left me behind like an old photograph, an image locked in the past.

I found their wife at the edge of the roof, in the shadow of that great carbon tube. She stood at ease, hands behind her back, and stared toward downtown. A strip of her brown neck showed below black hair shorn close to her scalp, above the collar of her khaki uniform. About my height, slender like a gymnast. When she turned at my approach, I saw delicate features, joined to a strong jaw by the elegant curve of her face. But her eyes, impossibly blue, commanded my attention. I'd never seen blue eyes on a South Asian before, yet hers didn't look out of place. They looked like the eyes of a goddess. I could see why my alts had fallen for her.

"Colonel Jain?"

I saw in her face an instant of joy, one that vanished when her subconscious caught up to what she knew to be true: I wasn't her wife. I was just her wife's alt. Nonetheless, she smiled at me, her teeth bright in the fading light. "You can call me Shanti."

We shook hands, her grip firm and businesslike. "Teri's told me all about you," I said.

Shanti raised an eyebrow. "Has she? That's too bad. I hope we'll get along anyway."

I laughed, feeling the grief float away, if only for the moment. "She said you have alts, but you don't work alongside them."

Shanti nodded. "I don't get along with myself like Teri does. She works better with herself than anyone else, the perfect balance between loner and group thinker. It's why she's so effective tactically. Did she tell you how she contained thirteen separate Hive incursions on Charon, kept them from escaping the moon, from spreading to Pluto Base, long enough for ninety percent of our ground forces to evacuate? I'd worked out the seismic stress points, the places she'd have to place the bombs. Even while holding off the enemy, she positioned herself perfectly."

She told me the story as we crossed the roof to the stairwell, her boots loud next to my sneakers. I wasn't used to picturing places I'd never seen, not even in still images, but as she spoke I felt as if I too had been there with my sisters-in-arms, fighting the Hive-infected people and aliens. The Hive weren't a species, like *Homo sapiens*. They were a collection of every species they'd absorbed. Some of the soldiers we'd fought had been human, but even more flew or hopped or slithered their way across the battle-fields of Charon, all bent on using the moon as a staging ground to infect Earth's main base in the Kuiper belt.

Shanti's face glowed with pride as she spoke of her joint accomplishment with Teri. She'd worked remotely with her other selves to plan the overall strategy, and the Teri Kang unit had executed it brilliantly. Then her face showed the next logical step: her wife's decision to sacrifice herself so that more of the other troops could escape. She broke eye contact and turned back toward the city. "I've never been to Chicago. I've been given a few days, so before I return . . ."

"I can show you around, play native guide. You can meet Dave."

She raised a quizzical eyebrow.

"My boyfriend."

"Ah." Shanti opened the door to the stairs. "Well, let's go below. How was she when you left?"

We exited the stairs on the first floor, then passed a checkpoint to enter the underground levels, and another one for Teri's floor. By the time we got back, we could see it wouldn't be long.

Shanti approached the glass and put her hand up as Teri had with me. My alt stood with effort to return the gesture. They stayed that way for so long I felt like an intruder. I sat quietly on the bench, barely even breathed. At length Shanti lowered her hand and sat down beside me.

Teri shuffled to her cot, where she lay still and closed her eyes, her breathing labored. Within minutes, she'd soaked her gown with sweat, so that bits of the material fell apart. Her chest rose and fell, its rhythm growing uneven. She began to thrash, to call out—names from our shared childhood, names I didn't recognize, from after we'd forked.

Safe on our side of the barrier, Shanti and I watched in silence. Sometime during that final hour, she took my hand.

Teri moaned and bucked, then lay still, unconscious at last. After maybe twenty minutes, she sat up and rubbed her eyes, as if she'd merely woken from a nap. She turned to face the glass, but she looked past us into the middle distance. "The sky," she said. "The sky is calling."

That's when the door to our room opened. The nurse returned, the MPs right behind him. In quiet, professional tones, he told us to say goodbye and leave. It was time, he said.

I took one last look at myself and followed Shanti out to the cold, empty corridor.


It's a curious thing to see yourself for the last time, to know you're truly alone again. When alt technology became affordable, years before the war, I felt drawn to the way it opened up possibilities. I could take different life paths, sync memories, and so explore them all. I knew intellectually a day like this might come, yet my new solitude felt stranger than my younger self—the self who underlay all my alts—could have imagined.

I took comfort in the mundane rituals of death. The funeral was short and dignified. Apart from the chaplain, only Shanti, Dave, and I attended. Afterwards, we took an aircar back to the apartment I shared with Dave, in the Hyde Park neighborhood near the university. Ever thoughtful, Dave asked Shanti what she'd like to do. We could have a simple meal, he said, or order in. Or he and I could go out for a bit and give her some space. He took care not to give the impression he'd prefer any particular option.

"Thanks," Shanti said. "But I've always been partial to wakes." She flashed us a sad smile that reminded me of my alt's. "Teri was always on about the pizza here. Though they gave me a few days, I've decided to head back in the morning. Too much needs doing up there. Still, I'd like to try this Chicago-style pizza thing before I go."

"I'll order take-out and bring it back," Dave said, "give you two a chance to unwind here." He called in the order, then bundled up and headed out, even though it wouldn't be ready for forty minutes. I dashed after him, catching him in the drafty hall that led to the stairwell.

"Why the rush, Dave?"

"I thought you might like some time together. I mean, it's not like I don't trust you."

It stung that he'd even thought along those lines. "She's her widow, not my wife."

He held up his gloved hands, surrendering. "Of course, but you both have a bond to the deceased I don't share." Dave's a good guy, but he's a singleton. He never even considered forking alts. He knew I had alts, but I'd met him after the war. Maybe for him they were a distant thing, a theoretical possibility. Teri and Shanti's appearance had made the theoretical uncomfortably real.

"Sure," I said. I hugged him briefly, then let him go. He headed downstairs without another word and out into the autumn night.

Back in the apartment, I found Shanti had helped herself to our scotch. She'd poured two glasses, though, and handed me one before raising hers.

"To Earth!" she said. "How I'll miss her!" We clinked glasses and drank. She downed hers, but I just took a sip. Dave and I usually drank wine, and we seldom had a second glass.

Shanti crossed to the living room window. That side of the building overlooked a small park. "You know what makes Earth great?"

I shrugged, though she couldn't see the gesture. "Stuffed pizza?"

"Naw. I haven't even had it yet." She used her empty shot glass to point to the trees outside. "Life! It's brimming with life. In space we make our bubbles, build our habitats, but here it literally bursts out of the ground. And humanity—hell, that was quite an achievement."

She turned back to me, her face unreadable. "Okay, Homebody, it's truth time. Did Teri tell you what's happening up there, what it's really like?"

"Some."

"I'll tell you the rest, but first a question: before you had clearance, when you were just another civilian, what did you know or guess?"

I frowned and took another sip of scotch. "People . . . wonder. It's no secret the Hive first showed up at the Oort cloud, infected a few miners, and then swarmed its way inward to the Kuiper belt."

Shanti nodded. "That much is declassified. I imagine everyone on Earth knows about Pluto Base."

"Yeah, and Charon too. It's not like you could hide an exploding moon from all the amateur astronomers."

"As you say."

"What I've been wondering—what I still wonder—is this. As the name implies, the Oort cloud's a rough sphere. The Kuiper belt, like the asteroid belt and all the planets, lies in the plane of the ecliptic. It's not talked about, but if you do any digging, you find the first comet miners attacked were in a part of the Oort cloud forty degrees north of the ecliptic."

"And?" Shanti crossed the room to the bottle and refilled her glass.

"If the Hive wants to infect humanity, why is it mucking around fighting our forces in the Kuiper belt? Why don't they just fly in from the Oort cloud directly to Earth?"

Shanti downed her second shot. "Why indeed?"

On Earth the Hive was a distant concern, way out in the Kuiper belt. We knew they were gunning for us, wanting to make us their latest acquisition, but we had faith, faith in our united armed forces, faith in the human spirit. Teri'd had that faith as well, and she'd had a much more informed view of our chances.

Shanti seemed to follow the trail of my thoughts. "You're just like her." She scowled, as if the very idea angered her. "I can see Iwo Jima in your eyes."

I cocked my head sideways, studying her. "You mean the statue of the marines raising the US flag?"

She snorted. "The military history prof gets it in one. You think we can beat the Hive, don't you? We just need the kind of spirit embodied by that image, and we can beat them, stay human."

"Teri thought so," I said quietly.

She didn't reply, but I saw in her face I'd just entered a long-standing argument between them.

Shanti put down her glass and strode to the apartment door. "Come on. We've got a few minutes till Dave gets back. Let's go outside."

Shrugging on my coat, I followed her out to the park. She didn't bother with her own coat, wearing only her dress uniform. Leaves crunched under her boots as she hiked to the clearing in the center. There she stood, waiting for me to catch up.

"Do you know how cold it is out here?" I said.

"I'm okay. It's colder on Pluto." She pointed up at the sky. "Look. There's a break in the clouds."

It was true. Most of Orion floated above, twinkling. "See anyone up there you know?" I asked, trying to lighten the mood.

She shook her head. "Too few remain."

"Then why are you going back so soon? I've lost a piece of myself, sure, but it's not the same. You lost your wife—*all* of your wife." I suddenly felt embarrassed, knowing myself a mere doppelgänger.

She looked at me. Even in the cloud-obscured moonlight, her eyes shone blue. "You think I need more time to grieve, is that it?"

"Why not?"

She turned back to the stars. "I'm not grieving. You heard Teri there at the end, same as I did. The sky called to her. That was her Hive nanobots making a connection, despite all the EM blocking fields and two dozen floors between her and the rest of the Hive. The army killed her, put her down like a rabid dog, but not before part of her uploaded to the Hive. Maybe only a small part, but a part." She turned to me, her jaw set. "No offense, but it wasn't worth most of her dying just to talk to you."

I could see it then, almost as if Teri and I'd synced, how she'd urged my alt to go AWOL when she'd been bitten, despite knowing that when the Hive took her over, she'd give them all her military secrets.

"Charon's not the only time we engaged them," Shanti said, still watching the sky. "We'd lose someone, someone would get bitten, and we'd shoot them, take them out completely, head shot and all. Then a week or a month would go by and we'd see them again, maybe looking just like before, maybe in some crazy body with tentacles and fish eyes and an exoskeleton, but the thing would speak in their voice, their speech patterns, know stuff only they knew. We'd blow it away, but then sure as anything they'd be back again the next time we fought."

I didn't know what to say to that, or even how I felt about it. Violated, maybe. Relieved. That ghastly combination silenced me, while wheels within wheels spun in my head.

"They're up there," Shanti said, "waiting for you, me, and the rest of humanity. You want to know why the Hive didn't just skip the Kuiper belt and go straight to Earth? They don't want to miss anyone. They're here to make us all Hive. Everyone. Certainly every human, but maybe every animal too, or at least every mammal. For all I know they might integrate the trees." She gestured at the ring of oaks around us. "They preserve everything, link it all up. And really, is that so different from what we do, splitting our minds among multiple bodies? Did we become the Hive even before we started to fight them? Who's to say it's not humanity who'll wind up running the place once we're onboard?"

"But we won at Charon," I growled, sounding to my own ears like all my military alts. "We saved Pluto Base. We're fighting them still."

Shanti waved a hand, dismissing the notion. "A rearguard action. A delaying tactic. They're coming, Homebody. They'll take Pluto Base, maybe next week, maybe next month. Then they'll take Titan and Europa and Mars. They'll swallow Earth and keep going until they've got the whole damned solar system." She smiled, then, looked back at the sky. "After that, they'll move on, only we'll be there too. Humanity's oldest dream: to touch the stars."

I followed her gaze to the deceptively quiet night sky. The clouds had broken apart and blown away, leaving a vast starscape arching above.

"Do all the troops feel like you do?" I asked.

Shanti shrugged, as if such concerns were irrelevant. "Everyone at HQ."

"Then why fight them at all? Why not give in and let your-selves get taken over, become a bunch of marionettes?"

"Believe me, I thought about it. Teri did too, though her stub-born streak won out, her insistence on 'staying human,' as she called it. Still, I thought there might be more than one way to merge with the Hive. Who says we have to do it on their terms? They'll take us in, pull our strings, as you say. That's inevitable. But before they do, right up to the last moment, even as we get absorbed, we can show them what Teri showed them: the human spirit."

We stood in silence for a minute or two while I followed her logic, digested her philosophy. I felt the latter infect me as if it too were a Hive nanobot swarm, though I fought against it. I doubted the human spirit would survive inside the Hive. That's when my path—and the path for all my future alts—unfolded before me.

"Take me with you," I said.

I didn't think about Dave before I spoke. I loved him, had figured someday I'd marry him, but now I couldn't see it, not un-less I went up there and turned the tide of the war.

Shanti raised an eyebrow, though she didn't say anything. I wondered if Teri had even told her she'd offer me that new batch of alts if I joined the cause.

"Not as a soldier," I said, "and not as your wife. As a civil-ian advisor. I've already got clearance, and I've got millennia of military history under my belt. I bet I can come up with a thing or two."

"I bet you could, but it's out of the question. Stay here. En-joy your time with Dave. We'll all meet up again, one way or another."

Colonel Shanti Jain was brave, a good soldier, no doubt a brilliant strategist. But she wasn't a hero, not like Teri had been. The war had gotten to her. Maybe I couldn't help her—or any-one else at HQ, if they truly thought as she did—but I could try. I could make a difference. So I pulled out my trump card, one I hoped still had weight with her.

"Teri believed in me," I said. "That's why she came home."

Shanti frowned. "You really think you can find a way to de-feat the Hive?"

"We'll find it together."

She stared at me with those eyes like twin blue suns. "All right." Her gaze flicked back to the apartment building, and she hugged herself, as if the cold were finally getting to her despite her protest. "Let's go back inside. I want to catch the morning car up the shaft, and you need to pack."

# The Last Human Being on Earth

## Kyra Worrell & Theresa Barker

The Grafton machine woke her up. Lifted her eyelids off her eyes. Opened them. Focused them. Turned her face towards the screen so she could see videos, still images from the feed, and finally the text-based experience. Everything she was supposed to do. It was right there.

Sharah was not pretty and she was not plain. What she watched suited her, made her pretty and plain and all sorts of things, made her more than she was. And sometimes, this was too much.

She stretched a finger out of its gentle constraints and hit a button.

Her companion robot rolled forward, a steaming cup in hand. "Tea?" The robot's voice had a pleasant accent that mirrored the dialect from Sharah's youth.

"No." She spoke into the headset, momentarily stopping her feed. Though Sharah couldn't fault the machine for jumping to conclusions. Tea was what she usually wanted. Tea requests abounded in the robot's databanks.

"No, today I think I want something different." This was more words than she had said in any number of days.

The unit rolled sideways in a show of shock. Then it then rolled back into place, ready to serve.

"I think today, I think today I want to walk." Sharah was suddenly tired. She couldn't think today, too tired. She let her hand and finger drop. "Never mind," she said. "The tea is fine."

And tea would be fine. Fully restored by the Grafton machine's deft manipulations, the tea would be as if it were the original in all its leafy glory. And she, Sharah, the last human being on Earth, she deserved every bit of it. The robot would hand it to her, and she would sip. Just as she had every day, day after endless day, for countless days gone by. Just a taste, sitting up, unclamped from safety restraints that otherwise contained her, and then she would fall back onto her bed, the bed responding, as it always did, by re-clamping her fingers, hands, limbs, and torso into the holding cocoon.

As she lay in the restraints, unable to move—it was, of course, for her safety—she felt as comfortable as an inert person might be. There was no need for comfort, really, when you were the last living human being on Earth, was there?

The feed began again. All the uploaded minds, thoughts, memories and reflections, of all the dwellers of this desiccated planet flowed into, over, and through her mind. It was a burden, but she had the repository space, vast auxiliary memory stores that were fostered, maintained and kept in order by the Grafton machine. This was her purpose. If only one person on Earth was to survive, it was the duty of that person to hold the entire recollection set for all of humankind, and hadn't they worked fast and furiously in the final days to make an enormous deposition entity, one that would live indefinitely, tended by the Grafton machine, one that could retain the uploaded memories of millions, of billions, from infant and child all the way to old age and senility. And hadn't she been the most fortunate being on Earth, the human that had won the most desired role on the planet, the opportunity to be tethered—for life—to that deposition entity that contained the planet's entire consciousness.

The intelligence of a world. What that meant was even beyond Sharah. At first. But now, now after days upon days, days upon more days, and more days, she felt nothing like the human she had been. She was, perhaps, a Gaia, the ancestral mother of all life.

No. She was only Sharah. Human joined to machine, machine joined to human. What had it been like to be human, to walk upon the Earth, to eat and drink normally? To be with family.

The feed flowed over her.

"Tea?" The robot had returned.

Shara considered. "No." She was tired, yes. But today she felt so, so utterly non-human, that she could not just lie here inside the cocoon's restraints. She had the right. She had the right to get up, to walk. To behave as more than a tethered-machine's extension.

"Today I will walk." It had been a long time. Would she remember how?

The restraints relaxed, after a pause, she noted. Was it her imagination, or did the Grafton machine hesitate to obey her wishes? It had been so long since she had done this, she could not remember if it was customary for a pause before relaxing the restraints. No matter. She had enough to simply remember how to walk.

The bed tilted, gently, ever so gently, gradually bringing her to a standing position. Her companion robot appeared with a mechanical device, a rolling sort of cage that she could enter, her hands on the bars, her form protected from hazards above and below, side to side. She must be protected. That was primary. Last human on Earth. They were not about to let her die accidentally.

She shook her head. "No." The robot, again startled, did its little sideways roll of shock. Then it rolled back, again ready to serve.

"You will guide me," she instructed the robot. Another hesitation, another pause, this one a bit longer than the previous one. The Grafton machine's intelligence. Was it testing her? She had just made up her mind to restate the command when the companion robot rolled into place at her side. She put a hand on the smooth round surface of the unit, and gently stepped out of the cocoon. Well, not stepping, exactly. More like shuffling. But it would do.

The light cotton shift she wore brushed the sides of her legs, draped comfortingly around her calves, moving as she moved. It was piercingly obvious to her that she had waited too long. When had she last walked? What had kept her motionless for so long?

The feed. The everlasting, ever-present feed, the flow of a million billion thoughts in the Grafton machine's repository. Sitting there, or lying there—no difference to her—was her job, wasn't it?  She had the responsibility to have the consciousness maintain its presence even in the absence of every single other human being on Earth.

The feed.  Early morning breakfasts of rice cereal and edamame . . . cold cut deli sandwiches eaten in a cafeteria . . . sunset walks on a distant beach . . . the birth of a first child . . . the radiance of ice crystals on bare winter branches.

Wait.

The frailty of illness . . . a parent's loss of sanity . . . the killing of an innocent . . . the death of a beloved child.

"Stop." The robot, all obedience, halted. Sharah looked up. It was only a short distance further to the observatory viewer. She had been here before, she remembered. Perhaps the robot had led her here.

But the viewer held no interest for her.  What was there to see but the brown-gray husk of an abandoned planet, a planet that had killed its inhabitants after being stripped of its protective shell of forest, trees, rivers, lakes, stone, sand, ice, oceans. She could not watch it again.

A tear began to form behind Sharah's eyes. What was this? She did not have time to cry. Her need was to filter, to relive, to experience, to stand in the place of every human on Earth and to preserve their right to be remembered. She could not waste time with small emotions like sadness, like sorrow. No. No time for that.

She turned, shuffling carefully so as not to lose her balance even with the robot's guiding bulk beneath her hand. She would go back to the cocoon. It was only what she deserved. Living was for those who had already perished, perhaps.

The Grafton machine grunted as she arrived back at the starting point. Well, grunted is not, perhaps, the right word. There was a noise, a sound, that came from the device. She had been right. It was glad to see her back within its controlling, surrounding, cushion.

Her muscles, unused to movement, had begun to tremble. She reached out her free hand to grasp the side of the cocoon. Then—

Collapse.

Sharah lay in a heap, micro-inches from the safety of the restraint-cocoon. Whiteness, whiteness all around her.

The robot stood waiting. What was her command?

The Grafton machine grumbled again.

This had happened before. Eventually the robot, guided by Grafton machine programming loops, managed to negotiate Sharah's form into a position near enough to the pod that she could be drawn into the restraints, gently, ever so gently, then the bed rotating, slowly, ever so slowly, from its vertical standing position to the reclining position she was accustomed to. The finger rested inside its restraints again, ready to lift itself and press a button if the need arose.

The feed began again.

This time there were no tears.

# ESCHER'S HANDS
## JEFFREY STEVEN ABRAMS

When I resigned from the Physics department in 2072, I vowed never to return to the Neutrino Detection lab. Now, sixteen years later, I'm standing in its control room, waiting to witness the validation of my life's work.

From behind, I hear a diminutive voice. "Good morning, Professor Walker. You honor me by attending our demonstration."

Turning, I see Dr. Weng Li's smiling face. Current director of Cal Tech's Time Energy Department, Dr. Li is fifty years my junior with an MIT doctorate and dozens of influential papers to her credit. Colleagues had difficulty accepting this tiny woman when she first replaced me, but once they witnessed the intellectual powerhouse within her slight exterior, their fears evaporated.

"No, I'm the one who's honored," I reply respectfully. "Tell me Wen, what do you have planned?"

"With the improvements we've made to your Time Compression Chamber, we hope to detect accelerated radiation from the neutrino stream," she begins excitedly. "Once the super electrons strike the chamber's photovoltaic lining, they should drop back to ground-state levels, but not before releasing their excess energy."

Pointing at the thick cables that protrude from the chamber and exit into the floor, I ask, "With wireless transmission, you're still using cabling?"

Li smiles. "Yes., For the output we expect, high-voltage transmission lines are still the safest and most dependable. They are linked directly to the storage arrays at Scholl Canyon Landfill."

Suddenly, a device on Dr. Li's wrist begins to beep. "I'm sorry, Dr. Walker, but I'm needed elsewhere."

"Of course," I say, inwardly thanking her for answering my

unasked question. I settle into an unoccupied chair, and with nothing better to do, reminisce about Galen Troth, and the fifty-seven twisting years since we met.

At the freshmen orientation in 2030, my first glimpse of Princeton's ivy-covered buildings left me speechless. The University's history saturated everything, but for me, it was heaviest outside Jadwin Hall, the physics building where I'd dreamt to follow in the footsteps of giants like Feynman, Turing, and Compton. Near the entrance stood a distinguished older gentleman. With a full head of silver hair, wire-rimmed spectacles, and neatly trimmed beard, he fit the stereotype of an Ivy League professor. While the sharp wrinkles on his forehead suggested advancing age, his eyes remained sharp, penetrating.

Catching my gaze, he gave the slightest nod, but I turned away, embarrassed by a tear trickling down his cheek. When I looked back, he was gone.

I spent my first semester obsessing over this vanishing man. Whenever I encountered a pod of faculty, I sought him out. If there, he was well disguised.

Over the eight taxing years that followed, I never saw him again. I graduated with a Ph.D. in particle physics, but with East Coast academic jobs nonexistent, I accepted a position at Occidental College in Southern California. It was there, while rail commuting to Pasadena, that I ran into him again.

"Mind if I join you?" he'd asked.

I'd been grading papers and didn't look up. "Um, it looks like plenty of other seats are open," I mumbled.

Ignoring the hint, he eased himself into the seat, and after drawing a long breath, said, "I don't believe we've met. My name is Galen Troth."

I said nothing.

"I see you're grading finals from Physics 1b. Let's see, 2040, isn't this your third year at Occidental?"

My workpad slipped through my fingers, bouncing off the train's floor. "How do you know that?" I sputtered, but then, after a closer look, added, "Do I know you?"

"Ah Michael, you're still so young, and there's so much to tell you."

"Uh, how do you know my name?"

Rather than replying, Galen gave me a wistful smile, shimmered, then disappeared. In his place was a small package.

I looked around, but not a single passenger seemed to have noticed this extraordinary event. I slipped the bundle into my pocket, hoping further examination would reveal some clues about its mysterious owner.

I spent that morning in my office reflecting. Galen Troth frightened me. Being old and frail, he posed no physical threat, but his knowledge about me was unsettling. Was this illusionist the same wizened professor I'd seen all those years ago? If so, why was he following me?

The Brown paper package had no discernible markings. I shook it carefully, and hearing no ticking or anthrax shifting sounds, tore away the wrapping. Inside, a thick layer of bubble wrap yielded to my penknife, revealing an unusual object—a miniature replica of the traveling device from the eighty-year-old movie, *The Time Machine*. Stuffed into its leather appointed chair was a note which read, "In time, I hope you appreciate this gift. All I ask in return is your promise to stop me in fifty years."

A chill settled over me.


Two years later, on the same commuter shuttle, our paths crossed again. When he sat beside me, I recognized his eyes immediately. Less forlorn, Galen looked oddly younger, his face tan and radiant.

After the shock of seeing him wore off, I asked, "So who are you? I did some searches on Galen Troths, and from what I couldn't find, you don't exist."

His shoulders drooped. "Yes, well that's my burden." Then, regaining his composure, he added, "You have quite the memory, Dr. Walker . . . Didn't we meet in 2040?"

"Don't play games with me! You're the one who initiated the contact."

"Yes, of course . . . What exactly did we talk about?"

Annoyed at this clumsy fishing attempt, I replied, "We barely spoke to one another. You were here and then you were gone. However, you did leave behind an interesting present."

"Ah yes, but remind me, what was it?

"You don't remember giving me that model time machine or the odd note stuffed inside?"

Galen fidgeted at the question but recovered quickly. "Sorry, just testing you. By the way, did you like it?"

"As a matter of fact, I did, but how is it that you know me, and why do you keep popping up?"

"Strange as it might seem, Michael, we have a shared history. As such, I know many things about you. For instance, you're thirty-one years old, an associate professor of physics at Occidental, and you're interested in alternate forms of energy. Sadly, your teaching duties allow little time for research."

"How . . ."

"I don't have much time, so please let me finish. A groundbreaking paper, which I believe you'll find fascinating, is about to be published." Galen pulled a note from his coat pocket and handed it to me. "Here's a list of websites referencing that study."

I raised my voice. "That's great, but you're avoiding my questions. WHO ARE YOU?"

As if on cue, the train ground to a halt. "I have to get off here, too many people," he said, moving toward the exit. Before stepping onto the platform, he turned. "The next time we meet, I'll tell you the whole story."


Galen's note referenced a controversial study dealing with time to energy conversion. While attempting to explain the universe's matter and antimatter imbalance, Lithuanian physicists had observed neutrinos within deuteron nuclei traveling faster than the speed of light. After breaking that impossible barrier, the particles vanished. The popular explanation theorized that once neutrinos exceeded lightspeed, they began moving backward in time, thus appearing to wink out of existence.

The implications of unbounded light speed were staggering,

calling into question fundamental laws of physics, Einstein's theory of relativity included. In order to keep E = MC2 balanced, increases in velocity required either an increase in energy or a decrease in mass.

The findings, which hinted at a new energy source, became the darling of venture capitalists. They poured billions into research but saw little return on their investments.

Until my breakthrough.

It took three years to conceptualize and create the Time Compression Chamber. Throughout that period, Galen's role in my success gnawed at me. The time machine replica and the websites—it was as if he'd been purposely shaping my career. At the end of that third year, when he'd asked to meet at Café Panda, I hoped to finally get some answers.

Sitting in a booth far from other patrons, Galen looked different, like someone who'd recently shaved his beard or lost weight. I had to admit, he looked better.

Recovering, I said, "Before we go any further, you're going to tell me how you know so much about me."

Galen's eyes sighed. "Perhaps it would have been better if we'd met at a bar. A few drinks would have taken the edge off. But to answer your question . . . you told me."

"I told you?"

"Yes, I believe the year was 2065."

"Right. 2065, twenty years from now!"

"Your math is excellent, professor."

Irritated, I stood to leave, but his pleading face stopped me.

"Michael, when I met you, you were already an old man, and I was only twenty. That's when the time reversal started."

"What are you talking about?"

Galen glanced at his watch then frowned. "Something happened forty-five years ago, I mean from now. I was, will be caught in an experiment that went badly. Ever since that moment, I've been living my life backwards. It's not that I'm getting younger; when I wake up tomorrow, I'll be a day older, but my tomorrow will be your yesterday."

"I see . . . Let's say, for the sake of argument, that you're telling the truth. If you're living in reverse, how is it possible that we ever meet? At best, we should be like ships passing at sea, close but never seeing each other."

"This is way out of my league, but ten years ago, I mean from now, you explain to me how this happens. Apparently, the reverse timeline I'm living in is stable, but my presence there isn't. On random occasions, I'm ripped back into my original reality. The durations are short, but those are the only times we can interact."

His words had an undeniable logic, but . . . "Something still doesn't make sense. How do you know when these intersections will occur? The odds of our lives lining up on those occasions are infinitesimal."

He pulled an old sheet of paper from his shirt pocket and handed it to me. "Forty years from now, you'll give me this list. It's served its purpose for me; now it's yours."

On the paper was a list of dates, times and locations of future meetings. Hard as it was to accept, the handwriting was undeniably my own.

Galen's voice broke my train of thought. "Michael, have you ever seen M.C. Escher's painting called 'Drawing Hands'?"

I looked at Galen blankly.

"Pity. It's one of his more notable works. That sketch captures the essence of our lives. It depicts a hand rising from a sheet of paper, drawing a similar hand which also rises to draw the first. Each hand affects its counterpart. A line in one becomes a line in the other; if one wrist bends, the other matches the angle.

"Our lives are similarly intertwined. When we're in contact, what I say to you is often based on something you said in my past. What I'm telling you now will impact your future. Like it or not, we control each other's destinies."

Ill-prepared as I was for a discussion like this, the conversation turned out to be one-sided, because I heard, "Too short . . ." as Galen faded away.


On April 23, 2046, I turned thirty-six and found out what happens when dreams come true. Galen's spoiler muted some of the excitement, but it was a small price to pay for the offer of a tenured position at Caltech.

I'd like to think that my work, along with the NSF and industry money I brought, secured the promotion, but the possibility of Galen's intervention plagued me.

For over sixteen years, I'd spent only a few hours in his presence, but that time had been life changing. While our meetings had always been productive, they'd been too short for bonding on anything but a superficial level. Too many mysteries still existed.

With my back blocking the view of other Café Panda patrons, the space in front of me began to shimmer. Within seconds, Galen materialized.

"Congratulations, Professor," he said cheerily. At sixty-four, his hair was graying, but his eyes sparkled with youth. He reached into his pocket and withdrew an item which he handed to me.

"A fortune cookie?"

"Open and read it."

The paper inside the cookie read, "Fame is in your future."

"I had it made special," Galen said, then his tone turned serious. "Michael, I have to tell you something very disturbing, something I doubt you'll ever forget. It's something that happens fourteen years from now."

"Galen, I know you love being dramatic, but get to the point."

"You're right. Anyway, in 2060, I'm going to shoot you."

"Excuse me?"

"My life was unbearable back then. No friends, no career, and not much hope for improvement. I started a one-way swim into the Pacific but turned back when the epiphany hit; if I killed you, things would return to normal."

My hands started to shake. "If that's true . . . why warn me?"

"Like I said, I was in a bad place. Over the last nine years, I've turned my life around. I also realized how selfish I'd been. Undisturbed, your work will have a profound effect on the world. Who am I to derail such advancements?"

I held the fortune tightly in my hands, staring through it like I'd stared through Galen at Princeton. Before I could reply or ask other questions, he was gone.

\*

My fiftieth birthday marked the point when Galen and I were the same age. It felt like the passing of a torch, the time when mentor became mentee.

It was also Galen's warning date. Not that I needed to be reminded; his words had haunted me for fourteen years. Although we'd met several times during that span, I never broached the subject, fearing I'd break the tenuous thread that connected us. In the strangest of circumstances, we'd become friends.

To celebrate our matching ages, I'd reserved an hour in the Neutrino Detection Lab to show him my work. Explaining the technical details to a lay person presented serious challenges, but I believed Galen would be more than up to the task.

When I arrived at the lab at 9:00 that morning, Galen was already waiting outside the door. His calm demeanor was both reassuring and disconcerting. As I shepherded him through the lab, pointing out arrays of specialized electronics, he stared at the equipment with frightening intensity.

"I didn't think you'd find this so interesting," I remarked.

"Interesting? . . . More than you can imagine."

Then he began to shake violently, as if trying to exorcise unseen demons. When he finally settled, he said, "A few years ago, you asked me how I deal with living in reverse. At the time, I didn't have an answer, but I've had a lot of time to think about it.

"When the accident occurred, I lost everyone. They didn't die or move away; they just weren't there. That was hard at first, but over the years, I've met new people, had relationships, you know, gotten by."

Galen bit nervously at a fingernail before continuing. "The hardest part . . . It's when I'm back here. Things have changed in the thirty years since the accident. I can't say which of my worlds is better or worse, they're just different."

Keeping my voice as calm as possible, I asked, "Given the choice, would you return to normal or continue in both worlds?"

He jolted, then with a look of hatred that jerked me backwards, replied, "I'd do anything to live normally again."

Then he broke.

Extravagantly waving his arms like a hustler enticing patrons into a club, he announced, "Ladies and gentlemen, come see the magical doctor. Before your eyes, he will make a man pop out of thin air."

I wiped away sweat from my suddenly slick forehead.

Abruptly, his tone shifted from demonic to docile. "Jeez Michael, I almost forgot. Happy birthday, doc. Welcome to the fifties club. Here's your present."

Galen had always been a gift-giver, but when he pulled out a Glock .45, I froze.

"My God, it's true," I moaned.

"Huh? What's true?"

"Fourteen years ago, you warned me this would happen. I didn't want to believe it, but …"

Completely unhinged, he shrilled, "I told you? God, what a pathetic creature I am."

I lunged forward, heard a loud blast, then the world went black.

As Galen and his weapon receded into the past, my own journey limped forward. While the protective vest I'd been wearing had foiled Galen's murder attempt, his wish for me to cease my research had been granted. As an unwilling guinea pig, he'd shown me how easily my work could ruin lives. Only Gods should wield that kind of power, and being no deity, I made the not too painful decision to discontinue my work.

I quit that day.


My next meeting with Galen occurred ten years later. Not knowing when murderous ideas had first blossomed in his mind, I approached our rendezvous cautiously, surveying the location from across the street. He was sitting under an Italian umbrella outside Café Panda, drinking alone.

From my vantage point, his younger years looked joyless. Shaking badly, he needed both hands to steady his cup. Even so, liquid sloshed out, creating smoky plumes of steam that turned his wrists red. He never flinched as the scalding drink burned his skin.

Recognizing me, he jumped out of his seat, but after recovering, a calmer, curious look graced his face.

"Hey Professor, what's cranking? For an old geezer, you're looking pretty spry."

Up close, Galen looked worse than from across the street. The pupils of his bloodshot eyes were pinpricks, and his skin was a sickly gray. "I wish I could say the same about you," I replied. "You're only forty but you look like death warmed over."

Staring at me, he set his cup down. "Nice to see you, too."

"I'm serious. What's going on?"

After a long sigh, Galen replied, "Nothing. Nothing's wrong, I've just been watching the vid-feeds. In my timeline, they're buzzing about how your new energy source is saving the world. Everyone's talking about it. You'd think that after twenty years I'd be over the trauma, but it's still too raw. Oh, and by the way, calling it Troth Energy was a nice gesture. I shrug away questions whenever anyone asks, they wouldn't believe the truth anyway."

"That doesn't explain why you're letting yourself go like this."

Galen flailed his arms. "Jesus, are you that dense? Look at me! Isn't it obvious that I just don't give a shit? I've lost everyone, my parents, my sister, all my friends . . . I'm living in a world filled with strangers, and I'm fucking lonely."

The effect of his words bit deeply but paled before the sight of needle marks on his exposed arms. "Ah Christ, Galen, you're a junkie?"

"Congratulations Professor. As always, your insights are spot on." As he reached toward the heavens in mock victory, his arm struck the coffee cup, sending it flying across the patio.

It was hard to believe that this disheveled individual would become the silver-haired, distinguished gentleman who greeted me that day in Princeton. Worse, I knew his lowest point was yet to come.

Without thinking, I blurted, "Galen, this won't make any sense to you right now, but I forgive you."

\*

In 2067, twenty-five-year-old Galen's mental state was a train wreck. In order to cope with constantly escalating disorientation, he'd rock and moan for hours, collapse into sleep, then repeat the cycle. One day, I tried to gain a better understanding of his world by asking him what it was like to live in two timelines.

"At first it was bad, really bad," he'd said, shaking his head. "It was like a dream I couldn't wake up from. I'd be here, then there, then back again. It wasn't until I started spending more hours in the alternate timeline that life became tolerable."

The topic must have triggered a memory because he abruptly changed the subject.

"Y'know, when I was in college, I learned about this psychology experiment where the participants wore these glasses that made the world look upside-down. They spent the first few days bumping into things, getting dizzy and sick, generally being miserable. Then, after three days, most of them woke up to find the world had flipped right-side up. Apparently, our brains acclimate to new environments. I guess that's what's happening to me."

After a pause, his expression darkened. "I couldn't have taken it otherwise. I'd have slit my wrists by now."

Every word from the Galen-to-be stabbed at me like a knife. I knew my interactions with him would soon end, while his journey was just beginning. Reaching into my pocket, I withdrew a barely legible remnant of paper, the one he'd handed me years before. After selecting a new sheet, I copied the old lines onto their new home and handed the note to him.

"We'll be meeting each other a lot in your future. Here's a list of all the times and places."

"What if I forget, or just don't want to see you?"

"You won't."


I'm shaken back to the present by an ex-colleague who's trying to engage me in conversation. "Amazing, isn't it?" he says. "I mean, we're about to witness history being made."

When I grunt in reply, he frowns, then walks away. I probably should apologize for my rude indifference, but right now I'm too preoccupied to care.

By 11:00, the lab's overflowing with faculty members, science reporters, and graduate students. There's electricity in the air, partially from chamber emissions, but mostly due to excitement. As I meander through the crowd, Dr. Li's microphoned voice cuts through the buzzing hordes. "I think we're about ready. Everyone, please move behind the yellow line on the floor." Thick walls from each side of the lab begin to move outward. Slightly offset, the two barriers slide past each other after meeting in the center, continuing until they lock into opposite walls. Equally spaced portholes allow viewers to watch the proceedings. After students perform a final safety check, Dr. Li presses a button, then announces, "Process initiated."

Outside Batavia, Illinois, the underground particle accelerator at Fermilab spins into action. After the generated proton stream smashes into a beryllium target, the resulting neutrinos are directed to Pasadena where they feed into the Time Compression Chamber.

Rumbles beneath my feet release floodgates of memories: hours spent working on equations, discussions with staff at Fermilab, the trip to Geneva, where I spoke to particle physicists at CERN. I can't believe this is actually happening.

"Neutrino stream detected," a graduate student announces. The output monitor displays temperature change, absorption rate, voltage increase, and a myriad of other measures. Of particular interest is the battery charging rate because it shows how much energy is being captured. All eyes, with the exception of mine, are fixed on the screen. Unable to stay any longer, I slip out of the lab, unnoticed.


Twenty frightening minutes later, after speeding through red lights along the eight-mile stretch between Pasadena and Glendale, I arrive at Shoal landfill. Piecing together bits of conversations I'd had with Galen over the years, I know that, because he's too poor to own a car, he'll take the 181 bus to get here. I also know that after the explosion, he'll be found near the landfill's south side.

Right on schedule, I see a man with the youthful bounce of a twenty-year-old walking towards me on Figueroa Street. A large canvas bag hangs from his overall covered shoulder, but his face is obscured by a Dodger cap atop his head. I move across the sidewalk to block his way, and when he looks up, my knees go weak. Untouched by life, and not yet wrecked by my intervention, Galen Troth stands before me.

"Who're you?" he asks irritably.

My lips move, but only a whisper emerges. "Hello, Galen. My name is Michael Walker."

He looks perplexed before responding. "How the hell do you know my name?" Full of boyish energy, his eyes are clear and blue—a far cry from the black dullness I remember.

"It's an unbelievably long story," I reply. "But for now, you've got to stay out of this landfill."

"What the fuck . . . What makes you so sure I'm going there?"

Remembering my own misgivings when I met Galen on the commuter train, all those years ago, brings tears to my eyes.

"Dude, what's the matter with you?"

A sense of déjà vu strikes me so powerfully that I grab onto Galen's arm to avoid passing out. I recall that time at Princeton, sixty years earlier, when his tears had confused me. It's amazing how little I understood about comradery back then. Galen faced what I now face, the irreversible ending of a friendship.

Only now do I realize how much I'll miss him. Over the years, he changed from a father figure to a friend, and finally to a son. From this point forward, my life may be filled with happiness, tragedy, fulfillment, or loss, but it will all come as a mystery, no longer dictated by his sphere of influence.

Galen rips my hand free as he shouts, "Get away from me, you crazy old fuck."

While our lives may have been similar, mine was one success after another, thanks in large part to this young man. In exchange, I gave him a life filled with lonely days and suicidal thoughts. This is my one chance at redemption.

I grab at his bag, trying to wrench it free, but he counters with a shove that sends me sprawling. At seventy-eight, I'm no match for this young man, but with a strength he can't understand, I wrap my arms tightly around his leg. Ignoring the curses,

I accept his punches and kicks as long deserved punishment.

Suddenly, a flash, followed moments later by an ear-piercing boom, freezes Galen. I look up, drawn toward the landfill where a bluish fire burns out of control. I go limp at the sight and begin to sob. "Galen, I did it. You're free," I say before the world goes dark.

"Professor Walker?"

Opening my eyes, I see a man hovering over me. "Who are you? Where am I?

"It's good to have you back. We've been worried. I'm Dr. Francis, and you're at Huntington Hospital recovering from quite a beating. You have several broken ribs and a hairline hip fracture."

I try shifting positions to better view my surroundings, but straps have me locked in place.

Answering my unasked question, the physician says, "Sorry professor, but we have to keep you immobile; at least until your ribs stabilize."

Cyndi's hand shakes as it takes mine. "Michael, you were mugged outside the Scholl Canyon landfill. Why on earth were you there?"

The familiar touch of my wife's hand is a lifeboat amidst this sea of confusion. "I . . . I don't know. I can't remember anything. How long have I been here?

"They brought you here two days ago," she replies, her grip tightening to the point of pain.

"Because your MRI showed no concussion," Francis interjects. "Your memory should return to normal in a day or two."

The physician moves from my field of vision, replaced by a larger man. "Dr. Walker, I'm detective Burrows, and I've been assigned to investigate your case. Obviously, this isn't the best time, but I do have a couple of questions. First, the man who attacked you was chased down, and we have him in custody. His name is Galen Troth. Do you know him?"

"No, I don't think so. The name isn't familiar."

"You were carrying several eCash cards, but he didn't take

any of them. In fact, he had nothing of yours in his possession when we brought him in, so this doesn't seem like a typical mugging. Do you have any idea what might have prompted his attack?"

"I don't have a clue."

"I see . . . A witness told me that you appeared to be hanging onto one of Troth's legs while he was kicking you. Why would you have done that?"

I stare past the detective, mesmerized by the tiles on the ceiling. I just want to go home. Back to the bungalow that Cyndi and I have shared for the last forty years. Maybe get a chance to see the grandkids. Anything to put this unpleasantness behind me.

Galen Troth, what an odd name.

# THE MOTH GIRLS

## E.E.W. CHRISTMAN

**SOPHIE**

I don't like grandma's house. It's stuck in the '70s, with its wall-to-wall shag and wood paneled television set, knobs half-falling out if you jiggle them too hard. A dilapidated homage to the past trapped between Someplace and Someplace Else, too far away to be in town, too close to truly be in the country.

Grandma's house creaks in time with her body, the floorboards cracking like old bones with each step I take. The windows rattle in their panes when the wind blows. It is always too cold in grandma's house, with the chilly night air coming through every loose board.

I don't like grandma's food. She doesn't ever order pizza or make spaghetti. She makes dry meatloaf with ketchup and cornflakes, ambrosia salad, tuna casserole that fills the house with its fishy funk. Even when she makes things I like, they don't ever taste like dad's. When I say this, grandma looks heavier, the weight of words pulling her down into my own despair, and I feel a quiet, angry guilt.

I don't like nighttime, out here between civilization and the wilds of nature. It is far too quiet, without the sound of cars and sirens and people staying up too late drinking at the nearby bars and the sound of music. The auditory void augments every tiny creak, every hoot of an owl until it's deafening, so scarce are the sounds. I wake up in the night to something shrieking in the woods, and I can no longer sleep, even after grandma reassures me it's just the howl of a coyote (which isn't as reassuring as she thinks it is).

**EVELYN**

My earliest memories of father are of his absence. Home is an empty place, inhabited by the people father pays to care for me while he stays away on business. When he is home, he doesn't look at me, nor does he speak to me. I am less a daughter and more a side effect of mother's death. Father never says so, but he makes sure I know. Even I understand his aloofness for what it is: punishment.

There is a painting of mother in the parlor. She is bright and beautiful, smiling down on us from the mantle. I stare at her often, and although I never met her, I think she must have been kind. I wonder if I will grow to be half as vibrant as she was.

The servants tell me she used to walk through the woods often, so I, too, begin walking through the woods. I search for mother in the trees and the creek. I try to retrace the steps of a ghost in order to understand her. I enjoy the forest. It does not suffocate me the way the house does; it doesn't reek of death and grief the way father does. The woods sing. Sometimes, I sing back, and hear the answer in the gurgling brooks or the gentle breeze ruffling the leaves.

One day, father is waiting for me as I return from the forest. He had just gotten home after being away for more than a month. I can see Freddie tending to the horse and cart in the drive. Father's arms are crossed and he scowls at me, neither of which are unusual. But as I walk up the hill, I can feel the anger emanating from him.

"What are you doing?" he demands.

"Walking, father."

"You are not to go in those woods again." His voice is loud, and his eyes are stone. Freddie turns from the mare, watching.

"But why, father?"

He answers with a slap across the face. It is the first time I can remember him touching me.


**SOPHIE**

I don't like grandma's stories. My room, the room she lovingly keeps for me, with all my stuffed animals and children's books even though I'm too old for them now, the room she thanklessly cleans and that I take for granted and know I take for granted and yet, I still take it for granted, guilt and all, is full of shadows and moonlight. She likes to sit in the rocking chair by my narrow bed and tell me stories.

"This house was built over a hundred years ago."

"Yes, grandma."

"By a man who made his fortune on the canals."

"I know, grandma."

The story goes that the mogul built this house for his wife, who loved the rolling Appalachian foothills. She loved the forest of sugar maples and yellow birches; she loved the nearby creek where, in the summer, one could hear the ceaseless song of frogs. Grandma says the wife would walk through the woods each day, no matter the weather. Even when she was with child, her belly heavy and cumbersome, she would still walk to the creek and sit at its banks and watch the cardinals flit through the branches.

"She gave birth and died shortly thereafter."

"And the husband was heartbroken."

Grandma taps her nose with a grin. "He blamed the child for her death. A daughter, who also grew to love the woods. The father stayed away on business often, not wanting to be near his daughter. As she grew older, it was more than the blame he placed on her; she was a strange child. Heard noises in the night, and said someone was in the forest, watching her. Folks called her a witch, some with awe, others with fear."

The next part of the story is the "scary" part. The part where the adult tells the kid some horrible ghost story nonsense, then says, well, goodnight, and creeps out of the bedroom with a smug smile.

"She was about your age, you know. When she disappeared." Grandma pauses, letting the gravity of the statement settle over me. As if my being fifteen were a death sentence. "She walked off into those woods right outside one night, and never returned. No body was found. Some say they can still see her at night, walking between the trees, waiting for someone to wander in to keep her company. In the afterlife."

"Uh huh."

"Well," grandma stands up stiffly, wiping her hands on her pants. "I'd better be getting to bed. Oh, and if you see any lights in the woods, don't follow them. It could be her out there."

"Ok, night."

Nothing could thwart grandma's enthusiasm for ghost stories. She held onto the door a little too long, enjoying the slow goodnight that she said in harmony with the creaking hinges. I listen to her footsteps as she walks down the hall to her bed.

### EVELYN

What shifts in him, I cannot say. But the change is undeniable. All my life, father has been a mountain on the horizon: stoney, unfeeling, distant. Something changed the day he found me leaving the forest. Now, instead of feeling nothing toward me, it seems I do nothing but inspire rage. Even if I stay in my room when he is home, he finds ways that I have crossed him. I left a book on the porch, I didn't eat enough, I ate too little; I spent too much time trying to get his attention, I ignored his presence; I was disrespectful . . . the reason mattered little. There is no logic, only anger. And punishment. My body is a patchwork of bruises. Marie, who has been my au pair since I was a baby, tries to stop him and receives a black eye and dismissal for her trouble. I watch her leave from my bedroom window, carpetbag in her clenched fist. I cry for hours.

After that, no one stops father. They learn to lower their heads and cover their ears.

And still, I do not stay away from the forest. I learn to stay near when he is home, for I fear what he would do if he found me there. But when father leaves, I barely stay in the house. Even as summer ends and the world grows cold, I walk the paths my mother once walked. Sometimes, I swear I can hear a woman singing, her voice as faint as a distant wind.

Perhaps it is not a ghost, but merely a shadow that remains. Like a footprint in the ground, or ripples on the water. Mother is still here.

If only I could find her, I think. Then, perhaps, father would be happy again.

### SOPHIE

I dream of the funeral again. Only this time, mom was there. I don't remember what she looked like, and she must look different now. In the dream, she had long blonde curls. She ignored me as they put dad in the ground. This time, I didn't even cry.

I wake up in a bad mood at 3 am. The house is dark and still, save for the ambient sounds of the forest. The shrill squeak of a mouse as it is whisked away to its doom by some unseen predator cuts through the night, and I can't help but think the stars above are strangely ominous in their silent observation of the carnage of nature.

The house is quiet. The familiar funerary dream is fresh and palpable, like the lingering aftertaste of diet soda.

For a time, I watch the stars above, twinkling in galactic rivers and eddies that were invisible in town. It is almost peaceful.

Then I see the light. So faint, and yet it is a beacon in the absolute blackness of the nearby forest. It is small, like the sputtering flame of a candle. It moves between the trees, coming toward the house, but stops short of our yard. It is not very close, but I can see the tall tower of wax, and the hand that grips it. I forget to breathe until the invisible figure turns and leaves, and the light shrinks out of view.


### EVELYN

I will take father into the woods. He will hear mother's voice, and he will be happy. Perhaps he will even learn to stop hating me. We can be a family.

I wait patiently for his return, the plan taking form in my mind. I cradle the wrist he broke before he left. He told the doctor I fell while climbing a tree, which the doctor believed. I dared not contradict him. The cast itches, but it is mending well enough.

It is a desperate plan, but I am a desperate girl. If I don't do something, father will eventually do worse things than leave bruises and broken bones.

**SOPHIE**

Grandma sits with me as I push my corn flakes around, drinking her coffee slowly.

"Hey, grandma," I start cautiously. "Does anyone live nearby?"

She shakes her head, eyes down. "Just the McCarthys up the road a way."

They were about a mile in the wrong direction. "No one in the woods?"

"Nope."

"Campers? Hikers?"

Grandma's eyes narrowed. "No. There's no campsite or trail. Why? Did you see something?"

"No!" It comes out a little too fast, a little too eagerly. Grandma grins, convinced her ghost story has successfully taken root in my mind.

"Just remember not to follow the light," grandma calls after me smugly.

After the sun sets, I watch for the light, despite myself. I stare into the black forest, waiting for movement. When nothing comes, I pull the covers over my head, embarrassment eclipsing any lingering fear.


**EVELYN**

The voice is clearest at night. I sit beneath the red and gold foliage of the maples at dusk, listening. I hear the crunch of leaves nearby. I follow the sound, the wordless song growing louder as I move deeper into the dense forest.

I can make out the clear, crisp tones of a woman's voice. Though I have never heard this wordless tune, nor have I heard this voice, it immediately feels familiar. Like something whispered in one's ear while sleeping. Like a half-remembered dream. Like someone else's treasured memory.

"Mother," I whisper to the trees, proceeding forward through the thicket. The moon is high and full, and I do not miss my lantern. The woods are a silvery hue, as if everything is coated in fairy dust. One can almost believe in magic in such a forest, with the haunting voice of a ghost leading my way.

I make out the orange glow of a nearby lantern ahead. I run to it, images of the painting of mother flooding my mind. Will she be as kind as I had dreamed? As beautiful? Will she love me, or blame me as father does? No matter. Once she returns to the house, all will be mended. I am so sure.

When I find the source, it is not a woman. The voice is moving away from us, deeper into the woods. It is barely discernible now.

Father stands before me, the lantern swinging in his hand. The fire dances in his dark eyes.

"You."

I say nothing. I suddenly start shivering and can't stop. I want to speak, but my tongue is dry and heavy. I can only watch the flames lick his pupils.

"It was you all along, wasn't it?" Father continues. "You used her voice to bring me out here. Black magic. Witch." His voice is so quiet, I can barely hear it. He takes a step forward, crouches. I see him pick up the rock.

### SOPHIE

I don't like sleeping through the night. I miss the sounds that could distract me from sleep. When I sleep through the night, I dream, and it's always him I dream of. Not dad as he was, but dad the corpse. Dad the memory. Dad who is no longer here. Dad in the shuttered garage, the engine of his car running, his body cold.

Worse still, I dream about mom. I was a baby when she left. I don't even know what she looks like anymore. And yet, she is often a fixture of the dreamscape. Lingering in the background like a bad omen. And when I wake, I don't feel rested at all. I only feel the vague sense of dread she instills in me.

### EVELYN

The woods are so cold. The voice is gone. Father believes I have tricked him. Perhaps I can explain, I think frantically. It is not too late to find her.

"Father, please—" It is a feeble plea. He will not even give me the dignity of finishing it.

"You will torment me no longer." This time, there is no shouting. No fists. No spittle in my face or insults thrown. His quiet voice is so much more frightening than his outbursts.

I turn to run, knowing I can't get away. Still, my legs attempt to flee. I try to save myself. I have that, at least. Something collides with my head and I feel my neck snap. I hit the cold ground. The life saps from the hole in the side of my head; something hot runs down my neck.

And even as I die, I feel the rock come down again and again. Even when I can no longer feel it, even as I stare forward with dead eyes, still I can hear the sound of stone crushing bone. Father isn't satisfied until my head is pulp in the dirt. He stands up, breathless, the stone falling from his limp hand. When father speaks, I am not sure it is to me, to the ghost of mother, or perhaps God. It is a cryptic farewell, even for him:

"It could not be helped."


### SOPHIE

Grandma has a phone call early in the morning. She sits me down, and I know it's about him before she says a word. She doesn't say who called (the lawyer, the cops, the morgue, what difference does the who make anyway?), but tells me what we all know: it's been ruled a suicide.

I cry. Just when I think there is nothing left to squeeze out of me, the world manages to extract one more little drop of grief.

I spend the rest of the day alone, wondering why everyone leaves. I wonder if grandma will leave me, too.

Night comes again. Grandma has no stories to tell. She whispers goodnight from the hall, and I wonder briefly if she hates me, too. Do we share grief, or does she blame me? Like the dad in her story. Did I take her son away? Fifteen years is a much slower death, but the end result is the same.

Maybe that's why she told me the story in the first place. Maybe she just wants me gone.

As if answering my question, the beacon appears in the

woods. Flickering between the trees like an amber phantom. I swallow my hesitation and grab a jacket and my shoes. I would do the leaving this time.

### EVELYN

Death is not the end. Death is new terrain. Life is the egg, and death merely the hatching. As my body grows cold, something new emerges from it. Something powerful takes my place as father turns to leave. His eyes grow wide at the sight of the second daughter he has created. Sex made me, but violence made me this.

Father tries to run. He always tries to run. But he always finds his way back to me.

### SOPHIE

It feels colder out here, despite the summer heat during the day. I pull my jacket tighter and hurry forward. I wield my phone flashlight against the shadows, being sure to move quickly from the yard so grandma doesn't see. Grass and twigs crunch beneath my feet as I chase down the light. But it never seems any closer, always moving deeper and deeper into the forest. Grandma's house disappears quickly, and I can no longer remember which direction I came from. My phone flashlight does little to alleviate my anxiety; every shadow is a monster, every noise not made by myself is a potential threat. But I still follow the light, moth-like. Even it runs from me. Yet I keep chasing.

The gap closes, so slowly, with no one to witness our chase but the crescent moon. The light brightens, and as it does, the forest changes. Summer is in full swing; the trees should be laden with green leaves, were in fact laden with leaves only moments ago. But the crunch of autumn leaves beneath my feet is unmistakable. The green aura of summertime is replaced by the golden hue of fall, many of the trees completely bare. The air chills, and my teeth begin to chatter. Above, the moon is full and bright.

But still, the light beckons. I follow. My feet move faster, heedless of the many roots and pitfalls around me. I call out, and the light pauses, finally, in its path. I catch up to it. A man in a dark suit and wide brimmed hat holds a lantern. His mouth trembles at the sight of me stumbling through the trees. The fire reflected in his eyes glows red.

"You . . ." the man mumbles. "You should not be here. Who are you?"

"Sophie."

"Sophie . . . " the man says the word slowly, as if turning its flavor over and over in his mouth. He looks down at me like a man dreaming. "You look like her. Did she bring you here?"

"Who?"

"She must have brought you here," the man says, ignoring me. "Conjured you up from the woods to torment me. To remind me of my sins." He casts his lantern from side to side, searching the treeline. "Begone, witch! Leave me be!" I can't tell if he's shouting at me, or the woods. Both thoughts are terrifying. I take a few slow, cautious steps back.

"I just came from my house," I point behind me. "I saw the light from my window."

"Send this demon away!" The man cries, tears in the corners of his eyes. Then he turns his attention toward me. I can see the familiar rise of mania in his eyes. "I have been here so long. How long has this night gone on? How long have I been punished?" His voice trembles. He takes a step toward me. "It is not a crime to kill a witch, is it not? It is not a crime in the eyes of God, certainly. And what are you? Another hellspawn?" He stretches his hand toward me. "Are you flesh or mirage?"

I've seen grown men like this before. Wild, on the verge of falling over the precipice and slipping into violence. Dad had been like that, towards the end. He'd ultimately inflicted violence upon himself, but there was no telling which direction the rage might be directed. And if I wasn't losing my own mind, he'd just admitted to murder.

I don't wait. I run. I can hear the man behind me, his panting like a beast. The creak of his lantern rings out in time with each galloping step he takes, like a metronome ticking down to my own demise.

Then he gasps. I hear the sound of his body falling behind

me as he trips over a root I'd narrowly jumped over. Glass shatters in the dark, the man swears, but I keep going, not even sure if I'm running toward the house or deeper into the woods. The man screams behind me. An anguished cry, a sound like a mind cracking.

When I can no longer hear him, when my heart is humming in my chest and I feel like my lungs will burst, I dare to stop. I gasp for breath and try not to notice the autumn leaves still at my feet, still unexplainable.

It takes me a moment to see her. I have stopped near the creek, and look up at the sound of the babbling brook. Grandma had told me it dried up years ago. The girl stands at its banks. The man's daughter does look a bit like me, I think, but in vague ways. We are about the same age, the same height, the same build, both with long mousy hair. Hers is matted at one side, something dark and wet clinging to the strands. I don't dare shine a light on the blood, not really wanting to confirm with my own eyes what I could smell hanging in the air: the smell of death. Her hands rest on her dress, pulling the fabric in nervous twists against her palms as she eyes me with those lifeless eyes.

"I'm sorry," I tell the girl, not really knowing what else to say. "I'm sorry he did that."

Her cracked lips open. Her voice is a croak, a death rattle given life: "You cannot stay here. He will kill you, too, given the chance." She raises a narrow, pale arm and points to her left. "Keep away from his light. You will find the way home as long as you keep away from his light."

"But his lantern broke."

The girl shakes her head slowly, a horrible snapping sound coming from her neck with each motion. "It is fueled by his belief that what he did was good and noble. It won't extinguish for good as long as he sees no wrong. Only when he accepts what he really did can he leave. Just keep away from his light, and he can't trap you here."

I nod, half-comprehending. And indeed, as I squint into the woods, I can see the lantern, once again. Distant, but undeniable.

"Hurry." I run in the opposite direction of the light. Not in the panicked, fight or flight gallop from earlier. I keep a steady, careful pace, maintaining the distance. The air begins to warm, and the light grows hazier, less vibrant. The leaves are back in the trees, full of life and vigor. And faintly, I hear someone calling my name in the dark. Grandma.

### EVELYN

Father doesn't find the girl. I watch her from the winds hugging the branches as she reaches home—her home, now. Her grandmother is waiting. It is nice to see a family brought back together. To see tears of joy rather than dread. I linger until they are inside. The girl turns back once. Does she hesitate? Does she perhaps see me floating through the trees? But no. She turns and goes inside. I leave them to their lives.

Father is not difficult to find. He stumbles through the undergrowth, as he always does. His feet have not grown as accustomed to the eternally dark forest as they should have; my doing, of course. The ground shifts beneath him ever so slightly. I have taken away his sure footing. He screams for the girl until he is hoarse, then he only moans. There is no rest for him. No sleep. No dawn. Only an endless autumn night, and the body of his daughter he cannot stop finding.

Some would call this punishment, but I no longer see it that way. Father is simply not used to consequences. But he is growing accustomed to the idea, slowly.

I linger in the air above, and slowly, I begin to sing.

# BEING A VAMPIRE
## RAMONA RIDGEWELL

*Author's Note: Seattle Vampire Tales Book One: Being a Vampire (coming October, 2024) follows a Seattle vampire, Rix, as he navigates employment and housing challenges that only grow worse when the pandemic strikes. This excerpt takes place on the eve of COVID-19. Rix is looking for safer housing in a new part of town.*

**ovember 15 to 17, 2019**

I'm outside the basement door when the rays of the sun fall below the southwestern horizon. After rushing over to the mailbox service, half a mile away, I find my check in my box. It's only sixteen hundred dollars—they take out twenty percent for taxes—but it'll hold me over for a while. On this contract, I'll get at least a couple more checks. If I can find a studio for less than a thousand a month, which is doubtful, I'll be able to pay rent for three or four months. It's a start.

I head north. After crossing the Lake Washington Ship Canal, I peer around as I walk, watchful of local vampires. A cheap motel on Aurora Avenue North is seventy-five a night, plus taxes and fees, but if I pay for a week, one night's free. My need for a few days respite, and to escape from Capitol Hill, overpowers my penurious grip on my cash. I slide five hundred-dollar bills across the counter, and in return get a pocket full of change and a room key.

"That's enough quarters to run two loads of laundry and get everything dry." His mouth smiles, but not his face. "No laundry after midnight."

"Thank you."

As soon as I'm in my room, I put the *Do Not Disturb* sign on the door and secure the lock, a deadbolt that appears brand new. The original lock in the doorknob is punched out, leaving a peephole which a wad of toilet paper plugs. I'm relieved to find a strong wifi signal. When my VPN connects, I login to work, pull a ticket and begin to relax. I close a third ticket and check the time. Oh. I've gone over my four hours for the day. After closing the lid, I unpack the rest of my things. Then, I take a long, hot shower.

Clean and warm, I slip between crisp, white sheets in the safe quiet of my own room. The stress and tension from the autumn chaos that cling to my muscles, like the yellow and brown fall leaves on a bigleaf maple, begin to let loose and drift away.


Two afternoons later, I struggle to pull myself from a bad dream. It must be a dream. My brothers died a century ago. Alan, the eldest, pins me to the ground. I try to squirm, to get away, but he's so much bigger than me. My other brother, Gareth, holds down my arms and grasps my head between his knees. Why is he helping? Now, I can't move at all. "You listen when I speak, you little freak," Alan barks. He raps his knuckle against my chest. Hard. He knows it won't show. A lesson from Father, before he left for the war. Where's Mama?

I jerk awake. I still can't move. Oh. The sheets are wrapped around my arms and legs. The desperate feeling stays with me. Did my fear of what Robert might do trigger this? Will James turn on me, like Gareth did? I need to get him away from Robert. Or maybe I should leave town, but I need more cash to do that. I'm trapped here, as much as I was with my brothers. A move to this new neighborhood may be enough to keep me safe.

I try to work for a while, but can't focus. My hunger drives me outside. The bright pink remains of the sunset make me squint as I head north toward Green Lake, spurring me to walk in the relative shade of the buildings that buffer Winslow Place from the traffic noise on Aurora. Overhead, a raucous band of crows rushes toward their evening roost, maybe up in the park. On a picnic bench outside a small office building lie the abandoned remains of someone's dinner. The white paper bag holds half an order of still-warm fries, and a scrap of bun, drenched in grease from the hamburger it once enveloped. I take it with me. It never hurts to befriend the neighborhood crows.

At Fiftieth, approaching sirens capture my attention. My entire body tenses, preparing to bolt. Calm down, Rix. They're not police sirens. Two firetrucks rush toward me, lights flashing and horns blaring, forcing me to cover my ears. I shake off the panic as their howls diminish, echoing in the tunnel that passes under the highway. After crossing the busy street, I pass through a parking lot and into the maze of trails in the wooded parkland of aptly-named Woodland Park. Sure enough, crows fill the air, swooping and calling to one another before settling into the trees. I stop at a picnic area to watch them, and begin to relax. When I dump the contents of the bag onto a table and caw to get their attention, one spies me and darts down to take a look. As I back away, he cautiously drops to the other end, eyes me suspiciously, then sidles toward the food. Several more of his mob join him. "Bon appétit, mes amis."

As I continue deeper into the park, the landscape transitions to grassy rolling hills. A few joggers and walkers hurry along the trails in the waning daylight. Near a pedestrian overpass that crosses the highway, I loiter in the shadows until a lone walker strides out onto the path, and fall in behind him. He stops and turns toward me. His pale face glimmers a soft lavender, similar in shade to the French herbs my mother grew, which she brewed into a tea to ease my anxiety. She always had some, too. I could use some of that tea. This man is not anxious and shows no concern for my presence.

Walking up to him, I smile. "A little cool tonight, isn't it?"

"Do I know you?"

"No." I take a step nearer and touch his cheek. "Let's go over here where it's more private."

Smiling dreamily, he allows me to lead him into the shrubs that line the highway. Cautious of an encounter with a neighborhood vampire, my eyes sweep the area around us. I only feed for a short time. After covering the wound with my hand, I swab everything clean with a sanitizing wipe. "Are you all right?"

"I . . . I think so." He blinks at me. "Do I know you?"

"We haven't met." As I retrace our steps to the path, he follows. I pat his arm. "Take care out here. It's getting dark."

"You, too." He takes off down the trail.

By the time I return to the picnic bench, nothing remains of the fries. "Kuck, kuck," a crow coughs. He dives toward me, but pulls up before striking my head. The last blush of daylight glints from a mylar ribbon as it flutters to the ground in front of me. After stooping to pick it up, I scan the sky, but he's already disappeared into the darkness.

### *November 17, 2019*

Ahead of me on the path, almost to the parking lot, a woman kneels beside someone. They're hard to make out in the soft light that filters through the trees from the streetlamp. At first, I think I'm interrupting a couple having sex right there on the trail, but then I see she moves in the steady rhythm of CPR. As I begin to turn away, she looks up. Her intriguing eyes, sparkling black jewels, draw me toward her. The maize glow of her cheeks expresses concern, but for the man on the ground, not because of me. I stop a few feet from them. What am I doing?

"Do you know CPR?" Her pumping punctuates the words. "Will you help me?"

"Um." Moving nearer, I kneel on the other side of the man. "I can do compressions." I take over, thankful with all the worry over communicable diseases that mouth-to-mouth is no longer required. I'm uncertain I could manage that much breath. In the distance, sirens howl like coyotes. Neighborhood dogs join the chorus. I know help is coming for the man, but my gut tightens regardless.

The woman picks up her phone from the ground beside her knee. "Still no response, but I've got someone here to help now." She watches me. "He seems to know what he's doing. Oh, I hear the sirens. I'll keep you posted." She sets the phone back down. "Are you doing all right?" I nod as I try to keep rhythm with the 'Staying Alive' playing in my head. Around her slight

smile, her aura cools to a less-concerned soft ochre. "You're doing great. Sorry it's taking so long. The local station's out on a
call or they'd be here already." Several choruses later, she puts
her hand on my arm. I almost jerk away, but keep pumping. The
warmth of her hand permeates the sleeve of my hoodie. I hope
she doesn't notice the hole in the elbow. "Stop for a sec while I
check for a pulse." When I sit back on my heels, she presses her
fingers to the man's neck. Shakes her head. "Let me relieve you."
As she pumps, her thick curls spill loose from whatever was rein-
ing them in. "Not again." She keeps pumping. "Not now."

I pull the crow's gift from my pocket. As I gather her hair,
my fingers linger on her neck for a moment. Her life's blood
gently pulses beneath the surface. I swallow the saliva that pud-
dles in my mouth, and slip the ribbon around her dark tresses,
securely tying it, all while she continues to pump without missing a beat. Good thing I just fed or letting her go would be more
. . . difficult.

The sirens grow louder. When two firetrucks race into the
parking lot, the wailing stops. An EMT dashes toward us from
one of them. I hop to my feet and move out of his way, allowing him to kneel across from the woman. While he sets up the
defibrillator, she keeps pumping. I can't hear their words over
the sound of another approaching emergency vehicle, this time
the Medic Unit.

When the paramedic rushes to the downed man, the woman
grabs her phone and gets to her feet. With all the people, I'm surprised she spots me. Holding her phone to her ear, she comes to
stand beside me. "They're here. I'll let you go. I hope he's okay,
too. Thanks so much." She pockets the phone. I only notice this
peripherally. The flashing lights mesmerize me. She touches my
arm, making me start. "Are you all right?"

My head spins toward her. "I . . ." The world fades to only
her face, and I lose myself in her eyes.

One of the firemen approaches, breaking her thrall. "They got
a pulse. It's a good thing you were here and knew what to do."

"I'm a nurse." She glances at me with a little smile. "But I
had some help. I'm so glad you folks arrived when you did."

"It's busy tonight, or the Number Nine would've been here

even sooner. Thank you both. You two have a good night." By the time he heads back, the medics are loading the gurney into the ambulance.

The woman turns to me. "Thank you for stopping to help."

"You're welcome." I love looking into her eyes. "I'm Rix." Why did I say that? I never share my real name with breathing folks.

"I'm Maggie." She smiles again, her face carrying a soft carnation glow. Whoa. She's interested in me. "Will you walk me home? It's not far."

"Um." I really should go back to my room to work. "All right." My weak-voiced agreement is a surprise. What's going on with me? I follow her out to Fiftieth, where we head up the hill to the other side of Highway 99. Her voice enchants me, but I barely hear her words.

"The CPR'll have to do for my aerobic exercise today. I was just heading out when I ran across that man." She pants between the words as the hill steepens. "If it's busy in the ER tonight, I'll probably make up for it." Without breaking her stride, she unzips her jacket. As I gaze at her, I nod, although I'm only vaguely listening. I draw in a deep breath. She smells good, even her sweatiness. "Do you come to the park often?" Her voice, raised in a question, draws my focus.

"Um." My mind stumbles through what she was saying. "Sometimes?"

When we stop to wait for a light, she looks me over. "Are you sure you're okay? You seem a little rattled." When I only blink, she frowns. "He'll probably be all right. Did you know Seattle's one of the safest places to have a heart attack? We had the very first Medic One in the country. Half the people who live here know CPR."

"Oh." Noticing my mouth still hangs open, I bring my lips together. What *is* wrong with me?

"You did a really good job. Most laymen need some instruction, but you jumped right in."

The light changes, and we head down Fremont Avenue. I struggle to construct a coherent sentence. "I . . . um . . . have some medical training." My reaction to her is unsettling, to say

222 \ RAMONA RIDGEWELL

the least. Normally, *I'm* the one who does the charming. "So, you're an ER Nurse?"

"Nurse Practitioner. The ER needed extra help tonight"—she shrugs—"so I signed up for a shift." As we approach Marketime Foods, the anchor of the small Upper Fremont commercial district, she slows. "It's not like I have a lot else going on." She frowns and looks away, as if she shared more than she should have. Stopping completely, she turns to me. "Hey, I need to grab something at the store. Thanks for walking with me." She seems to have as much trouble looking away as I do. "Let's have coffee tomorrow, and we can talk some more. Meet me at Lighthouse Roasters at five?"

"I'd like that." I'm not sure what's going on. A date? I break eye contact, since she hasn't, turn my back and walk away.


### November 18, 2019

I don't sleep well. Every noise awakens me: a big truck rumbling past on the highway; the rattle of the housekeeping cart; the crows cawing outside. Each time, the first image in my mind is the woman I met last night or, more precisely, her amazing eyes. When I look into them, the world—and all its worries—just melts away.

A little after noon, I give up on getting any more sleep, and take a shower. I wish I had something other than an old, faded t-shirt to wear, but at least it's clean. What am I doing going on a date? I've never been on a date . . . well, not in almost a hundred years. And I can't get involved with a breathing person. Will I be safe inside a coffeeshop? It may be crowded. But I told her I'd be there.

I read news headlines and a couple of stories. I don't usually pay attention to the news, but I don't want to sound like I live under a rock. Outside of pre-primary politicking and the impeachment hearings, the only news is the record-breaking cold back East and the continuing drought in the West. I guess I'll talk about weather.

When the sun sets, I hike over the pedestrian walkway that

spans Aurora. Misty rain dampens everything, except under the trees where none of it reaches the sidewalks. As soon as it lets up, the streets are dry again. The coffee shop's only half a mile away, and I'm a little early, so I drop by Marketime to buy a package of peppermints. Even though I brushed my teeth, I worry about my vampire breath.

At Lighthouse, a rush-hour line reaches to the door. I pause with my palm on the handle, suddenly reluctant to enter such a public place. What if someone notices me? A man approaches, sipping his fresh to-go coffee. We peer at each other through the mist-clouded glass. I open the door to let him exit, and edge inside, barely able to swing the door shut behind me.

The heavy aroma of coffee tumbling in a loud roaster at the rear saturates the warm, steamy air. I glance through the throng. Tightness clenches my stomach, reaching into my chest, shoulders and groin. She's not here. I'll wait outside to see if she comes. Pivoting, I reach for the door, the escape from this noisy, crowded place, but the space has filled with more customers. Nausea wells in my belly as bodies press me from all sides. Swinging my head back and forth, I try to find an opening where I can squeeze through without bodily contact.

When a cool gust of air ruffles her dark hair, the woman three people ahead of me in line turns. "Rix!" She waves. A brilliant smile competes with the brightness in her eyes. They draw me like a beacon. My muscles release. She makes her way back to me, somehow managing to stay a few inches from my chest. "You made it."

"Were you worried?" I return her smile, and the residual tension in my jaw flees. "I'd never turn down a cup of coffee. You're buying, right?"

"Sure." She giggles. "I'm buying. What're you drinking?"

"Tall Americano."

"A couple of seats opened up." She points with her chin. "Go snag them for us."

At a tiny table with one side pushed against a wall covered with local art, and four chairs clustered around the other three sides, I ask the couple who huddles at one end, "Are these seats open?"

The woman barely glances at me. "All yours."

I sit and look around. At every table, and the stools at the bar, people are reading or conversing—mostly, conversing. Even the readers occasionally turn to the person next to them to chat. As people enter, the folks behind the bar greet them by name and ask if they'll have their usual. I understand why it's so crowded, and why Maggie suggested we meet here.

As my eyes return to the line, Maggie—back in her original position—reaches the front. I watch her until she sets the cups on the table and sits. With the tight squeeze, her knee bumps mine. I try unsuccessfully to move my leg to give her more room. "Sorry," I murmur. The pair at the other end scoot over, old wooden chair legs scraping on the floor. This is all so pleasant and . . . mundane. I haven't done mundane in a while. When she's settled, we sip our beverages.

"Careful, it's hot." She smiles, upper lip pencil-mustached in white froth that offsets the rosy radiance in her cheeks. "How was your day?"

"I can't get 'Staying Alive' out of my head, but otherwise, okay."

"I use 'We Will Rock You.' I actually like that song."

"You were amazing last night." I take another sip from my cup. She turns unexpectedly demure, the glow of her cheeks intensifying, and won't meet my eyes. Even though she's dressed in a floral blouse, I ask, "Are you working tonight?"

"No." Looking up, she licks away the foam. "I worked all day. I usually save the extra shifts for the weekends, unless the ER's really short-handed. What do you do for a living?"

"DevOps." When she stares blankly, I add, "I keep computer servers up and running."

"Nice. Do you live around here?"

"Sort of." Was that too vague? I swirl my coffee. "I can't believe the weather back East."

"It's so surprising." She sips her latte. "They're setting record cold temperatures, and here we are with a dry and balmy fifty. My yard could sure use some rain."

"It may rain tonight."

"I hope the next time it rains, it *actually* rains. A good soaking."

"Right." I've liked the weather. Rain and cold limit my hunting.

When our cups are empty, she smiles. "This was really nice. We should do it again."

"Maggie, may . . ." I get lost in her eyes.

She looks at me curiously. "That's what my dad called me."

"Maggie May? Like the song?"

"Oh." Her face lights up. "You were going to ask me something. Nobody uses *may*. It's so old-fashioned. What is it?"

"Am I allowed to call you Maggie May?"

"That wasn't your question." She rests her chin in her palm and gazes at me with glimmering onyx eyes. "But yes, you are."

"May I treat you to coffee next week, Maggie May?"

Opening her phone, she hands it to me. "Put in your number so we can text."

# A Volcano Walks into a Bar

## Seelye Martin

That Halloween, Sparrow worked as a bartender at the Tangletown Tavern, dressed as her namesake, Captain Jack. She wore a tricorne hat, a black greatcoat, a puffy white shirt, black tights, and calf-high floppy-cuffed boots. One of our busiest nights, she thought, watching the crowd as a werewolf and a coronavirus entered the tavern holding hands, headed for the dance floor.

As the room heated up, she replaced her tricorne hat with a red bandanna, removed her coat, and rolled up her sleeves. When she looked up, there it was, the volcano. It stood about five-feet high and was conically shaped, a narrow plume of steam rising from its crater.

"Hey Toots," its rumbly voice echoed from deep in its interior. "Wanna dance?" A smoke ring puffed out of its cone and floated upward, disintegrating as it hit the ceiling.

Sparrow shook her head. "No thanks. The last time we danced, I got third degree burns, ruined my clothing, and my left foot still hasn't recovered."

A big man with a thick dark beard, at least six feet tall and dressed in a plaid-wool shirt, work pants, boots, and red suspenders, stepped forward. "What happened to your foot, Toots?" he said sarcastically. "Did you crack-a-toe-a?" He snickered.

Sparrow grimaced. "That's it, lumberjack, go away. I'm not serving you."

Three witches walked in, not the sixteenth-century Shakespearian hags, but twenty-first century young women out looking for trouble. Dressed in black, they wore tall pointy hats, short skirts, low-cut tops, high-heeled boots, sheer stockings, and face paint.

They circled the volcano. "Ohhh, aren't you adorable." It emitted a puff of steam, and its crater glowed red. "Can we use your caldron for our ritual?"

"Of course!" said the volcano. "Just use plenty of beer."

"Hey ladies," Sparrow said, "Can I get you something to drink? How about a nice saucy chardonnay?" The witches nodded with enthusiasm. "But no alcohol for the volcano, it's allergic." She winked. "But you can give it all the eye of newt it wants."

They laughed and got their wine. As they returned to the volcano, the lumberjack pushed through the crowd toward them. "I'm the lumberjack," he said. "Can I buy you sweethearts a drink?" They ignored him. He flushed and stepped back.

"My name's Wicked," said the green-faced witch to the volcano. "What's yours?"

It bounced a little, shaking the floor. "I'm a stratovolcano, Vesuvius-class. My eruptions are infrequent but cataclysmic." More steam.

"And your name?" asked Wicked.

"In volcanese, my name is Orcdruin, which in English, translates to Fire Mountain. But you might know me better as . . ." It paused dramatically. "Mount Doom."

As steam and ash shot toward the ceiling, the witches stepped back. They blinked and wrinkled their noses at the sulfurous fumes. The bar shook and a crowd gathered.

Wicked started to speak, but Sparrow interrupted. "You're not giving it booze, are you?" The witches shook their heads. "The last time someone gave it booze, my ceiling got scorched." She pointed up at the burn marks. There was another jet of dense ash.

Wicked danced on her heels with her need to speak, but Sparrow continued. "Hey, volcano or whatever you call yourself, you set off my fire alarms again, you're banned for life, not just for a year." Another steam burst, but the ash stopped. She turned away and as she took an order, the lumberjack returned. He stayed on the edge of the crowd, listening intently, hiding from Sparrow behind the witches' hats.

Wicked immediately spoke. "Mount Doom! You mean . . . *Lord of the Rings*?"

"Well, yes. You could call me Mount Doom of the rings.

Back in the day, I worked really hard with that halfling dude Frodo and his pal Sam to get the ring from the shire to my crater, which turned out to be pretty important for Middle Earth.

"I also consulted with Tolkien and Jackson on their books and films, and gave them my eye-witness account of what really happened at the crater. But did they listen to me? No.

"Remember that scene in the Jackson film, where Gollum bites off Frodo's finger, then he and the ring fall into molten lava?"

"Sure do," said Wicked, her eyes bright. "Gollum burns up and the ring dissolves." The crowd nodded.

"Not true! Even though Jackson and Tolkien greatly benefitted from my eye-witness account of what actually happened, they would not listen. Oh no, to close their story arc, they needed the ring to melt. But unlike their stories, the ring remained intact. Just as it fell into the lava, I encapsulated it in pumice."

"You mean . . ." said Wicked.

"Yes," said Doom. "The ring survived, and I have it."

The lumberjack moved forward. "Hey, you glorified lava-lamp. Are you saying that the 'one ring to rule them all' is right here, in a second-rate Tangletown bar? Gimme a break!"

Sparrow bristled. "Don't insult my bar, don't insult my customers."

"Doubt it if you wish," said Doom, "but it's the truth."

"Why shouldn't I doubt it? Just look at yourself! Aren't you kind of short?

"You're not even a halfling volcano! Or a quarter-ling! You might be a one-thousandth- or milli-ling . . ." He paused. "But what I'd call you is a ding-a-ling!"

"Them's fighting words, lumberjack!" said Sparrow. "You're banned for life!" She pushed a button to alert the bouncers, but it was too late.

There was a loud screech, a thunderous explosion, and a series of explosive flashes as a jet of high-pressure steam erupted from Doom's summit. Within the crowd, a purple wombat clutched its paws to its ears, and a gorilla gave a deep guttural scream. Temblors shook the bar, rattling the whiskey and brandy bottles. Some shattered. Sparrow gasped as the alcohol vapor and gaseous sulfur burned her throat and stung her eyes. The lights swayed overhead, then went out, replaced by the dim emergency LEDs.

If this volcano erupts, thought Sparrow, Tangletown could be the next Pompeii. She had to act fast.

Sparrow locked eyes with Wicked, then flicked her head toward the ice-water pitchers at the end of the bar. With a sweep of her arm, Sparrow cleared the bar of toothpicks, napkins, and menus, then vaulted over it. The bottom of the crater had just started to turn a dull red, the first sign of molten lava.

She grabbed a beer pitcher, then stood, indecisive. She shrugged. Needs must, she thought and poured the beer into the crater. There was an enormous hiss, the smell of burnt hops, and a cloud of superheated steam. As it scalded her hands, she cried out, almost sobbing at the pain. But the lava, instead of going cold and black, got even hotter. It had been like pouring gasoline on a fire. She dropped the empty pitcher and stepped back, defeated.

Then Wicked, breathing hard, ran up through the crowd, holding two pitchers of ice water. Her hat was gone, and her purple hair in disarray. "No more high heels for this witch," she said, pouring the ice water into the crater. As she briefly disappeared in the steam, the lava glowed red, then went dark. Except for a residual hissing, the volcano was quiet. The crowd cheered.

"Yes!" said Sparrow, pumping her fist into the air. As the ice and water drained out of the crater through its vents and fumaroles, she and Wicked broke into hysterical laughter and hugged. There was a bubbly hiss.

"Doom," said Sparrow, patting the volcano on its flank, "We're not laughing at you."

The lumberjack stood back from the volcano, his face pale. Sparrow straightened, pointed her right index finger at him, and said, "You, go!"

She turned to Doom. "You have to leave, too." She and Wicked moved to opposite sides of Doom, each placing a hand on its slopes. They walked toward the exit, the crowd parting before them.

"Best Halloween costume ever, dude!" said a giant pink rabbit, and the crowd cheered and applauded. A bouncer opened the door.

While they stood with Doom in the exit, a quiet voice said, "Sorry about your hands," then a small rock fell into the top of her pirate boot. As she and Wicked watched Doom disappear into the light rain and twisted streets of Tangletown, Sparrow felt light-headed, her hands burning, her skin cold and clammy, her pulse accelerating.

When they turned to step inside, Wicked took her arm. "Those burns look bad. I'm taking you to the emergency room."

Her manager agreed that Wicked should accompany her to the ER, not the best place to be on Halloween night. It took until dawn before she was treated and sent home. Although she never saw Doom again, Wicked was a different story.

Sparrow kept the small cube of pumice that she found in her boot on her dresser and used it to buff her nails. Sometimes she saw a flash of gold within the gray stone, and just once, the glowing outline of a ring. If there were mica, pyrite, gold, or God forbid, an elfin ring inside it, she had no desire to know. It had caused enough trouble.

# THE SANDWICH SHACK
## PATRICK HURLEY

Chicago doesn't have much time for magic anymore. Packed with practical Midwesterners having little use for the offbeat and mysterious, it has become a stolid, solidified place, every street mapped out on Google and every shop reviewed on Yelp.

But before the north side was hit by the gentrification tsunami, before its streets were rebuilt, over-policed, and white-washed, the Windy City was a different world, far more dangerous and far stranger, riddled with hidden nooks and crannies.

Most of the secret places are gone now. The bodegas, stew houses, and record shops have been replaced by brunch cafes, fashion boutiques, and upscale pubs serving the latest Belgian craft beer.

There are some secrets left, though. For example, every once in a great while at summer twilight, when soft lamps have filled the tree-lined streets with a faint silver glow, someone with the right combination of kindness and curiosity might decide to stroll down an alley they've never been through before.

As they walk, they will begin to smell the delicious aroma of baked bread. They'll hear an old transistor radio playing the blues. If they're smart enough to follow their nose and ears, they'll find themselves walking up to a singular diner with a glowing neon sign that reads *Brady's Sandwich Shack*.

If you happen to find yourself in the Shack, you'll notice that your smartphone has lost its signal. Attempting to document the retro interior on Instagram causes the app to crash. Twitter and Foursquare will be unable to triangulate your location, and reviews on Yelp mysteriously refuse to upload.

Don't panic. Relax. Enjoy the blues. Savor the smell and order some food. If you're with someone, enjoy each other's company.

There is a simple menu tacked onto the wall listing five sandwiches. Only five. Do not question this. Don't ask whether the bread is gluten-free, there are no gmos, or if the vegetables are local. Such questions will be met with puzzlement by the man behind the counter.

In every profession there is a maestro whose skill is so complete that others can only admire their greatness, and so it is with Brady Jones and sandwiches. He uses only the most savory and succulent meats, the best corned beef, just lightly spiced with mustard. His cheeses are the stuff of legend: the sharpest cheddar, a subtle provolone, a Pepper Jack so delicious it makes men weep.

In the 1970s, Brady's Sandwich Shack was a regular place where anyone could go. It opened at 11:30 in the morning and closed at 10 at night. If he was busy, Brady sometimes hired a local kid to run the register, but mostly he ran the shop himself. He worked hard, only taking a half-hour lunch at 3 and a 15-minute break after the dinner rush, when he allowed himself one cigar and one shot of rye whiskey while sitting on a folding chair in the alley behind the Shack and listening to BB King on the radio.

The Shack served everyone, provided they could pay. Brady didn't do hand-outs, but he was willing to barter goods for services. A nearby plumber and an electrician received one sandwich on the house every day, and the Shack never had any maintenance problems. Brady Jones had only two rules: everyone waits in line and no special orders.

But there were few long waits because Brady put together sandwiches like a man possessed. Half the fun was watching him hunched over in the kitchen, his hands blurring as meat, peppers, onions, and tomatoes flew as though being tossed by a juggler.

One hot day at the end of August, a long, black limousine pulled up. Two gentlemen in dark suits and mirrored sunglasses got out and looked around. Once they were satisfied the area was secure, they opened the limo door and accompanied an elegant, pale old man into the Shack. The man waited in line like everyone else, and smiled when given his sandwich: a #4 Reuben, with corned beef, sweet pickle relish, wheat bread, and the best damn sauce the old man had ever eaten. When he finished, he wiped his lips and gave a satisfied smile.

Later that evening, as Brady sat out back on his folding chair, staring up as his cigar smoke disappeared into the wooden El tracks above, he was surprised to hear a voice.

"Good evening, Mr. Jones. If you've a few minutes, my employer would like to speak with you."

Brady shrugged, then followed the driver to the limo. He sat across from the elderly gentleman, who shook his hand.

"Don't mean to be rude," Brady said in quiet voice, "but I need to get back in 'bout 15 minutes."

The gentleman smiled. "Of course. This won't take but a moment. I've a proposal for you."

"Oh?" Brady asked.

"No doubt you think I'm going to ask you to become a chain?" the old man said, a shrewd look on his face.

"Happened a few times," Brady said cautiously. "Ain't got the time. And this one suits me fine."

"And I would never want you to cheapen your art for the sake of money. No, my offer is somewhat different. My name, Mr. Jones, is Carapachi. You probably have never heard of me."

Brady admitted that he hadn't.

"That's as I like it. I'm a behind the scenes man. Without boring details, let me say that I am one of the richest men in the world."

Brady raised his eyebrows, but said nothing.

"I've kept careful track of any would-be challengers, and I'm on top because I'm the best at what I do. And that is where we come to you, Mr. Jones. I would like to offer you a job."

Brady put down his cigar. "Like I said, man, all I want is to run my shop, not be someone's personal cook."

"No, no, no. I would never dream of making a man as skilled as yourself a mere servant. This would be a special, one-time contract. I would like you to make me the greatest sandwich in the world. All the time in the world to devote to finding the perfect mixture of ingredients: the best breads, cheeses, and meats all at your disposal. None of this repetitive clap-trap of giving the ragamuffins their five sandwiches, but new, innovative, extraordinary pieces. You would have unlimited access to any exotic ingredient in the world. No financial worries, no constraints on your time."

Brady's mouth fell open. Finally, he answered, "I'm not sure what to say."

"My driver shall come by tomorrow to hear your answer."

Brady watched the limo drive off into the twilight, then returned to the Shack and began taking orders and making sandwiches. The next day, Mr. Carapachi's driver was waiting for him in the alley as the train rattled by.

"Stayed up late last night thinking about your boss's offer."

"And?"

"Tell him I said no."

The driver nodded. "If you don't mind my asking, sir, why not?"

"Why fix something that ain't broke? I like making food for them as enjoys it. I sleep well at night. Your man says I'm the best. If so, it's only 'cause I love what I do. If I changed things, stopped serving 'the ragamuffins,' I'd lose that. Tell him he's welcome in the Shack, and that's the best sandwich he's like to get."

Brady went back to work and nothing changed, except his sandwiches seemed to get a little better, if that was possible.

A week later, Brady's Sandwich Shack received another visitor. Though most didn't notice him, nearly everyone in the Shack felt a chill down their spines the moment he entered. The man didn't order, but stood quietly in a corner, waiting until everyone had left and Brady had begun to close up. Just then, in the middle of Robert Johnson's "Crossroad Blues," Brady's faithful radio fizzled out.

"Good evening, Mr. Jones," the stranger said, his voice as smooth as an oiled knife. Brady looked up, startled.

"Please allow me to introduce myself," the stranger said, licking his lips and offering his hand, "as one man of taste to another."

The man wore a long gray coat, dark trousers, and a brown derby cap. A ruby ring gleamed on his right index finger. Brady shook his hand, then gasped as he looked into the stranger's eyes.

The stranger grinned. "For the purposes of this visit, you may call me Mr. Reel."

"Reel? Don't mean to be rude, but I got no business with you, sir."

"Ah, but I have business with you, Brady Jones."

"And what's that?" Brady asked, calculating how quickly he could get to the snub-nosed revolver he kept hidden beneath the register.

Mr. Reel raised his hands. "To talk about your fine sandwiches, that's all. Those who I do business with say they're nothing short of miraculous."

"How do you know if they're really any good? Don't recall you orderin' one." Brady said, trying not to meet Mr. Reel's eyes.

"A trifling detail. Let's talk about what I have to *offer*!" Mr. Reel pulled out a briefcase from nowhere and set it on Brady's counter. Elegant hands with long tapered fingers deftly released the case's clasps.

"Now then, Mr. Jones, though money, power, and fame don't seem to interest you, I have with me several items that might."

He pulled out a small glass jar filled with an orange paste. "A special sandwich spread. Spread this on any one of your sandwiches, and the sandwich will taste so good those who eat it will be forced to come back for more. And more. Eventually they will be able to think of nothing but your sandwiches. They will do anything to get their hands on more. And then I—that is you—will have them in the palm of your hand. What do you think?" Reel's eyes gleamed in the soft light of the diner.

Brady snorted. "My customers come back anyway. Not that you'd know. You still haven't ordered a sandwich."

Mr. Reel laughed and shook his finger at him. "Very good, Mr. Jones, very good. To be honest, I would have been disappointed if you'd taken the sauce. Perhaps the next offer will prove more to your liking—a partnership."

Mr. Reel pulled out a deck of cards, shuffled, and began laying them out. The king of hearts changed to the picture of a chest x-ray. "I know about the pains in your chest that have you worried."

A jack of spades became a taxation notice. "I know about the city raising its property taxes."

The king of clubs became a Chicago City Council bill. "I know about the alderman's plan to rezone your shack into a parking lot. Partner with me and I can make all that go away."

Mr. Reel waved his hand and the papers turned back into playing cards. "You don't even have to change the signage. I'm perfectly content being a silent partner. All you have to do is take my money and say 'yes.'"

"Doesn't sound quite right," Brady said.

Mr. Reel appeared irritated. "Do you have any idea of what's coming, Brady? Let me show you which way the winds of change are blowing." And Mr. Reel put a hand on Brady's shoulder and showed him the Chicago of the future, a little private picture show in the sandwich man's mind.

When the vision passed, Brady stared at Mr. Reel, wide-eyed, as if he couldn't quite believe what he'd seen.

"You have no place in that Chicago, Brady," said Mr. Reel, pity in his voice.

That may have been his mistake, for when Brady heard Mr. Reel's pity, his own face hardened.

"Maybe so," Brady said. "But if that's what's in the cards, I'll play the hand I'm dealt." Brady stared at the ground, then into Mr. Reel's face. "You've taken enough of my time. If you're not gonna order anything, I'd appreciate it if you left."

Mr. Reel's mouth worked in surprise and fury. His eyes began to spark. Then suddenly, he shrugged and packed up his suitcase. As he was leaving he turned and said, "I do have one final offer." He reached into his sleeve and pulled out another playing card, the ace of diamonds. With a wave of his elegant hands, it changed into something else.

Brady's eyes widened. In a voice barely above a whisper, he asked, "Where'd you get that?"

"What, this? Merely a photograph. You can get them developed at the drugstore around the corner. Why is your mouth trembling, Mr. Jones? Surely, you recognize your ex-wife. The woman who wanted the finer things, things a small sandwich shop owner couldn't afford. She can be yours again. Just say the word."

"Get out," Brady said, pleading.

Reel placed a clawed hand on Brady's shoulder. "Why should I leave now that things have gotten so interesting? You do want her back, don't you? I can make that happen."

"Enough!"

Mr. Reel's face darkened. "Or, I could show you other pictures. Photographs where your woman is, how shall we say, in flagrante delicto? Perhaps that would be more to your taste?"

Brady pulled his revolver from beneath the register. Mr. Reel's smile grew impossibly wide, showing sharpened teeth. "Perhaps I'll even pay her a visit myself."

Brady pulled the trigger. There was a dry snap. He stared at the gun, then pulled the trigger again and again. Misfires each time.

The Shack darkened as Mr. Reel plucked the gun from his hand and pulled Brady across the counter. "All I want is just a tiny piece of the pie. Is that so much to ask?"

"Just leave me alone," Brady pleaded, his face inches from Mr. Reel's glowing eyes.

The Sandwich Shack rumbled. Beyond the windows, the city had vanished, leaving only darkness and a howling wind. "Just give me what I want, Brady, and I'll go away."

Almost without thinking, Brady said, "What if I give you a sandwich instead?"

For the first time Mr. Reel appeared uncertain. "What?"

That touch of uncertainty gave Brady a little of himself back. "Don't you want to know what you're buying into? Try one, then maybe we can talk."

Mr. Reel stroked his sharp chin. "Very well, I shall try one of these little delicacies. It is only fitting, I suppose."

Brady Jones smiled grimly. "You have to order."

"What?"

"You have to pick one from the list right there on the wall."

"Very well. The #2 Turkey on Rye." Outside, the darkness seemed to dissipate slightly.

Brady Jones returned to his kitchen. He didn't know if he'd ever concentrated so hard on making a sandwich in his life. Coming back up to the counter, he said, "That'll be a $1.25."

"What?" Mr. Reel said, shocked.

"We ain't in business yet. You gotta pay, just like everyone else."

Mr. Reel growled, dug into his pocket and slammed five pieces of silver on Brady's counter. The sandwich man didn't recognize the denomination, but they looked close enough to quarters that he decided to leave well enough alone.

Mr. Reel sat at the counter and looked at the sandwich, as if uncertain what to do next.

"You gotta put it in your mouth," Brady said helpfully. "And chew."

Hesitantly, and almost, Brady thought, a little timidly, Mr. Reel brought the turkey sandwich to his mouth and took a bite.

Brady watched as Mr. Reel's eyes closed. He watched as Mr. Reel chewed slowly. When the stranger opened his eyes, there were tears of blood and flame running down his face. For a moment, Brady thought Mr. Reel looked almost angelic.

"You— you—" Mr. Reel began, but he could not finish. He closed his eyes and took another bite. Now, the fiery tears of joy were streaming down his face. "Such beauty. Such exquisite beauty." Wiping his eyes, he stood, placed the card back up his sleeve, and began to leave. "Damn you, Brady Jones. I cannot do this."

The darkness outside the shop lifted. Brady released a breath he hadn't realized he'd been holding. Mr. Reel was almost out of the shop and he called out, "Those cards?"

"Don't think on them," said Mr. Reel. "Lies and parlor tricks. Nothing like . . . that." He pointed to the remains of the sandwich.

"You gonna finish it?" Brady asked.

"No," said Mr. Reel smiling. "I believe if I did, I'd renounce too many things, and I'm not ready to walk those crossroads just yet. I will leave you in peace. Until your next visitor that is."

With a blast of hot wind he was gone. The radio came to life again, still playing Robert Johnson's song. Brady stumbled with relief as he closed up shop.

The next three days passed as usual, though there was a noticeable drop in violent crimes around Chicago. Then another visitor of note came in. Her dark skin, black hair, and deep green eyes gave her the look of a wandering Traveler queen.

"What can I get for you?" Brady asked.

"I'd like a number #3, Italian hero please," she said. Brady was not quite sure who he was seeing, but he said, "That'll be one dollar twenty-five cents.

Her face fell. "Unfortunately, I don't carry money."

Brady smiled. "Tell you what, you sweep the floor, take out the trash, you got yourself a number #3."

She ate the hero with relish. After finishing, she began sweeping the floor. And for the next half hour customers felt a little less worried and left the shop smiling, eager to face the rest of the day.

When the woman returned from taking out the trash, Brady inspected her work and blinked. His floors sparkled as if brand new.

But everyone in the Shack had frozen. Folks were paused mid-bite, faces filled with bliss, crumbs half-tumbled out of their mouths frozen in the air. A single drop of cola from the soda-machine floated mid-fall.

"Suppose I should have expected it," said Brady, as if time stopped in his shop every day. "Everyone wants me to stop making sandwiches for people. So who're you?"

"I think you know who I am, Brady Jones."

Brady looked into her eyes and saw eternity: the beginning and ending of universes, planets of sentient crystals and oceans of purple and octarine. He cried out. He was only one man, and behind those eyes lay the truth of creation.

"Oh my G— It's an honor," whispered Brady.

"Indeed it is, Brady Jones," the woman said. "I have heard tell of your good work, and have come to offer you a place at my right hand."

"What?" Brady sputtered.

The woman blazed with light. "You shall be the head cook of Heaven and live amongst the angels in a mansion of ivory and gold."

Brady looked at the floor, shoulders hunched, silent.

She glared at him, seeming to double in size. "MORTAL, I AM ALPHA AND OMEGA. INFINITE AND ENDLESS. DO YOU DARE REFUSE ME?"

Brady clutched his register in an effort not to fall over. He closed his eyes, took a deep breath, and managed a whisper. "Yes, ma'am."

The woman smiled, and shrunk back into herself. "Good. I had to know if you were sincere. True sincerity is one of the rarest qualities in all the universes."

"So this was a test?" Brady said, jaw tight.

"Everything is a test, Brady Jones. But I was also here to try one of these sandwiches I keep hearing so much about. And I have to tell you: I've never tasted the like."

"Thank you." he whispered.

She laughed. "So Brady, don't you want anything?"

Brady tried to smile. "Just want to make my sandwiches. Only . . . that vision, about the future. That's gonna come true, ain't it?"

For a moment, she looked sad. "Yes, I'm afraid it will all come to pass. In this, he did not lie to you."

"I hate the thought of Chicago—the real Chicago, getting wiped away. Hate the thought of the Shack disappearing. Might not be fine or fancy, but it's what I was made for."

"Indeed. People should do what they were made for, what makes them happy."

Brady was pleased that someone finally understood. "And what makes you happy, if you don't mind my askin'?"

The woman looked momentarily shocked and was silent a moment. "Stories, I think."

"World needs more stories."

She nodded. "And, if you don't mind, Brady, I think yours will go on for quite a while longer. Oh I'm not granting you immortality. Let's just say that every once in a while, whenever you feel like it, you can come back to do what you love and give others a taste of old Chicago."

Coming back every once in a while? That suited him fine.

"Brady, how do you make them taste so good?"

"Well, some folks will tell you the secret's in good bread. Others will say it's the meat or the spread. I think maybe a fine sandwich is like a good story: made to be enjoyed by other folks. Long as I keep that in mind, I do okay."

The woman smiled, shook Brady's hand, and walked out. After she left, time resumed, and Brady returned to his kitchen, a smile on his face.

Years later, as Chicago began to change, Brady took sick. While he lay dying in the hospital, the city council fiddled with its zoning requirements and the Sandwich Shack was closed. Or at least some days it was closed, but some days it was still there. As time passed, it seemed only to be open for those who needed it, those who remembered it, those who wished for it.

It has stayed that way to this day. If you hear the blues, follow your ears; if you smell the bread, follow your nose. Tell Brady Jones hello. Enjoy your time there. Brady will tip you a wink and ask what you'd like. The #5 is a personal favorite, but any of Brady Jones's sandwiches is a small miracle: good enough to make a rich man feel poor, the devil weep, and God Almighty Herself smile with pleasure. And as long as they're around, that old Chicago will never really die.

# ABOUT THE EDITORS

**NIB** (they/them) is a queer & non-binary speculative fiction writer who lives in Seattle. They're a cofounder of Two Hour Transport, which is currently virtual and welcomes writers from all over the world. They have an MFA in creative writing from Goddard College. Their flash fiction story "Strange Music" was published by *Fireside* in April of 2021. Their flash fiction story "Sold For Parts" is out in *Reckoning 6* and available on their website in both print and audio form. Their flash fiction story "Going Green" was published in the SolarPunk edition of the Flame Tree Press Newsletter in February of 2023.

**Ramona Ridgewell** is a Seattle writer and poet whose works include poems in Eccentric Orbits: An Anthology of Science Fiction Poetry Vol 4 and Vol 5. Her debut novel is a vampire urban fantasy due out in October, 2024 (from which her story was excerpted). She has been reading at Two Hour Transport events since 2016, and on the management team since 2019.

**Keyan Bowes**, a peripatetic writer of speculative fiction, is based in the US. With around forty short stories and poems published—some more than once—her work can be found online in various webzines, a podcast, and an award-winning short film; and in over a dozen print anthologies. She's lived in ten cities in seven countries and visited many others. They often appear as the settings for her stories. A member of SFWA and a graduate of the Clarion Workshop for writers, Keyan's been attending Two Hour Transport since 2016.

# CONTRIBUTORS

**Jeffrey Steven Abrams** received a BS and master's degree in physiological psychology, then began work toward a PhD in Neuropharmacology. At 24, his academic life ended when he could no longer stomach the hideous animal testing. He spent the next seven years as a sailmaker, a profession as far from science as possible. In 1982, after learning how to program an Apple II, he was hired by a large HMO to write pharmacy software. Later, he became a database engineer at Microsoft where he worked until 2013. He began serious writing when blindness forced him to retire. Now, eight years later, he has a small, but growing collection of work.

**Sarah Allen** is a Midwest to Pacific Northwest transplant, who's still unsure if the soil and climate are right for her roots. She enjoys any game that involves exploring strange new worlds and building a city of LEGO in her spare time. This will be her first published work and she is quite thrilled that it will be on the same shelf as those who inspired her to write in the first place.

By day, **K.G. Anderson** writes about home repair and cats. By night she writes about the futuristic and fantastic. Someday she will live in a home that repairs itself and have cats that will live forever. She's been reading at Two Hour Transport events since May of 2016.

**Elly Bangs** is a queer trans woman who was raised in a new-age cult, had six wisdom teeth, and once rode her bicycle alone from Seattle to the Panama Canal. Her debut apocalyptic cyberpunk novel, *Unity*, came out in Spring 2021. Her short fiction has appeared in *Lightspeed Magazine*, *Clarkesworld Magazine*, *Beneath Ceaseless Skies*, *Escape Pod*, *Fireside Quarterly*, and elsewhere. She's a SFWA member and a 2017 graduate of Clarion West. She lives in Seattle.

**Theresa Barker** is a creative writer and artist in Seattle. Together with co-founder NIB, she stewarded the Two Hour Transport reading series for five years. She also developed the Twenty Minute Transport podcast, featuring writers and their craft. Theresa studied fiction and poetry at Goddard College, earning an MFA in Creative Writing in 2015. Before that she graduated with a Ph.D. in Engineering from the University of Washington. Among her current projects are a hybrid novel entitled *One Step from the Sea*, and a near-future fiction project, *Scarecrows and Seed Bones*.

**E.E.W. Christman** (they/them) is a queer nonbinary writer and editor working in the Seattle area. Their work has appeared in a number of publications, including *The NoSleep Podcast*, *Uncanny Magazine*, *Diet Riot: A Fatterpunk Anthology*, *Tales to Terrify*, and others. They're an active member of the Horror Writers Association. Find him at www. eewchristmanwrites.com

**Andy Dudak** is a writer and translator of science fiction. His work has appeared in *Clarkesworld*, *Asimov's*, *Analog*, *The Magazine of Fantasy and Science Fiction*, and Year's Best anthologies edited by Jonathan Strahan, Neil Clarke, and Rich Horton. He believes in the healing power of *Dungeons & Dragons*, and he likes frogs.

Raised in Houston, **Rex Erickson** enrolled at the University of Houston. There, he was editor of the student newspaper and a freelancer for the *Wall Street Journal* during the 1969 moon landing. Following a stint in Vietnam, Rex moved to Seattle and enrolled at the Jesuit-managed Seattle University. There, he read and analyzed the styles of 16th and 17th century writers. Transferring to the University of Washington, he received his M.A. in International Communication Theory and Methodology. Accepted into the Ph.D. program, he was employed as a Research Assistant at the Center for Quantitative Studies. There, he assisted students in computer programming and statistical analysis. Restless, he dropped out of the Ph.D. program to start a small tech company which he eventually sold. Now with his lifelong partner and editor, Diane, Rex writes & composes. His current project is a SYFY series centered on the Texas Big Thicket National Preserve, where unexplained lights dart above the Thicket's Ghost Road and the plaintive call of the supposedly extinct Ivory Billed Woodpecker is occasionally reported by hikers. As Bubba would say, "Shucks, reckon that oughta do it."

**Louis Evans** is a writer living and working in NYC, whose fiction has appeared in *Vice, Nature: Futures*, *The Magazine of Fantasy & Science Fiction*, and many more. He's online at evanslouis.com. His sleep is seldom troubled by unpleasant dreams, he swears. No, really, it's true—

**Karen Joy Fowler** is the author of seven novels, including *Sarah Canary* and *The Jane Austen Book Club*. Also three short story collections, two of which won the World Fantasy Award in their respective years. Her novel *We Are All Completely Beside Ourselves*, won the PEN/Faulkner Award for fiction in 2013 and was shortlisted for the Man/Booker Prize. Her most recent novel, *Booth*, was published in March of 2022.

**Eileen Gunn** is a writer and editor living in Seattle. Her work has received the Nebula Award in the U.S. and the Sense of Gender Award in Japan, and has been short-listed for the Hugo, Philip K. Dick, World Fantasy, and Tiptree/Otherwise awards. She is the author of three story collections: *Night Shift* (PM Press, 2022), *Questionable Practices* (Small Beer Press, 2014), *Stable Strategies and Others* (Tachyon Publications, 2004). Her website is at eileengunn.com.

**Patrick Hurley** has had fiction published in *Factor Four*, *Galaxy's Edge*, *New Myths*, and *Abyss & Apex*. Patrick is a graduate of the 2017 Taos Toolbox Writer's Workshop and a member of SFWA, Codex, and the Dreamcrashers. Find out more about his work at www.patrickhurleywrites.com.

**Seelye Martin** is a retired ice scientist who writes science fiction and fantasy and lives in Seattle. His work has been published in *Lovecraftiana*, *The Periodical Forlorn*, and *Two-Hour Transport*. When he is not writing, he enjoys gardening, working on climate issues, and his family. He acknowledges the help and support of the North Seattle Science Fiction and Fantasy Writers Workshop.

**Tod McCoy's** work has appeared in *Asimov's*, *Felix Futura*, *Starward Tales II*, *The People's Apocalypse*, *Bronies: For the Love of Ponies*, and *AntipodeanSF. com*, as well as others. He is a graduate and board member of the Clarion West Writers Workshop, and is the publisher behind Hydra House Books. He lives in Montana with his wife the witch, a goblin child, and a variety of animal familiars.

**Evan J. Peterson** is an author and game writer whose works include *Drag Star!* (Choice of Games), the world's first drag performer RPG, as well as *METAFLESH: Poems in the Voice(s) of the Monster* and *The Road to Innsmouth: Arkham Horror*. His writing has appeared in *Weird Tales*, *PseudoPod*, *Queers Destroy Horror*, *Nightmare Magazine*, and *Best Gay Stories*. In 2024, Broken Eye Books will publish Evan's first novel, *Better Living Through Alchemy*, an occult noir mystery set in Seattle. Evanpeterson. com can tell you more.

**Dan Rabarts** (Ngati Porou) is an award-winning author and editor, living in Porirua, Aotearoa New Zealand. He is a four-time recipient of New Zealand's Sir Julius Vogel Award and three-time winner of the Australian Shadows Award. His short stories have been published worldwide, and together with Lee Murray, he co-wrote the Path of Ra crime-noir thriller series (*Hounds of the Underworld*, *Teeth of the Wolf*, *Blood of the Sun*) and co-edited the anthologies *Baby Teeth—Bite-sized Tales of Terror* and *At The Edge.*

**Mitchell Shanklin** lives in Seattle and enjoys writing stories with either magic or made-up science or both. He also writes code for companies (and sometimes for himself). In his free time he plays video, board and mind games, reads, hikes, and has rambling philosophical arguments. (No, not all at the same time. Yet.) He is a proud member of Team Arsenic, the Dreamcrashers, and Write of Passage. You can find him online at mitchellshanklin.com

**Nisi Shawl** (they/them) is the multiple award-winning author and editor of over a dozen books of speculative fiction and related nonfiction, including the Nebula Award finalist novel *Everfair* and its sequel *Kinning*, the first volume of the *New Suns* anthology series, and their acclaimed story collection *Filter House*, co-winner of the 2009 Otherwise Award. They've taught and spoken at Duke University, Spelman College, Stanford University, Sarah Lawrence College, and many other institutions. Recent titles include the horror collection *Our Fruiting Bodies* and the Middle Grade historical fantasy novel *Speculation*.

**Yang-Yang Wang** is a Chinese-American writer who's worked in film, commercials, and games. He attended Clarion West in 2014 and currently lives around Seattle. He is a lover of brevity.

**Genevieve Williams** (she/her) is a writer, librarian, musician, and naturalist based in Seattle. Her fiction has appeared in *Asimov's*, *Analog*, *Strange Horizons*, and other magazines, as well as several anthologies. "Song of the Water People" was inspired by the story of Tahlequah, the Southern Resident Killer Whale whose second calf died in 2018. You can find her on BlueSky, Mastodon server wandering.shop, and blogging occasionally at https://welltemperedwriter.wordpress.com/. Ask her about nettles and coyote scat.

**Cliff Winnig's** work appears on the *Escape Pod* podcast; in anthologies such as *Many Worlds*, *High Noon on Proxima B*, and the forthcoming *Scott's Planet*; and elsewhere. He is a graduate of the Clarion (East) writing program and has taught writing workshops at science fiction conventions. He hosts the SF in SF reading series and third Sundays for the B Cubed Sunday Morning podcast. When not writing, he plays sitar, studies aikido and tai chi, and sings bass in a local choral ensemble.

**Joshua K. Wilson** is an editor and journalist in San Francisco, and the publisher of *The Fabulist Words & Art*, online at www.fabulistmagazine.com. He is also a clawhammer banjo student, and an avid bicyclist on the streets, slopes and trails of the SF Bay Area and beyond.

**Kyra Worrell** wrote her first sci-fi/fantasy novel in 8th grade. This started a never-ending trend of sci-fi/fantasy writing in Kyra's life, even though *The Coin* was never published and sadly eventually lost. No matter—Kyra has continued her writing through Nanowrimo, writing groups, and story collaborations like "The Last Human on Earth," co-written with Theresa Barker. In addition, her poem "Water Babies" was published in the 2017 *Poetry on Buses* "Bodies of Water," and the novel excerpt "Flippin' Castles" was published in the *Two Hour Transport Anthology. 2019.*

# COPYRIGHT NOTICES

# OTHER TITLES FROM FAIRWOOD PRESS

www.ingramcontent.com/pod-product-compliance
Lightning Source LLC
Chambersburg PA
CBHW031058020726
47495CB00007B/1935